ARNOLD MARSDEN

Muir Trail Magic

A Bucket List Hike Novel

Contents

Author's Note

This is a work of fiction. The characters are fictional; any resemblances to actual persons are coincidental. I hiked nearly every mile of the trails described in the book and visited most of the facilities during my hikes along the John Muir Trail in 2021 and 2022. While I have tried to describe the trails, scenery, facilities, and operations accurately, I have made small adjustments to facilitate the story. In addition, conditions of trails and facilities and operational details of the facilities and regulating agencies change. Conditions described in the book may not reflect exactly what you have experienced in the past or may experience in the future. But then again, that's part of the wonder of visiting wild areas like John Muir Trail; each experience is unique!

As a special bonus for you, I have created a **Photo Album** showing many of the key scenes in the book. If you want to follow along as you read, you can download your free copy here.

(https://strivingforsafety.mailerpage.com/fiction)

Map

The John Muir Trail
Yosemite National Park
Tuolumne Meadows
Donohue Pass
Happy Isles
Garnet Lake
Red's Meadow
Lake Virginia
Silver Pass
VVR
Marie Lake
Bishop
MTR
Evolution Creek
Bishop Pass
Muir Pass
Mather Pass
Kings Canyon National Park
Wood's Creek Bridge
Rae Lakes
Independence
Kearsarge Pass
Sequoia National Park
Mt. Whitney
Lone Pine

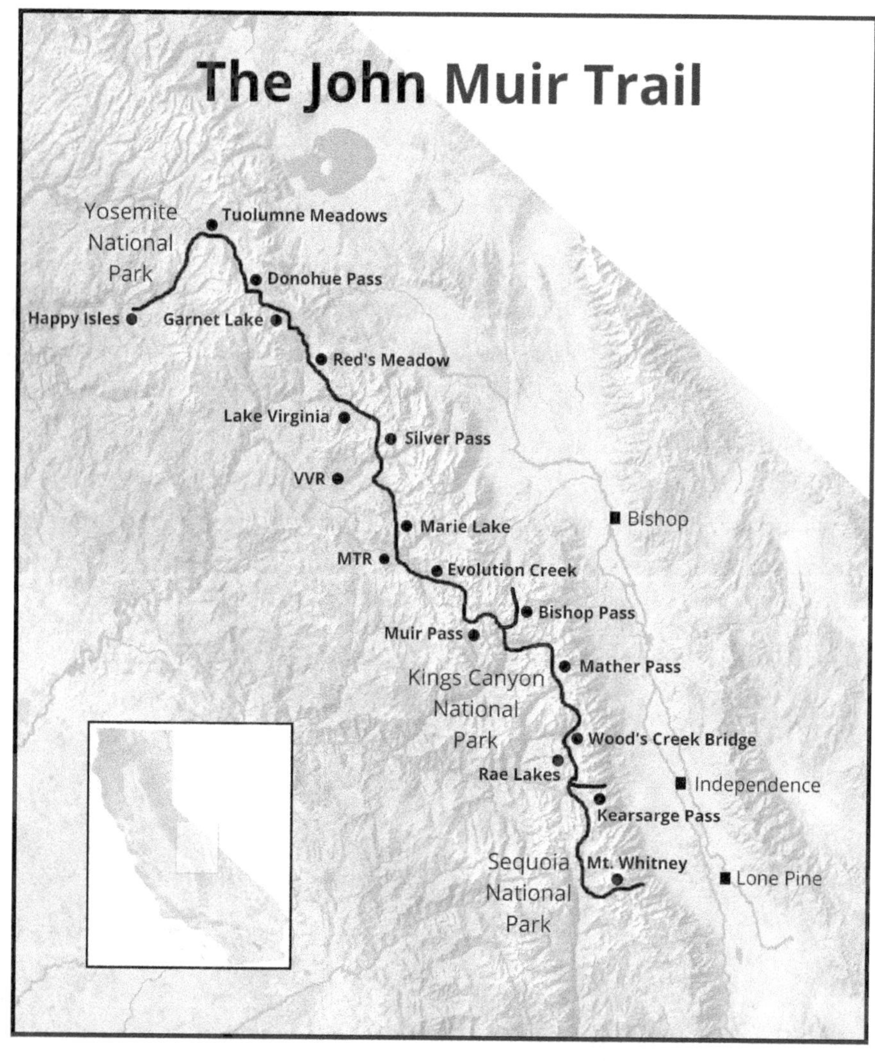

1

Abandoned

2021

July 8 - Houston, Texas

Bob was late—again! Cathy placed the tuna casserole in the refrigerator so it wouldn't spoil. She often ate dinner alone, but had hoped he would get home from work early today. She couldn't wait to share the good news about their upcoming hike on the John Muir Trail, which ran from Yosemite National Park to Mount Whitney, the tallest mountain in the contiguous United States. With little to no cell phone service for three weeks, maybe he'd pay more attention to her than to work for a change.

She was rereading parts of Elizabeth Wenk's *"John Muir Trail: The essential guide to hiking America's most famous trail"* when she heard the garage door opening. She hopped off the couch and headed to the kitchen to spoon out some lukewarm casserole into a bowl. Bob walked into the kitchen from the garage and kicked off his shoes. His shoulders drooped when he saw her put the bowl in the microwave.

"Sorry, another crisis at work," said Bob as he walked to the refrigerator and grabbed a beer.

"Let me guess. Someone cut their hand or twisted their ankle?"

"No. We had an emergency shutdown today, and the plant may be down for weeks. Smells good. What did you make?"

"Tuna casserole."

Bob nodded and Cathy continued. "Sorry to hear about the plant."

Bob sat at the counter and closed his eyes as the first cold sip slid down his throat. He opened his eyes just as the microwave timer hit 0:00 and beeped.

Cathy brought him the bowl and a fork. "Well, look at it this way. You only have to get through the next week, and the rest of your team can manage it while you're gone."

Bob shoveled two forkfuls into his mouth and gulped down his beer between bites.

"It's looking pretty bad at work, Cathy."

"But you said no one was hurt."

"Right, and I'm grateful for that. But now we face a bunch of unplanned work, which is when people tend to get hurt."

Bob moved the noodles around with his fork and took sip after sip from the sweating amber bottle.

"Well, that's why you have a team. Your title is Safety Manager, not healer of all woes at the plant, not overseer of every task of five hundred people. Beginning next week, you only have yourself and me to worry about—and a few other things, like bears and thunderstorms."

"But Cathy, I don't think I can go now. They're counting on me at the plant. Can't we postpone?" Bob gave in to his hunger and ate another bite of creamy noodles.

Cathy slammed her hand on the counter top, causing Bob to flinch and his bowl and beer bottle to jump. Why was she so surprised? He had backed out of hiking trips with her at least four other times. Somehow, he always convinced himself that a crisis at the chemical plant would only be averted by his presence. But this hike was different, over 200 miles, climaxing at 14,505 feet on the top of Mt. Whitney. Could she make it alone? Why can't he do this for me–just this once?

"You know how long it took me to get these permits. Three years! And we've done most of the work already. Our gear is ready, our itinerary is fine tuned, and our fitness is peaking just in time. All that remains is to show up and hike."

Bob laid his fork in the bowl. "Don't worry. I'll get us another permit. Or maybe we can get a walk-up permit."

"And waste all our efforts—that's what I wanted to tell you. Our last resupply bucket arrived at Muir Trail Ranch today. We are all set to go." Staging food supplies was one of the biggest challenges in planning such a hike. She and Bob had sent five-gallon plastic buckets full of backpacker staples, such as oatmeal, nuts, energy bars, and freeze-dried dinners, to three locations along the trail.

"Sorry, maybe we should wait until next year."

She threw the dish towel she had been using to wipe the counter across the bar, just missing his head and landing in the living room.

"Well, you can wait until next year, just like you've been waiting to retire for three years. I'm going to hike the trail this summer while I still can. You know how long my bucket list is. We won't be able to hike trails like this forever."

Bob's bowl was still half full, but he pushed it away. His bottle was empty.

"This is a tough hike," Cathy continued. "I am prepared to go alone, but I could use the kind of support you give the plant. What if I get hurt or sick? What if I run short of food? Don't you tell the people at work to have a buddy if they are doing dangerous work?"

"What if I go with you and someone gets hurt at the plant?"

"What if you don't go, and you die next month? I've waited long enough!"

She stormed off to the bedroom.

2

Anticipation

A year later - 2022

Day 0 (of Bob's hike)

August 4 - Tuolumne Meadows Campground

Bob hobbled off the bus when it stopped in front of a white canvas structure at Tuolumne Meadows in Yosemite National Park. The structure was a larger version of the tent cabin he had stayed in last night at Curry Village in Yosemite Valley and housed a store, post office, and grill. Thru-hikers congregated here during the hiking season. His entire body was stiff after a long day of travel yesterday and a steep day hike to Nevada Falls earlier today. He was ready to start the John Muir Trail, or JMT, tomorrow. Between here and Mt. Whitney, the trail crossed no roads. It wound its way around dozens of pristine alpine lakes and climbed nine mountain passes, all of which took hikers' breath away, some figuratively, others literally. Hikers typically climbed and descended 2,000-4,000 feet a day, causing many to curse the trail architects along the way.

The fast-moving, dark clouds were so low it seemed he could pierce them by holding up his hiking poles. After seeing the unappetizing burgers being devoured by a group of backpackers in front of the grill, he followed the convoluted path to the campground. He too would crave a burger of any kind in a week, but for now, he was eager to set up camp before the clouds opened up.

Signs led him through a maze of communal bathrooms, tent and RV campsites, parked vehicles, and bear-proof dumpsters in the drive-up campground. A short climb brought him to the section of the campground dedicated to backpackers. He wandered around the sites identified with numbers on small green signs, disturbing the established residents' dinners and conversations. Just before he turned to circle back for another pass, he spotted an empty site nestled against the dense, dark forest.

The rains came, but only after Bob had settled into camp, eaten dinner, and put away his food and toiletries in the bear-proof metal box assigned to his campsite. He relaxed in his tent on top of his sleeping bag and inflatable sleeping pad, still in his hiking clothes: khaki-colored, nylon cargo pants and a light blue, long sleeve, polyester shirt. He had worn them for two days now, but they were still clean by backpacking standards.

Now that his mind was free to wander, tears ran down his cheeks. He was about to embark on the adventure of his lifetime, but he would be alone. Cathy should be with him. He had abandoned her the week before their planned JMT hike last year. She went alone and never came back. He should have been with her. He could have saved her. Instead, he spent his time at the plant, telling himself he might be saving the life of an operator or mechanic instead of hiking in the mountains. He would never know if he saved a life. No one would. That was the life of a safety manager.

Bob was tortured by guilt after Cathy's death. If he had prioritized her safety as much as the safety of those at the plant, she would be with him right now. He retired immediately after her death and vowed to complete the hikes on her bucket list to try to atone for his misplaced priorities. He couldn't hike *with* her anymore, but he could hike *for* her. At the top of her bucket list, in both beauty and difficulty, was the JMT. Hiking this trail would keep his memories of her fresh and perhaps allow her to experience the epic mountain views, roaring waterfalls, and fresh forest scents through him—from wherever she was. He owed that to her.

A soft, "Excuse me," startled him just as he dozed off.

Cathy, is that you? What's wrong?

"Hello. Can you help me?" The voice was louder this time, less apologetic, more insistent. And it wasn't Cathy; it wasn't a dream. The voice was too high, too young. He wiped the tears from his face and opened the flap of his tent. A tall young woman with long, drenched hair hunched over just outside the door.

She continued when his head popped out of the tent. "Sorry to bother you. Can I share this campsite with you? My tent will fit right over there." She pointed to the other side of the picnic table with one of her hiking poles. "I promise I'll be quiet. I've made two laps around the campground and can't find any open spots. A lot of campers are doubling up." Her shivering body made her voice sound choppy.

"Sure. They should do away with the assigned numbers. Campsites won't be labeled when we're out in the wilderness. Are you hiking the JMT?"

She perked up and smiled. "Yes, I am, starting tomorrow."

Bob grabbed a shoe from the vestibule of his tent. "So am I. Let me put my shoes and poncho on, and I'll help you with your tent."

Her smile grew. "Oh, thanks. You don't have to do that, but I appreciate the help. My name is Hannah. I'm from San Francisco."

"Howdy, I'm Bob from Texas." He regretted the clichéd response; nothing about him resembled a cowboy.

* * *

Once Bob was settled in his tent again, he opened the voice recorder app on his phone and began speaking softly.

Dear Cathy,

I made it to Tuolumne Meadows! I haven't even begun the JMT, but I'm already exhausted. That's what a long cab ride, two flights, a three-hour layover, six hours on buses, and a tough day hike will do. I hope none of the days on trail are that stressful.

Since my flights were on time, I was able to hike the Mist Trail from the Happy Isles trailhead in Yosemite Valley to Nevada Falls this morning. What a wonderful hike. I returned to the trailhead via the JMT, where you started your hike last year. Part of me wishes I could begin my JMT hike there too, but Tuolumne Meadows was my draw in the permit lottery. I'm just grateful to get a permit so quickly after all the years it took you to get one. Hopefully, the exertion of the climb and the beauty of the waterfalls and granite domes will serve as a smooth transition to the rigors and views of the JMT.

I hope you enjoy revisiting your favorite sights along the first half of the trail and then experiencing our new favorites together. I truly regret not being there to help you finish last year. I know I can count on you to help me through the challenges I will face during the next few weeks—the steep climbs, cold mornings, thunderstorms, and gear failures. Ironically, it took losing you to get me on the trail you dreamed of completing together for years. One way or another, I will finish this hike for you.

I doubt I will sleep much tonight, but talking to you has soothed my mind, so I should try now. Talk to you tomorrow.

Love, Bob

* * *

Bob glanced at his watch for the fifth time since he went to bed. *Only 4 AM? Still too early to get up.* Hannah was quiet, as she had promised, and the rain had precluded any noisy games the teenagers in the car campground might have been scheming. He wasn't worried about bears and mountain lions. His permit was in hand. But the mild headache which had appeared after dinner was much worse. Each heartbeat pounded his temples. Each time he woke up, he took a couple of deep breaths to get more oxygen to his brain. Would altitude sickness stop him from fulfilling his commitment to Cathy before he even started? He shouldn't be sick yet, especially after spending a day acclimatizing in Yosemite Valley. Cathy never mentioned having such problems at this elevation. Maybe at 10,000-12,000 feet, but not at 8600 feet. *Maybe I'll get better when I start hiking and stop worrying.*

He heard screaming. "Bear! Bear!"

"Get. Go away!"

"Go, bear, go!"

Something sounding like a bass drum joined the ruckus. One of his neighbors must be banging on a bear box. Then someone shrieked, "Help! Help!" piercing his eardrums. *That was close. Hannah?*

He grabbed his headlamp, slipped on his sandals, and stumbled out of his tent. Once he regained his balance, he turned on the headlamp and swung his head around. No bear. No cougars. Hannah's tent was still standing. Screams pierced his eardrums again. He cupped his hands over his ears and ran to Hannah's tent, while yelling, "Hannah! It's OK. I don't see any bears."

He squatted next to the zipper on the vestibule of her tent. "Can I open your tent?"

"Yes. Please help!" Still loud, but at least the pitch was lower.

Bob opened the zippers of her tent. The light from his headlamp forced her eyes shut, squeezing out a flood of tears.

"Hannah. It will be OK. Let me find out if anyone saw the bear leave. I'll be right back."

"Don't leave."

As he stood up, the young man from the adjacent campsite yelled to him, "Tell her the bear ran into the woods. I saw him two sites over that way." He pointed to his left. "It bolted when I pounded on the bear box." He cradled his right hand with his left. "I hope I didn't break anything."

"Thanks a lot. I had just gone to sleep and was dreaming. I would've slept through it if not for all the commotion." *Sometimes, you don't want to know what's happening outside your tent.*

Bob poked his head in Hannah's tent again. She must have heard the entire exchange, but was still crying. "Can you stay with me a while? I don't want to be alone."

"The bear's gone. I'll be in my tent, twenty feet away."

"Please, please," she said, as the sobbing resumed.

"OK. Let me get dressed, and I'll sit here until you calm down."

He sat outside her tent in silence for fifteen minutes, but it seemed much longer. Two nights in a row with hardly any sleep. Last night in Curry Village, a group of teenagers had roamed the tent city playing hide and seek until two o'clock. He was wide awake now, thanks to the chaos created by the bear, but he feared he would crash in the afternoon. Hopefully, the excitement of the first day on trail would ward off the fatigue and headache. He couldn't wait to get to the backcountry, away from the crowds.

Hannah sniffled once every couple of minutes now. "What am I doing out here alone?" Bob assumed the question was rhetorical and let her continue. "I was supposed to hike with my boyfriend, but he accepted a job in Qatar and left me. He wanted to come back for the hike, but the permit was in my name. He told me I could never do this alone, so I should transfer the permit to him and his buddy. Maybe he was right."

"No, no, Hannah. You can do this. What can I do to help?"

"Don't leave me alone." Her sniffles became more frequent. "When I was growing up, my father would only take me on the easy hikes that he and my brother did. He thinks I'm crazy to try this by myself. That only made me want to do it more. I'm in the best shape of my life, but I'm terrified of wild animals. And a bear visits my campsite before I even begin the hike! What if the next one comes when I'm by myself?" Her sniffles turned to sobs.

Bob chose not to mention the less common, but more dangerous, mountain lions. "You'll find plenty of people on the trail to hang out with if you want." Even though permits were hard to get, JMT hikers were rarely alone for more than an hour or two at a time, and many congregated at the more popular campsites. The dialogue continued in his mind.

You are more likely to get hurt from falls, lightning, rock slides, falling trees, or contaminated water than from bears. True, but she didn't need to hear that now.

"Hannah, it's almost five o'clock. Neither one of us will get any more sleep, and it's not raining, so let's get up and start hiking. When I picked up my permit, the ranger told me Tuolumne Meadows and Lyell Canyon are the most likely places to encounter bears. Just focus on getting through today and tonight."

"Thanks. I wish my father was as supportive as you."

3

Companion

2021

July 13 - Houston, Texas

Cathy filled her backpack for the last time before heading to the airport in the morning. Before every trip, she worried about forgetting something crucial. She usually dismissed the concern quickly, knowing she could replace most items at her destination. But when backpacking, especially for three weeks, she had to get it right the first time. Fortunately, she had a thorough list based on years of experience and dozens of gear review videos, complete with the weights of each item to the nearest ounce.

Bob walked into the living room with a grin and an arm behind his back. They hadn't spoken for two days after he had backed out of the trip. He had left her to travel alone on many trips, but not one of this magnitude. The JMT had been at the top of her bucket list for years, but she had patiently waited for his retirement to schedule it. When he kept working and declining trips after his sixtieth birthday, she took matters into her own hands. His active involvement in planning the trip made her think he might have changed. But in the end, work came first. Work always came first. However, she tried to put the disappointment behind her. She wouldn't allow his betrayal to cast a pall over the trip, obscuring the spectacular sights or distracting her from taking care of herself and her gear.

Cathy zipped up her backpack. "That's it. Everything I need to live for three weeks."

"Not quite everything," Bob said, as he tossed a brown, floppy object her way.

She caught a small, plush animal in one hand. After a glance, she smiled. "Is this a marmot? How cute!"

"Yeah. I know they're your favorite critters in the mountains."

Marmots were indeed her favorite trail animal. They thrived in rocky terrain at high elevations, where they darted in and out of the endless nooks and crannies at the first sign of danger. The JMT was full of such environments, so she expected to see dozens of them. They resembled woodchucks and beavers found at lower elevations. Despite being the size of a house cat, they had a shrill cry to signal each other of potential danger. Only the call of the pikas, her second favorite mountain critter, was higher in pitch.

"Thank you." She placed it on her palm and moved it up and down. "What's another three ounces." She grinned and placed it on top of her pack and took a photo before cramming it into the outer mesh pocket. "I'll call him Marty. Marty the marmot."

"I'm glad you're taking him with you. Small plush marmots are hard to find. I saw plenty of lions, tigers, and bears, but this was the only marmot that wouldn't fill half of your backpack."

She stood up and hugged Bob. "That's nice. You know, it's not too late to change your mind. The permit is for two, and your food is staged. All you need to do is buy another plane ticket."

She looked at him with a sliver of hope.

"Come on, honey. You've seen how late I've been working this week. Nothing has changed."

She pushed him away with both hands. "Work, work, work! At least Marty won't stand me up!"

She laid down on the couch and cradled a pillow against her chest while Bob walked away.

13

4

Solo

2021

July 15 - Happy Isles to Clouds Rest junction

Cathy crossed the Happy Isles bridge in Yosemite Valley at 6:30 AM. The unusual solitude in the area made it seem early, but her body was still on Houston time, two hours later. After yesterday's tiring day of travel, she slept well during the first night in her tent. Her travels had been on schedule, so she was able to pick up her JMT permit from the Wilderness Office just before they closed. She would have preferred to start hiking earlier, but she tossed and turned in her tent for an hour after she first awoke so she wouldn't wake her neighbors. The trail to Nevada Falls would be packed with people from all walks of life by mid-morning: filthy, bearded backpackers; perfumed teenage girls taking selfies; and grandma and grandpa forcing hurried sightseers off the trail to get around them.

A few hundred feet later, a large trail sign reminded her of the magnitude of the challenge in front of her. Twelve destinations were listed, ranging from the Vernal Falls Bridge at 0.8 miles to Mt. Whitney at 211 miles. What had she been thinking? Could she really do this? It was too late to turn around now; she wouldn't be able to face Bob if she quit so early. Nearly all JMT hikers stopped here to take a photo, so she gave Marty his first chance to pose on the trail.

The steep, paved trail was deserted except for the chirping birds and a few day hikers getting a late start on their Half Dome summit attempts. The JMT shared a path with the Mist Trail for the first mile before branching off to the right toward dozens of switchbacks. Those going straight on the Mist Trail climbed steep stone steps made slippery by the continuous mist from Vernal Falls. Sightseers would linger in the area during the warm afternoon to cool off. She took a photo of Marty on the Vernal Falls bridge with the tumbling Merced River in the background. Instead of stuffing him back inside her backpack, she strapped him on top so he could enjoy the views and fresh air.

Cathy had ten mountain passes to cross between here and Mt. Whitney. This climb wasn't one of them, but aside from the lower elevation, today's hike was just as strenuous. The trail rose 3,000 feet in just over six miles to reach her planned campsite at the trail junction to Clouds Rest. With each step, her legs lifted her 35-pound pack in addition to her 115-pound body. She briefly envied the JMT hikers starting at Tuolumne Meadows, who began with a flat 10-mile hike in Lyell Canyon, but knew some of the best views on the entire trail were just ahead.

Preparing for high-altitude, mountain hiking in the flat landscape of Houston, Texas was difficult, but she and Bob did their best with stair-steppers to condition their knees and thighs and lap swimming to build their lung capacity. On weekend mornings, they walked for two to three hours, early in the morning, before the sweltering heat drove them inside. For the last few weeks, they had even worn their backpacks stuffed with water bottles to prepare their backs and shoulders.

She completed the switchbacks and walked along a six-foot-wide notch cut into a nearly vertical wall of granite. A man-made stone fence protected hikers from falling over the left side of the trail. A few minutes later, she stopped and gazed at three wonders of nature, each of which would make the strenuous climb worthwhile. On the right, a wide, white ribbon of water fell over a cliff–Nevada Falls. Just to the left was Liberty Cap, a tall, slender mound of granite resembling a sorcerer's hat. Flecks of green speckled the gray-white rock where pine trees took root in the smallest of cracks. The rounded side of Half Dome was on the far left. She could no longer see the 2000-foot vertical face of rock on the other side which gave the formation its name.

She had attempted to climb to the summit of Half Dome last year using the chains and boards installed every spring on the forty-five-degree slope. It was a terrible and unsuccessful experience. Once was enough for her. She had declined the option of attempting the climb again as part of her JMT permit. Instead, she would detour from the JMT tomorrow to hike the safer and less crowded trail to Clouds Rest, which offered even better views of Yosemite Valley.

Marty posed for another photo on the stone wall along the trail. She wondered if she might wear a hole in the poor thing at this rate. As she resumed walking, the view became alive as the shapes of the granite domes changed with each step, and she began to hear the roar of the free-falling water. *How could Bob choose work over this? I sure am glad I didn't wait for him.*

When she reached the bridge over Nevada Falls, the rushing water created a breeze that threatened to push her over the edge. She thought she heard Marty pleading to skip this photo opportunity, so she left him securely attached to her pack. "I don't blame you, little fella."

She hurried past the trail cutoff to the Half Dome summit. Even if she had the desire to try it again, she did not have the energy after the steep climb. She arrived at the Clouds Rest junction shortly thereafter. Six miles done, only 205 to go!

Just like the previous night, Cathy ate dinner staring at Half Dome. An early start led to an early finish and the best selection of campsites. She had thought of Bob only briefly today, each time she took a photo of Marty. She had made a big deal about how they needed each other's support, but she hadn't needed him at all today. The splendid views and exhausting climb had preoccupied her mind all day. It was still early, but perhaps she had been over-dramatic with Bob in trying to hold him to his word.

She sent Bob a brief text message on her satellite communication device, from which she could also send an SOS message if she got hurt or lost. Even though she was still disappointed in him, she didn't want him to worry about her needlessly.

Message from Cathy: *At Clouds Rest Junction. Tough climb, but beautiful. Marty had a blast.*

5

Intervention

2022

Day 1

August 5 - Tuolumne Meadows Campground to upper Lyell Canyon

After three miles of hiking, Bob laid on a granite slab, resting his head against his backpack. The rock still retained last night's chill and sucked the heat from his back. A few hours later, it would become a heating pad as the rain clouds had given way to a sunny day. He and Hannah had left camp around six o'clock, and were now snacking. He nibbled on a mix of roasted nuts, and Hannah devoured an energy bar.

They had spread out their tents and groundsheets on boulders deposited by glaciers long ago. They would dry quickly in the sun after being packed wet at camp. Hannah's black nylon hiking pants were draped over a small tree since they had not dried in her tent during the damp night. She wore red shorts over her black sleeping tights and a royal blue polyester shirt. A white baseball cap shaded the pale complexion of her face. Now that her hair was dry, Bob saw that it was dirty blond instead of brown. It fell six inches below the top of her square shoulders. Since she had been walking ahead of him most of the morning, he had already estimated her height to be near his, just under six feet. She appeared to be in her early twenties.

The trail wove in and out of the trees bordering the meadow in the center of a wide canyon. He struggled to imagine the size of the glacier that carved this canyon. The creek alternated between a wide tranquil stream surrounded by tall grass to water rushing over slabs of granite and squeezing through occasional constrictions. The canyon would lead them to their first big obstacle on the trail, Donohue Pass.

The forested walls of the canyon were not quite high enough to be topped with bare, jagged peaks. Most blogs and videos raved about the beauty of Lyell Canyon. It beat the scenery in Houston and served as a gentle introduction to the trail, but Bob imagined it might be a letdown to the northbounders, or NOBOs, having hiked for two to three weeks over nine mountain passes. Then again, the flat trail must be a welcome relief for their exhausted and starved bodies.

"Hannah, how long did it take you to get your permit?

"You won't believe this, but I got it on my second try."

Bob raised his eyebrows. "You lucky girl. I got three weeks of daily rejection emails before getting mine. I had resigned myself to going NOBO from Horseshoe Meadow."

Their prized permits were also known as *golden tickets* in the backpacking community since they were issued through a lottery. After receiving rejection emails day after day for weeks, many entrants felt the odds of winning were lower than those of Charlie finding a golden ticket to the Chocolate Factory. The scenery on the JMT would not be as colorful and mouth-watering as Charlie experienced, but just as magnificent.

Hannah said, "It would have been nice to start at Happy Isles in Yosemite Valley, but you take what you can get."

"Yeah, me too." Bob sat up. "But I'll tell you what. I hiked the first part of the JMT yesterday as a warm-up and saw a lot of miserable hikers carrying heavy backpacks up that steep trail. Maybe we're better off starting here after all."

Hannah shrugged her shoulders. "Are you ready to go again?"

Bob rubbed his temples.

"Are you feeling OK?" asked Hannah.

"I've got a pounding headache. I thought a snack and a little rest might help, but I was wrong."

"Oh no. Sorry. I probably didn't help with all the screaming earlier. Do you want to rest a while longer?"

"No. Let's get going. If all our breaks are this long, we'll never make it to Mt. Whitney."

Bob's backpack was now about half a pound lighter, thanks to the small snack he had eaten and his now dry tent. He motioned for Hannah to start down the trail first. He sensed that she still felt vulnerable, so he had hiked behind her most of the morning. When he had stopped for a photo and the gap between them grew, she turned around and waited for him, sometimes taking a photo of her own.

Fifteen minutes after they resumed hiking, Bob spotted a park ranger waiting for them on the trail.

"Good morning. Where are you two headed today?" asked the ranger. She had a small backpack, meaning she might have camped just this side of Donohue Pass last night.

Bob spoke first. "Well, this is my first day, so I'm not quite sure. I may try to get over Donohue Pass today while the miles are easy."

"And you?" the ranger said with a quick nod to Hannah.

"I don't think I'll make it over Donohue Pass. A bear in the backpackers' campground this morning cost me a lot of sleep. Maybe near the Lyell Fork bridge. Have you heard of any bear sightings up ahead?"

"Bears are pretty common all the way from the campground to where the trail steepens after the upper crossing of Lyell Fork. You won't find many campsites above there. Speaking of bears, would both of you let me thump your packs to check for your bear canisters? And I'll need to see your permit." JMT hikers are required to store their food in hard-sided bear canisters to prevent bears from associating food with humans.

Bob and Hannah removed their packs. They didn't need another pack break yet, but their shoulders wouldn't complain. The ranger tapped on Bob's pack with her knuckles and heard the loud thud she sought. She was about to knock on Hannah's pack, but pointed to the ridges of her bear canister bulging through the pack fabric. "You're good."

They handed their permits to her. "Oh, I thought you might be traveling together."

Bob said, "We are for now, but we just met last night. The bear in camp caused some quick bonding." Bob smiled at Hannah. Hannah looked at the ground.

"I see you're both headed to Mt. Whitney. Good luck and be careful. The forecast calls for a clear afternoon and evening." She looked at Bob. "It's about ten more miles to Donohue Pass. Before you begin climbing, keep in mind that you'll need to hike a couple of miles beyond the pass to find a good campsite. You should consider camping around the upper crossing of Lyell Fork. Then you can climb the pass with fresh legs in the morning."

"OK, thanks for the tip." Bob said as he swung his pack over his shoulders and groaned.

After the ranger walked away, Hannah said, "Bob, sounds like you're not keen to take the ranger's advice. Headaches are one of the first signs of altitude sickness. You don't want to ruin your hike by getting sick on the first day or two."

Bob wondered if he was that obvious or she was just very perceptive. He had hoped to take advantage of the easier terrain today and climb over Donohue Pass. The trail would only get rougher and higher as he journeyed south. But he thought about the stakes. He didn't know how many shots he would get at this. Cathy only had one. Since she started at a much lower elevation at Happy Isles, altitude acclimatization was not a big concern of hers. She had crossed Donohue Pass, at 11,000 feet in elevation, on her fifth day versus her first.

"Thanks. You're right. I guess I was a little ambitious. Another day of acclimatization should help."

Hannah said, "And from the videos I've seen, the camping area she suggested has epic views."

* * *

After ten miles of hiking the flat and smooth trail in Lyell Canyon, the switchbacks on the first small climb knocked Bob out of his rhythm. Hannah crept farther ahead; before long, she wasn't visible before the next hairpin turn. She stopped at several of the turns to wait for him, but by the time he caught up with her, she had caught her breath and was ready to go. It didn't seem fair. They had different hiking styles: the slow and steady pace of a senior citizen versus the enthusiastic bursts of youth. However, they would end up at the same destination this afternoon.

The switchbacks led to a bridge over a creek shaded by tall lodgepole pines. The breeze on his eyes was refreshing when he removed the sunglasses he had worn all day.

Hannah stopped in the center of the wide wooden bridge. "This must be the Lyell Fork bridge."

Bob checked the map on his phone. "Yep, you're right."

She looked left and right. "The ranger said we'd find camping sites here, but I don't see any. Plus, it's a bit dark and creepy here."

Bob joined her on the bridge. "I think the spot she referred to is closer to the tree line, maybe another mile ahead. That will make eleven miles for the day, not bad for an old man." Bob winked. Hannah shoved him gently, causing him to lose his balance and almost fall into the creek. She grabbed his arm with one hand and put the other over her mouth to hide her giggle. They both walked forward to solid ground.

"I'm glad you talked me into stopping before Donohue Pass. My headache is worse now that my heart rate is up. And this little climb is just a teaser for the main push up Donohue Pass."

"Do you need a break, or should we finish this off?"

To save his breath, he pointed ahead with his hiking pole, and they continued hiking. After a brief reprieve of a flatter and softer trail, the climb resumed. Hannah must have been anticipating the view, because she stopped less often to wait for him. She was out of sight when he heard her shout, "Wow! Bob, you have to see this!" Hannah's enthusiasm encouraged him to concentrate on breathing deeply so he could increase his pace. So what if he overexerted himself for a while; the end of the day's hike was near.

Hannah didn't move when he joined her. The mountains and glaciers straight ahead stopped him from slumping against his hiking poles. Emerging from the dense forest into wide open space seemed to make it easier to breathe. The light green grasses surrounding the creek provided a beautiful contrast with the grayish white granite boulders and ledges. After staring ahead for several minutes, he regained control of his body and let his hiking poles fall to the ground while retrieving his phone for photos. He had already learned that the poles would fall no matter how he leaned them against his body. Even a panorama shot couldn't capture the full extent of his view. He also photographed a smiling Hannah against the stunning backdrop—a far cry from the terrified young lady he sat next to before dawn.

They didn't see any campsites nearby, so they walked toward a small clump of trees in the middle of a meadow along a faint footpath, or social trail, usually a good sign of a campsite or a viewpoint ahead. As they approached the trees, Bob saw room for three or four tents, and Hannah said, "This is perfect."

She trotted over to one of the flat spots and set her pack down. "I'll take this one."

Though campsites were identified by signs the previous night, they could camp nearly anywhere for the rest of the hike, as long as the sites complied with wilderness regulations and were safe and comfortable. For the most part, campsites needed to be at least 100 feet from water and the trail and not disturb any of the fragile vegetation. Nearly all hikers preferred sites that were flat and reasonably close to water, with no dead timber overhead. Some preferred shade over sun. Some preferred privacy over the company of others.

Bob dropped his pack thirty feet away and wiped his brow with his sleeve. "I'm glad we started early this morning. I bet this site would be taken if we had left an hour later."

Bob set up his tent and changed into his shorts and sandals. He walked to the creek and soaked his aching feet in the icy water, which had been part of a glacier less than a day ago. He even rinsed the socks and underwear he had worn yesterday and his hiking shirt. He never knew when he would have the time, energy, sun, and easy access to water like he had today. He only wished he could soak his head to get rid of his headache.

* * *

A couple of hours later, Bob added some corn chips and taco seasoning to his refried beans, which were now rehydrated. Hannah was making something a little healthier for dinner: couscous, chicken soup mix, dehydrated vegetables, and olive oil. She added boiling water to the mix and placed the plastic bag in an insulating pouch, or cozie, so it would rehydrate quicker.

Bob picked at his dinner. He wasn't as hungry as he should be after eleven miles of hiking, but he knew he needed to finish the meal.

"You don't look very hungry," said Hannah.

"Nope. Another sign of altitude sickness."

"How is your headache?"

Bob closed his eyes tight, then opened them. "Still pounding. Thanks for making me stop. I might have gotten really sick if I had kept going."

Hannah nodded. "It's been nice to have a hiking companion on the first day. Everything is so new." Hannah took a small bite of her dinner and must have been satisfied that it was done because she kept eating.

"How are you feeling?" asked Bob.

"Pretty good. Just sleepy. But no headache, and as you can see, my appetite is good."

"It's nice to be away from the crowded car campgrounds. Should be nice and quiet tonight."

"I hope so." Hannah crossed her fingers.

* * *

Dear Cathy,

Our journey has begun! Hannah and I made it to the head of Lyell Canyon after a bear cut our sleep short at the campground. No one was hurt, but it sure didn't help my raging headache.

Between the headache and trying to catch my breath all night, I didn't sleep very much. I also couldn't finish my dinner tonight. All signs of altitude sickness. I don't remember you having such problems during your hikes. How do I know when it turns from an inconvenience to a danger? Should I turn back in the morning or spend another night here? I'll check back with you in the morning. Maybe all I need is a good night of sleep. I can't let you down again.

The hike through Lyell Canyon was the perfect introduction to the trail, letting my legs become accustomed to walking all day and my shoulders and hips used to carrying an extra thirty-five pounds. But the wall of mountains in front of us is just as intimidating as it is beautiful. I can't believe we have to cross that tomorrow. Marty enjoyed the view while I ate dinner, but even he looked nervous. I thought he would be excited about meeting some other marmots on Donohue Pass.

Hannah hiked with me all day and insisted we camp together tonight. Her fears seem to go beyond bears. You backpacked alone many times. Were you afraid? What worried you the most? Bears, other hikers, getting hurt off the trail? She made me realize how much I let you down. I realize now that it was more than having someone to enjoy the sights with and to split up the chores. If you felt that way, I am deeply sorry. I hope you can provide me with that support, even if it's from a place far away.

Love, Bob

6

It's Only Fair

2022

August 6 - Sacramento, CA

"Dad, have you seen the portable Bluetooth speaker?"

Mark breathed deeply, intentionally delaying his response. His son, Brock, took every opportunity to remind him that this trip was Mark's idea, not his own.

"Dad! Did you hear me?"

"I'll be there in a few minutes. I'm helping Jessica right now." Mark hoped that would hold him off for a minute or two.

What began as a father-son trip to attempt to correct Brock's downward spiraling path to adulthood had turned into a family expedition on a portion of the JMT. Brock's twelve-year-old sister, Jessica, insisted she come along. Mark didn't know if she was motivated by a secret love of nature or was protesting against all the attention Brock received after his brushes with school administrators and the police. Linda, his wife, hated the outdoors, but couldn't bear the thought of waiting for the *Safe at Camp* message every evening, or even worse, no message at all. Perhaps some time together as a family would help bring back the Brock of years ago.

"Go ahead, Dad. Brock won't drop it until someone reacts," said Jessica.

"Brock, where are you?"

"In my room, stupid." Mark winced.

Mark walked into Brock's room. His bed was covered with layers of camping gear, clothes, game systems, shoes, cameras, and items too buried to be identified. Enough stuff to fill two backpacks. "Come on, Brock. What did I tell you about your packing list? You can't carry all that."

"But Dad, I need it all. Don't worry about it."

"You can only take one backpack, so if it won't fit, it won't go. I'm already carrying some gear for the group. I'm not carrying any more of your stuff."

Brock lowered his voice. "I got this. So where is the Bluetooth speaker?"

Mark shook his head. "I don't know, but you don't need it. Other than being heavy, it will disturb other hikers. This is a chance to get away from all that."

Brock rolled his eyes. "Okay. I got that already, but I want to watch my downloaded videos at night. I'll ask Stan if he has one I can borrow."

The conversation ended as most did with Brock these days, with Mark walking away, murmuring things he had said aloud in the past to no avail.

When Mark returned to Jessica's room, Linda was sitting on the bed with one arm wrapped around her shoulders. Tears filled all four eyes. Neither noticed him in the doorway. "Honey, are you sure you want to do this? It's not too late to change your mind," Linda said.

"I'm not changing my mind. It's not fair. I deserve the same opportunities as Brock."

Linda wiped her eyes with her sleeves and stood up, noticing Mark in the doorway. He stepped aside to let her pass, but she tugged on the bottom of his shirt and led him down the hall. "I don't like this for so many reasons. The bears, the dirt—pooing in the woods. That's so gross! And what if Jessica can't handle it? She's so small."

Mark held her hands. "I understand. Remember, this began as a father-son trip, but I heard what she just told you. She has a point, you know. Brock gets a lot more of our attention than she does. I love her determination. She may even teach Brock a thing or two."

She leaned forward, and Mark gave her an extended hug. "Are you sure you can take care of all three of us?"

"Probably not, but we can all lean on each other. Brock and Jessica probably won't want much of our help anyway. So that just leaves you." He grinned, and Linda gently pushed him away and walked away.

Mark walked back to Brock's room. Brock was on the phone, still talking about the Bluetooth speaker. Must be Stan. Brock's physical appearance had changed as much as his behavior during the first two years of high school. His dark brown hair stood straight up on the top of his head, but was shaved short on the sides. The chubby cheeks and fat rolls he had as a baby had returned after being thin for most of his childhood. Unfortunately, he had inherited his dad's body type. They would both likely lose a bit of weight as a side benefit of the hike.

"Brock, be ready to leave at six tomorrow. We have a five-hour drive to the trailhead, then six miles to hike."

7

Kidnapped

2022

Day 2

August 6 - Upper Lyell Crossing to Garnet Lake

Bob continued to move oatmeal around in the plastic bag long after it was fully rehydrated. He raised a half-spoonful to his mouth every few minutes.

"Still not hungry, huh? How's your headache this morning?" asked Hannah.

"My headache is a little better. I think the coffee helped. But I have no appetite." Bob placed his right hand over his stomach.

"Maybe you should hang out here until you feel better. I'll stay with you if you want."

"No. Let's keep going. Like I said, I feel a little better. If I can just get over the pass, it will be mostly downhill to Red's Meadow."

"You need to eat. Donohue Pass is no joke."

"OK. OK." He shoveled three full spoons of oatmeal into his mouth. He gagged after the last one, but held it all down.

An hour later, after packing and repacking their backpacks, they walked across the meadow toward the trail. Things never seemed to fit in the pack like they did at home, but he had plenty of days to practice. Almost immediately, the trail crossed Lyell Fork again. A sturdy bridge had made the lower crossing easy yesterday, but this time they either had to hop across widely spaced rocks or walk through knee deep water rushing around the rocks. Bob wasn't expecting such a challenging water crossing so early on the trail. There was at least one crossing where he would have to walk through the water, but this wasn't supposed to be one of them.

"This water crossing looks tricky," Bob said, as Hannah hopped across from rock to rock.

Hannah turned around once on the trail again. "Piece of cake."

Bob unbuckled the waist belt and chest strap on his backpack. Hannah turned her back to him and started walking down the trail. "Hannah, can you please wait for me?"

She turned around and shrugged her shoulders.

Bob walked across the stream, placing both feet on each rock before moving to the next. Before putting his full weight on his forward foot, he tested the stability of the rock while both hiking poles were planted in the streambed. Once he had both feet on the opposite shoreline, Hannah said, "You OK?"

"Yeah, this one was a lot scarier than the water crossings we made yesterday."

Hannah tilted her head, raised her eyebrows, then pointed to Bob's waist belt. "Why did you unbuckle your straps? That just puts more weight on your shoulders."

"If you fall in the water, your pack can turn into an anchor. If you unbuckle the straps, you'll be able to free yourself more easily."

Hannah tilted her head back. "Oh, I see. But this one really wasn't that bad. Ready to go?" Bob nodded his head up the trail.

The trail crossed water a couple more times in the next thirty minutes. First, a small waterfall landed directly on the trail, getting their shoes and pants wet while they crossed the slippery rocks. Then the trail crossed Lyell

Fork again, but this time the water was shallow and the stepping stones were close together and stable.

After an hour of hiking through the rocky head wall of Lyell Canyon, Bob could finally identify Donohue Pass, only ten to fifteen minutes away. A pass is a trough, or low point, between mountain peaks where hikers can cross over the ridge into an adjacent valley. From their campsite yesterday, many peaks and troughs had been visible, but Donohue Pass was hidden by some hills off to their left. He was grateful that his previous guesses on the location of the pass were wrong, since they all appeared to be at least a thousand feet higher.

When the trail flattened out, Bob put his pack down and removed Marty from the top compartment. He placed Marty on the top edge of a sign indicating entry into the Ansel Adams Wilderness and Inyo National Forest. An adjacent sign indicated their departure from Yosemite National Park. "Hannah, can you take a picture of me and Marty with Lyell Canyon in the background? I can take your picture as well, with or without Marty?"

"Sure, I think he's cute. I don't mind plush animals, only the wild ones." She grinned.

After posing with Marty, Bob took Hannah's phone. While looking at the screen, a marmot darted into the frame and waddled toward his pack. He dared not tell Hannah until after he tapped the shutter button.

After handing her camera back, the marmot scurried away. Hannah noticed it and flinched, but then uttered "Aww" as it stopped a safe distance away.

"Keep an eye on those guys. They're darn cute, but will snatch loose food in an instant or chew a hole in your pack. Fortunately, any sudden movement will cause them to retreat, at least for a while."

Unlike many mountain passes, Donohue Pass was not a sharp point from which you could see both where you came from and where you were going. With the marmot planning a second attack, they both picked up their packs and walked over the desolate, flat top covered with large boulders to locate their path for the next hour. The descent appeared to be gradual and led to what looked like an oversized Japanese rock garden. Small pools were connected by meandering streams and lined with long grass. Stunted trees and granite features of all sizes and shapes dotted the landscape. Bob couldn't imagine anything he would change to improve the view.

"We won't be running out of water for a while," said Hannah.

"That's one of many great features of this trail. How about we eat a snack while admiring the view?"

"You must be feeling better."

"A little bit. You were right about the oatmeal; I really needed that energy. I need to catch up."

"OK. But I'm going to try to call my dad first. I heard cell service is sometimes available here. It may be my last chance until Red's Meadow."

Hannah wandered off to find a level rock to sit on a bit farther from the pass. Bob pulled out his daily food bag and grabbed a pouch of peanut butter and a bag of dried fruit.

A young couple approached from the south, and Bob welcomed them. "Congratulations. How was the climb from that side?"

The young man dropped his pack and breathed deeply. "The climb wasn't too steep, but after all the tougher ones down south, any uphill burns the legs."

"Well, your legs will enjoy the ten miles of flat, smooth trail in Lyell Canyon."

"Yes, we've been looking forward to that for days. We're finishing at Tuolumne Meadows, so this is our last day. Have to get back to work."

His hiking partner added, "There's a wonderful overlook of Thousand Island Lake up ahead. If I were you, I'd take my lunch break there. The view from above is even better than from the shore."

"Thanks for the tip."

* * *

A couple of hours later, Hannah turned around and said, "Bob, let's stop for lunch. I'm starving."

"I'm not very hungry, but sure could use a break from this pack. The couple on Donohue Pass told me about a great overlook of Thousand Island Lake. I was hoping we could stop there. Let's give it another thirty minutes. OK?"

Hannah's shoulders drooped. "OK. I'll take their word for it."

Bob must have misread his map. He thought the overlook mentioned by the young lady on Donohue Pass was only a couple of hours from the pass. He knew they had to cross Island Pass first, but they were descending again after a brief climb. Was that the pass? He hadn't seen a sign. Many backpackers thought Island Pass was a misnomer, given how easy it was, but surely it must be more than that.

A half-mile later, they both veered off the trail to the right, drawn by the vast blue water speckled with rocky islands of all sizes and shapes. "This must be the spot," Bob said.

They continued until their view was unobstructed by the dwarfed trees. Bob grabbed Marty and the food bag out of the top of his pack. Hannah removed several items before pulling out her bear canister. She looked at his food bag for the day and his intact pack and nodded her head. "Good idea. Keep the day's food at the top of your pack. Lesson learned for tomorrow."

While Hannah scraped tuna from a pouch onto a tortilla, Bob placed Marty on a boulder and took a photo with Banner Peak hovering over Thousand Island Lake. The lake's name was a little generous, but the view was impressive nonetheless. Many of the islands barely poked above the waterline. Some would make wonderful campsites if you could just get out there with a backpack–and if it were legal. *They have to take the fun out of everything.* Banner Peak resembled a broad pyramid with the peak lopped off at an angle, leaving a slanted top. Small patches of snow remained in the shaded nooks and crannies.

Hannah broke his trance with a shriek. "Bob, watch out!"

Another bear? Already? Cathy hadn't seen one during her entire hike, and now he and Hannah had encountered two in one day? Hannah pointed toward Marty. "A marmot!" she said.

A real marmot stood on his hind legs, sniffing Marty's face. When Bob tried to shoo the creature away, it grabbed Marty in its mouth and scampered toward the trail. "Come back, you damn marmot. That's not your kid. It belongs to Cathy."

Bob ran after the thief. He knew better than to run on such terrain, but the marmot was fast, despite all of its waddling. Who was he fooling? He would never catch that marmot. It rounded the corner of the trail and was out of sight. The trail was very rocky, so Bob stopped. Getting Marty back wasn't worth breaking his ankle. He returned to his pack, cursing himself for being so careless. He wondered if Cathy would be angry or amused.

What little appetite he had before was gone, but he vented his anger by chewing on a sausage stick. He thought Hannah was saying something, but he wasn't in the mood to talk. He heard it again, but the voice was deeper than hers. Two guys were walking toward them, one with a small, plush animal dangling from the tips of his fingers. "Is this yours? A marmot was running toward us on the trail. When we didn't stop, it dropped this and ran into a pile of rocks."

Bob leaped up. "Yes! It's mine. Or actually it's my wife's. Thank you so much." He grabbed the soggy plush with his fingertips and scrunched his nose. "Ooh. Marmot spit." One of many reasons hikers bump fists instead of shaking hands.

"I thought it was a baby marmot at first, but then realized it was a toy. Glad I was at the right place at the right time. Have a good hike."

Ten minutes later, Hannah asked, "Bob, why is Marty so special to you? And who's Cathy?"

"Cathy was my wife. She died on this trail last summer. She often hiked alone because I was always too busy with work. I should have been there." Bob sniffled.

"Oh, Bob. Sorry to hear about your wife."

"She loved marmots, so I scoured the internet to find one for her to take on the JMT. Marty helps keep her memory alive. I can't lose him." Bob wiped his nose on his shirt sleeve.

"Thanks for sharing, Bob. I sensed this might not be an ordinary hike for you."

"And it sounds like it's not for you either."

Hannah stared at her feet. "Nope. I didn't really want to hike solo, but I have to prove to myself that I can. I was really hurt when neither my ex-boyfriend nor my dad thought I could. Then, I started to doubt myself. I guess we both have ulterior motives out here."

"You can do it. Feel free to hike ahead of me whenever you're ready. It's been nice being able to look after each other for the first couple of days."

They both stared at the lake for a few minutes, then Hannah asked, "Can we camp down by the lake tonight?"

"We could. It's beautiful, but if I stop this early, I'll never make it to Red's Meadow tomorrow. I planned to camp at Garnet Lake tonight."

Hannah didn't respond. She must really want to camp here, but perhaps she's worried about being alone. He said, "Hey, don't worry about me. If you want to camp there, do it. It's a popular place, so you won't be alone."

"Are you sure you'll be OK—with the altitude and everything?"

Bob nodded.

"OK. I'll do that. I'm really looking forward to a shower at Red's, so I'll probably catch up with you tomorrow. How far is Red's from there?"

"Garnet is fourteen miles from Red's, so I'd say about sixteen miles."

"Ooh. Long day, but I think I can do it."

A few minutes later, Hannah walked across the trail into the trees without saying a word. Her pack still rested against the rock where she had been sitting. Bob figured she wanted to use the bathroom before getting back on the trail. He removed a rounded river rock, about three inches in diameter, from one of his pack's hip belt pockets. Bob carried two such rocks in his pack, and four others were in his MTR resupply bucket. Each was hand painted with a scene from the trail, scenes representing Cathy's most anticipated sights. The weight they added to his pack was a small price to pay for giving Cathy the opportunity to enjoy those sights forever. The first rock was painted with the view he had now. A perfect place to leave her first memorial rock. He scrambled down the steep, rocky slope below the viewpoint and found a pile of boulders. He slid the rock into one of the many gaps between them. The rock wasn't far from the trail, but he doubted anyone would come down here with such a wonderful and easily accessible viewpoint just above.

When he and Hannah reached the shoreline about thirty minutes later, they both filtered water. Though the water was clear enough to see every rock on the bottom, he knew it might contain microorganisms that could create havoc in his gut, severe enough to end his hike. After all, the wilderness was home to lots of wildlife that didn't follow all the rules about where to use the bathroom. All but the boldest hikers used a filter or chemical treatment as a precaution. The cold filtered water was refreshing and had none of the residual chlorine taste of his tap water at home. Bob used a two-liter plastic bag to gather the water and squeezed it through a small filter into a water bottle. The entire process took only a few minutes, a small price to pay for not getting sick.

He then took Marty out of the outer mesh pocket of his pack and dunked him in the lake a few times, squeezing out the marmot spit and water after each dunk. Bob held Marty in front of his face. "OK, Marty. I guess you can ride up top while you dry off. Don't jump off on the way to Garnet Lake."

Hannah giggled. "I'm going to find a campsite. I think most of the camping is over there." She pointed to the right with one of her hiking poles. "See you tomorrow."

"OK. Enjoy your evening at the lake."

* * *

Glimpses of Garnet Lake teased Bob through the trees to his right, but the blue water was far below the trail. His legs had pleaded for him to stop a mile ago; only his willpower kept him moving. The terrain between the trail and the lake was steep and rocky. If he didn't find a campsite soon, he'd either have to backtrack and walk down a social trail to the northwest corner of the lake or take a chance of finding a campsite on the other side of the lake.

The trail climbed toward a sharp turn to the left, worrying him even more about finding a tent site. He heard squeals and splashing in the water below, so he stopped and looked through the trees. His spirits rose and his legs rejoiced when he saw a flat rock shelf next to the lake. A young couple was leaving the water and wrapping their arms around their torsos. They quickly dried off with small camp towels and put their hiking clothes back on over their wet underwear. Only one tent was set up, but he saw room for at least two more. It would be close quarters, but his sore feet overcame any hesitancy to ask the couple about being neighbors for the night.

He was puzzled for a minute about how to get down there, but then noticed a faint trail heading in the right direction. As he slid down the steep, sandy trail, he noticed a small flat spot above the rock bench. The dense branches of a small tree would protect his tent from any wind that might develop overnight. When he reached the shelf, he realized how fortunate he was. Mt. Ritter and Banner Peak stared at him over the long lake. Most of the small islands he had seen from the trail were not visible from here, but a large one covered with trees sat under the iconic peaks. He couldn't see the bridge crossing the lake's outlet to the left, but he could just make out the trail climbing the steep ridge across the lake. A perfect home for the night.

The couple huddled together, facing the lake, and must not have heard him approach over the ripples of water hitting the rocky shoreline.

"Excuse me," Bob said.

Both of them jumped, then turned around.

"Oh. Hi. You surprised us," the woman said.

"What a great campsite!"

"It sure is. We're looking forward to a fabulous sunset and sunrise."

"Do you mind if I camp here as well? Looks like it might be the last campsite before the bridge. I noticed a small spot under a tree on the way down, so I won't be right next to you."

"No problem," she said. "We're going NOBO, so we know how frustrating it can be to find a good campsite when your feet have had enough for the day."

"Thanks a lot. I'll be a quiet neighbor, I promise. I wouldn't have even noticed this spot if I hadn't heard you two splashing in the water."

The guy said, "The water was freezing, but we were tired of being dirty."

"OK, thanks." Bob walked back up the slope.

About an hour later, the three of them sat on rocks near the shoreline enjoying their dinners. Bob's appetite was returning after descending 1500 feet from Donohue Pass. His neighbors for the night were Jerry and Cindy. Bob was impressed with their endurance; they had been averaging over fifteen miles per day. They shared a tip about Devil's Postpile near Red's Meadow. If he stayed on the official JMT, he would only see the National Monument from a distance and then have to backtrack to Red's Meadow after gaining a couple hundred feet of unnecessary elevation. Two SOBOs had made that mistake and shared it with them last night over dinner.

Just as they were finishing dinner, another hiker stumbled down the hill and slid down the final five feet on his rear end. "Whoa!"

Jerry stood up and headed his way. "Are you OK?"

"Yeah. I think so. That's not much of a trail." He unhooked his waist belt and chest strap and wiggled out of his pack instead of trying to stand up with it on. He opened his backpack and threw his tent body down ten feet from Jerry and Cindy's tent. Jerry looked toward Bob and Cindy, who both shrugged their shoulders.

The man appeared to be in his forties. His hair was long and scraggly. Bob had the impression it would be that way whether or not the man was backpacking. His cargo shorts had duct tape over the bottom of his stuffed pockets. His shirt had a hole on top of one shoulder and was covered in dark stains. *Does this guy ever wash his clothes?* He should only be a few days from laundry, regardless of which direction he was traveling.

Jerry held his hand out. "My name is Jerry."

The newcomer said, "I'm Nick," without looking up. Jerry walked back to sit next to Bob and Cindy.

Twenty minutes later, Nick joined them along the shore with his cooking and water filtering gear, but no food. "Do any of you have a dinner to spare?"

Jerry and Cindy looked at each other and raised their eyebrows. Bob turned his head toward Nick, but didn't reply. Jerry finally said, "You don't have anything left?"

"Just a few snacks. I'll go through the leftovers in the hiker buckets at Red's tomorrow."

Since most backpackers over-pack food, most of the resupply vendors dedicated buckets or boxes to collect the surplus for those who were short or wanted a change of taste.

Bob said, "I'm stopping at Red's tomorrow for my resupply, and I have an extra dinner." He walked up the hill to his bear canister and returned with a plastic bag containing instant polenta and a small pouch of bacon pieces. He handed both to Nick.

"What's this?"

"Instant polenta with some parmesan cheese and powdered milk mixed in. You can add the bacon bits if you want."

"Polenta?" Nick scrunched his nose and looked at Jerry and Cindy. "What about you two?"

Jerry responded immediately this time. "Sorry. We're heading north and donated our extras at Red's yesterday." He stood up and held his hand out to Cindy to help her up. They walked to their tent and began organizing their gear for bedtime.

"I guess this will do." Nick leaned over to fill a bag with water. Bob quietly made his exit up the hill.

* * *

Dear Cathy,

You won't believe this. I almost lost Marty today—to an actual marmot of all things. Perhaps it thought Marty was its long-lost son. During my brief but hopeless chase, I had two thoughts—don't break a leg and how will I tell Cathy. All was well in the end. I wish I could blame the incident on his wandering off, but it was just my carelessness. I promise I'll take better care of him for the rest of the trip. He's the most tangible reminder I have left of your love of hiking.

Fortunately, I am finally getting acclimatized to the altitude. My headache is almost gone, and I ate most of my dinner tonight. I am so grateful to Hannah and the park ranger for encouraging me to scrap my plans for climbing Donohue Pass yesterday. Did you play a role in that? I guess I am more susceptible to altitude sickness than you were. They say it affects people differently, and one never really knows how their body will react until they get there. Lesson learned for next time.

Other than the Marty incident, our lunch break overlooking Thousand Island Lake was splendid. I left your first memorial rock at the overlook so you can see the lake forever. I remember you telling me how much you loved camping there when you called from Red's Meadow. I think you can even see your campsite from there.

Hannah decided to camp at Thousand Island Lake, but I continued on to Garnet Lake so I could more easily make it to Red's tomorrow. It is just as breathtaking, but you already know that. A rude hiker joined me and another couple at a wonderful campsite overlooking the lake and made us feel very uncomfortable. I hope you didn't run into any such characters while you were all alone.

Love, Bob

8

Basking

2021

July 19 - Upper Lyell Crossing to Thousand Island Lake

Cathy left her campsite near the upper crossing of Lyell Fork early so she could arrive at Thousand Island Lake before the best campsites were claimed. Being within a day or two of hiking from the Mammoth Lakes area, thru-hikers and weekend backpackers competed for campsites at the beautiful lake. After eating a snack on Donohue Pass, she switched her phone out of airplane mode to check for cellular service. A couple of hikers she passed yesterday were able to call home from there. When two bars appeared, she called Bob. This would be one of the few opportunities to talk to him during the hike. He surprised her by answering on the first ring.

"Hi Bob."

"Are you OK? I didn't expect to hear from you until you got to Red's."

"Yeah, I'm doing great! I'm on Donohue Pass now. I hope you can hear me over the wind."

"I hear you just fine. How are you holding up?"

"Better now. Climbing out of Yosemite Valley was tough, but yesterday was pretty easy, and I'm getting my trail legs. The scenery is out of this world. Even better than I expected. And people are so helpful. My neighbors last night tipped me off about the cell service up here. I wouldn't have even thought to check."

"That's great. I'm glad you're enjoying yourself. Is all your gear working out? Do you need me to send anything to your resupply points for you?"

"The gear is fine, but this is a lot harder than I expected. The hiking is tough enough, but I have so many chores in camp. It takes forever to set up camp and pack up in the morning. I don't have any time to just sit around and relax."

"It should get easier as you become efficient with your chores."

"How are things at work?"

"Oh, not much has changed. Working more hours since you're not here."

"It's not too late to join me near Red's. I can even take a day or two off in Mammoth if it will help. I really could use your help."

Bob didn't respond right away. She looked at the screen on her phone to check the connection—or maybe someone had walked into his office.

"Bob?"

"Yeah, I'm here. I don't know, Cathy. Let's talk again when you get to Red's. Like I said, things should get easier with more practice."

Cathy was learning on the trail that things would get more difficult instead of easier. She would become more efficient with some tasks, but she could already feel the fatigue building. But clearly, Bob would not change his mind.

"I better get going. I want to get to Thousand Island Lake by early afternoon. Perhaps I'll even go for a swim."

"I'm glad you called. Love you."

* * *

When Cathy arrived at the lake, she stepped on the log bridge over the outlet stream and took a couple of pictures. Marty would have to wait until she got to camp before being set free from her pack. She backtracked to the social trail leading to the north side of the lake. Her quick pace had resulted in a pleasant dilemma. Which of the fabulous sites should she select? Closer to the lake for easier access to water? Higher up the hill for more privacy and a better view? Or sheltered from the wind behind trees or boulders? She found one meeting the latter two criteria and set up her tent.

She then headed straight for the water to clean up before the crowds arrived. They didn't need to see her wrinkled, pale skin. She stripped down to her underwear and let herself squeal as she dipped herself in the frigid water without fear of disturbing others or attracting curious eyes. She rinsed the socks and underwear she had worn yesterday, then let the intense sun dry her skin and wet clothes. Her hiking shirt and pants could wait for the washer and dryer at Red's Meadow tomorrow.

Banner Peak hovered over the lake. She knew the climb to the top was too technical and strenuous for her to attempt, but her eyes tried to find a route anyway. The view from the summit must be spectacular. From there, perhaps she could identify more islands than the two-hundred or so she had counted at lunch overlooking the lake.

After thirty minutes, her underwear was dry and her skin was on fire, so she put her hiking clothes back on. She discovered a cereal bar in her pants pocket while putting them on. While she nibbled on it, she watched a few trout swimming ten feet away, searching for insects on the surface. They were probably even hungrier than she was, so she tossed little pieces of the bar in the water. The water rippled as they snatched the pieces from the surface. The largest fish was eating more than its fair share, so Cathy tossed the last pieces toward the smaller, more timid fish.

As she walked back to her tent an hour later, she passed two tents which had been set up since she had arrived and saw a solo hiker and a young couple searching for their perfect campsites. The area would only become more crowded, but she had already enjoyed the shoreline in peace. A nap was next on the agenda, followed by dinner. Who knew, maybe one of the new arrivals would provide pleasant dinner conversation. Except for Bob's unwillingness to come and help, the day had been perfect.

Message from Cathy: *Wonderful afternoon at Thousand Island Lake. Believe it or not, much more beautiful than the photos. You would love it. Please reconsider.*

9

Roomate

2022

Day 3

August 7 - Garnet Lake to Red's Meadow

Bob slowly unzipped his tent and looked down at the rock shelf. Jerry and Cindy were already gone. They must have packed during his only deep sleep of the night, right before he woke up for good. He was grateful he had discovered this tent site above the rock bench. Even though Jerry, Cindy, and he had retired to their tents before Nick finished his dinner, Nick interrupted them with many nuisance requests and talked to himself while getting ready for bed. Being only a few feet away, Jerry and Cindy took the brunt of the abuse. Bob had heard Nick asking for hand sanitizer and batteries for his headlamp. Jerry and Cindy ignored him, which made him talk to himself even more. Several times during the night, Nick interrupted Bob's attempts to fall asleep by yelling, "Did you hear that?" and, "Is that a bear?" Bob had no intention of eating breakfast with him. Surely, he would ask for some oatmeal or coffee. Instead, he would pack quietly and eat somewhere else in peace.

Hiking the steep and slippery slope back to the main trail was difficult with stiff legs. His calves protested every step until he reached the flatter main trail. In ten minutes, he reached the bridge over the outlet stream. He put his pack down and removed the cooking kit and food he had placed in his side pocket for easy access. Nick would not be allowed to ruin sunrise over Garnet Lake. The pastel colors on Banner Peak and Mt. Ritter changed continuously as the sun rose over the mountains behind him. Their tips appeared to ignite as the first few rays of direct sunlight struck them. Bob didn't take Nick for an early riser, so he should have plenty of time to enjoy his breakfast with a view.

* * *

The shuttle bus from Mammoth Lakes arrived at Red's Meadow Resort after a forty-five-minute ride along a winding mountain road. Red's Meadow Resort provided services for hikers and horseback riders enjoying the many trails in the area. Many JMT hikers sent a resupply package there for pickup during their thru-hike. Mark and his family were starting their hike there, so they wouldn't be using that service.

Brock hopped off the shuttle bus as soon as the driver opened the door. Mark, Jessica, and Linda held the handrail as they stepped down carefully while their shifting backpacks disrupted their balance.

To their left was the general store where hikers could buy treats or replacement gear and pick up their resupply packages. Straight ahead was a building containing showers and a laundry room. Several hikers congregated on a small porch, waiting for an open washer or shower and charging their phones and power banks from a single electrical outlet. On the right was the grill.

Mark spotted the bathrooms in the distance between the shower house and grill. "OK. Let's hit the bathroom, then the trail. Remember, no more indoor toilets for twelve days."

Jessica rolled her eyes. "Come on, Dad. How many times are you going to remind us?"

They walked four-wide toward the bathrooms. Brock veered to the left toward the general store. Mark stopped and shook his head. "Brock, the bathrooms are over here. You couldn't fit another tube of chapstick in your pack. Let's go." Linda and Jessica continued toward the bathrooms.

"But I never found a Bluetooth speaker. They might have one here."

"I doubt it."

Brock grunted and sat at a picnic table as Mark continued walking toward the bathrooms.

* * *

Brock walked alone out front. Mark stopped to wait for Linda who was struggling up the hill. Jessica kept her company. Jessica's two brown pigtails dangled below her pink, wide-brimmed hat. Her legs, sticking out of her khaki shorts, were barely thicker than her hiking poles. Her pack and shirt were both royal blue, making it hard to tell where one ended and the other began. The backpack covered over half of her height and must weigh almost half her body weight. Mark cringed when he watched her put it on at Red's Meadow. He tried to help her, but she insisted on putting it on herself. Jessica looked much more like her slim and fit mother versus his pudgy self. Linda wore long black pants, instead of shorts, and a lime green sun hoodie. She was just old enough to notice what damage the sun could do to her skin. Though she exercised regularly, she hated the outdoors, like Brock.

They were hiking uphill in the sun through a forest of blackened tree stumps and young firs and pines. Mark was expecting the first retort from Brock—something like, "You brought us all the way out here for this! We have better views at home." But instead, it came from a winded Linda. "Where are all the beautiful sights you've been telling me about? I just see a bunch of dead trees."

"It will get a lot better tomorrow. I think a fire and windstorm cleared out this area a long time ago. Looks like we'll be in the shade soon." Jessica pointed to the intact forest on the mountainside in front of them.

"We have to climb that?" Linda dropped her chin.

"Yeah, but we only have six miles today, so it shouldn't be too bad," said Mark.

"Don't all the little fir trees remind you of Christmas?" asked Jessica.

Linda wiped her forehead with her sleeve and reached for her water bottle. "Not when I'm sweating my butt off hiking uphill in the sun."

"Come on, Mom. Let's go. You'll feel better when we get to camp." Jessica nudged her mother forward by pushing on her backpack.

After the trail flattened in another sunny section, Mark stopped when he caught up with Brock. When Linda and Jessica joined them, Mark pointed to the right. "Look. Those must be Red Cones."

"Cool. They look like small volcanos. Is there a trail to the top?" asked Brock.

Mark was surprised by Brock's enthusiasm. Brock was upset earlier when Mark told him to turn off the music blaring from his phone. The loud music was irritating him and other hikers passing them. He sympathized with the exasperation on their faces. Mark asked him to stop three times, but it took Jessica pointing out the piercing stares of approaching hikers to convince Brock to stop.

"I don't believe there's an actual trail, but I see some sort of path." Mark pulled out his phone to check the map.

"Can we go to the top of the cone?" Brock asked.

Mark didn't want to spoil the only positive vibe of the day, so he said, "OK, but I'm not going. Our first campsite is about three miles ahead, and I want plenty of time to set up."

He looked at Jessica and Linda. Before he could even ask, Linda said, "Are you kidding?"

Jessica hesitated before saying, "I'll go with Mom and Dad." Mark wondered if she was tired of walking or being around her obnoxious brother.

Brock hurried ahead. As he cut off the main trail, Linda said, "Be careful."

A minute later, the music resumed. Mark looked at Jessica, and they shook their heads in unison.

Jessica said, "Well. At least he won't surprise any bears with all the noise," and they both laughed.

"Bears? You think there are bears?" Linda asked.

Mark said, "Probably not, but they're usually only a problem if you surprise them or get between a mama and her cubs. Brock won't be surprising anybody or anything."

* * *

Three hours later, Mark sat on a log soaking his feet in the babbling Deer Creek, a short walk from their campsite shaded by lodgepole pines. He hoped the therapeutic benefit outweighed the sharp pain caused by the frigid water. He could only tolerate a couple of minutes at a time. Jessica and Linda were resting in their tent. Setting up camp on their first day seemed to take forever, even with Jessica helping to set up his tent after she put up hers in just a few minutes. She also had filtered enough water for everybody's dinner.

However, all was not well; Brock should have arrived an hour ago. Mark's first instinct was to hike back up the trail, but he was reluctant to leave Linda and Jessica alone on the first night of the trip.

Thirty minutes later, his resolve weakened. The climb to the summit of the cone could not have been long, maybe half a mile. Mark assessed the possibilities. He might be injured, lost, fighting with other hikers, or just being inconsiderate. The way Brock had been acting lately, the last two were the most likely, but could he count on that?

Mark sat next to Jessica and Linda's tent. "Brock should have been back by now. Should I go look for him?"

Linda shrugged her shoulders as she yawned.

Jessica rolled over. "Come on. He's just goofing around as usual."

"I know, but he could be hurt or lost. Or fighting with other hikers over that damn music."

"Well, you can go, but I'm staying here with Mom."

"Give him a few more minutes. He seemed pretty excited about going up there," Linda said.

"OK. I'm probably overreacting."

As Mark stood up and walked away, he heard the tent zipper open. Linda and Jessica left the tent and went over to their bear canisters to select their dinners. Linda was not enjoying her first day, and Mark had to admit he was disappointed in the scenery so far. But he was proud of Jessica. She knew more about the trail than he did and was trying to keep her mother's spirits up. He hoped the scenery improved tomorrow, or the second-guessing would resume.

Once Linda and Jessica selected their backpacker meals for dinner, they sat on a log across from Mark. Linda drank an electrolyte mix. Two male hikers veered off the trail toward them after crossing the bridge. They took off their packs, and one of them said, "Hi there."

"Hi. Where are you headed today?"

"Right here, actually. Shady, lots of water nearby. Mind if we join you?"

Linda and Jessica didn't object, so Mark said, "Fine with us. By the way, did you pass a teenage boy on the trail? Long gray pants, red long sleeve shirt."

The hikers looked at each other, and the one who hadn't spoken yet said, "Oh yeah. The one playing his music out loud? Is he one of yours?"

The other hiker tapped the ground with one of his hiking poles. "We passed him about thirty minutes ago. I asked him to turn the music down, but he just flipped me off. We sped up to escape the noise."

Mark bowed his head. "Yeah, that's him. I'm sorry. I told him how much it bothers other hikers."

"I think we'll move on to the next campsite."

The hikers put their packs back on and hurried away. Mark figured they didn't want another encounter with Brock. Mark looked over at Linda. She glared at him. "Are you sure this was a good idea?"

"I don't know. It's the first day. Let's give it a chance."

Fifteen minutes later, Mark heard music, its volume increasing before stopping.

Brock walked into camp. Mark, Linda, and Jessica stared at him.

"What?" He looked down at his shirt and pants, as if they had all spotted an open fly.

"What took you so long? I was about to head back down the trail to look for you. Two hikers just stopped by and told us you flipped them off."

Brock snorted. "Oh, those party poopers. Who cares?"

Jessica stood up. "I do. You make us all look like jerks. Have you seen how everyone looks at you? Looks at us!" She ran off toward the creek, and Linda followed.

"Brock, people come out here to get away from it all. Just give it a chance."

"Alright, alright, I got it. I won't play my music on the trail anymore, but you can't make me enjoy this hike. This was your idea, not mine. It's not my thing."

"Just give it a shot. Hey, why don't you set up your tent? It's getting close to dinner time."

Brock walked to the far end of the camping area and set down his backpack.

* * *

Hannah glanced at the trail sign for Devils Postpile and kept walking. As expected, she had caught up with Bob well before they got to Red's. This was their longest day so far. The anticipation of eating a fresh meal and cleaning up dulled the aches in his feet and shoulders. Rosalie Lake and Shadow Lake were lovely, and the short stretch of waterfalls along Shadow Creek was invigorating. Except for the steep switchbacks up to Rosalie Lake, the trail had mostly been downhill. He was now at the lowest elevation he would experience on the entire trail, 7,500 feet.

When Bob saw the sign, he stopped and hollered, "Hold on, Hannah!" She backtracked to join him. "We need to be careful here." Bob had heard the trails around Red's Meadow were confusing. "The couple I camped with last night told me to be careful with the trails around Devils Postpile."

"What's that?"

"Some cool rock formation. I want to stop and take a close look."

Bob had looked at his map every evening for a preview of the next day, but hadn't needed it while hiking until now. After looking back and forth between the sign and the map, he pointed to his right. "The official JMT goes that way, but they said we get a better view of Devils Postpile if we go straight. I'm going to take the detour. How about you?"

"The shortest route to a shower." She retraced the steps she had just taken, and Bob followed.

While it didn't rival Garnet Lake in beauty, Devils Postpile was intriguing. Bob stared at the wall of hexagonal rock columns 200 feet high and a foot in diameter. They seemed much too symmetrical to be created by Mother Nature and looked almost alien. But they resulted from volcanic activity, similar to Devils Tower in Wyoming. A massive pile of column fragments sat at the base of the formation. Most of the columns were vertical. However, on the edge of the formation, some curved like downspouts ready to spray hikers with water during the next rainstorm.

Bob looked at the sign marking a trail to the top of the landmark. He turned to Hannah and had just opened his mouth to speak when she said, "Go ahead, but I'll pass. I'll watch your pack and enjoy the view from here." She took off her pack and sat down on one of the column segments, grinning at him. Was he that predictable after only three days?

Bob smiled back and set his pack next to hers. "Thanks. It shouldn't take long." He was only a few steps away when he returned to retrieve Marty.

Without his pack weighing him down, he felt like he was walking on the moon. He was on top before he knew it. The hexagonal shapes were even more evident here, and they resembled a polished tile floor. Only glaciers could have left such a smooth surface. He took small steps to prevent his feet from slipping. When he looked over the edge, Hannah pointed her phone at him, so he posed with Marty held close to his face.

* * *

Upon arriving at Red's Meadow, Bob looked at the small building containing the laundry room and showers. A dozen hikers congregated on the porch. They appeared to be in good spirits, sharing stories from the trail over a cold beer or soft drink and looking forward to being clean, if only for one day. During his long downhill hike, Bob had debated the order in which he should eat, shower, wash clothes, and retrieve his resupply bucket. The trail provided plenty of time for such internal debates. He could charge his electronics later in his cabin; it didn't have a bathroom, but it had electricity.

The wait for the washers and dryers would only get worse, so he took the next available washer. His clothes were filthy, but he had so little that he asked Hannah if she wanted to throw hers in. She tossed her clothes in rather than waiting for an open machine. Then they both hopped in the showers, which operated on five-minute timers. What should have been a soothing experience was more of a race to scrub everything without being left covered in soap when the water stopped.

They enjoyed their first fresh meal in three days while their clothes were drying. His burger and beer almost filled him up; he would top it off with a milkshake when his clothes were dry. Since they each carried only one set of hiking clothes, he wore his sleeping top and shorts, and Hannah wore her rain jacket and rain pants.

Their resupply buckets sat on the ground next to the table. Other hikers were sorting their new food and toiletries on picnic tables or on the ground. He had the luxury of doing so in his cabin later that night. Just as Cathy had done last year, Bob had sent resupply buckets to Red's Meadow, Muir Trail Ranch (or MTR), and the Mt. Williamson Motel and Basecamp in the town of Independence. Red's Meadow Resort and Muir Trail Ranch were a short detour off the trail. The town of Independence required a 15-mile round trip detour over Kearsarge Pass. Unfortunately, his pack would be about seven pounds heavier in the morning.

A couple of solo hikers shared a table with him and Hannah. They were NOBOs taking a day off from hiking. Backpackers called such days 'zeros.' Bob had considered doing the same here at Red's or in nearby Mammoth Lakes, but dismissed the idea since it was only day three. If he had been going NOBO, he would be desperate for a day off to recover for the final stretch to Yosemite.

Bob asked, "Where was your favorite campsite so far?"

Janet said, "Marie Lake, by far. It will be right before Selden Pass for you, maybe three days ahead."

The other hiker, Skeeter, using his trail name, said, "Marie was great, but I preferred Rae Lakes. It was crowded, but I couldn't stop staring at the Painted Lady and Fin Dome." Skeeter showed Bob and Hannah a few photos of Rae Lakes on his phone.

Janet said, "And watch out for Glen Pass afterwards. It's beautiful, but a butt-kicker."

Hannah asked, "Did you stay at the Red's campground last night?"

Janet nodded.

"How was it?"

Janet shrugged. "OK. It's hard to readjust to crowds. I needed the day off, but I'll be glad to return to the wilderness tomorrow."

Skeeter added, "Janet, you left out the most exciting part, the bear! We were forewarned that bear sightings were common with so much food around. Sure enough, around 5 AM, everyone started yelling and banging their pots and spoons. The bear didn't threaten anyone, but took its sweet time walking back into the woods."

Hannah leaned her head back in exasperation. "Not again! He has a friend at the Tuolumne Meadows campground. You might want to pass through instead of staying there."

Bob was curious about something else. "So, Skeeter, how did you get your trail name?" Thru-hikers often gave each other trail names, or nicknames, based on some quirk or unique experience of theirs. Bob knew there must be a story behind Skeeter.

"Janet gave it to me a few days ago. We haven't seen many mosquitos, but if they're around, they'll be on me. I think that's the only reason she hangs out with me." Janet smiled and raised both of her thumbs.

Skeeter stood up. "Speaking of camp, time for us to get back down there. If we don't see you in the morning for breakfast, have a great hike."

Janet and Skeeter weren't ten feet away when Hannah looked at Bob. "Here we go again. Just when I begin to feel more comfortable. Bob, I realize this is getting weird, but can I stay in your cabin tonight? I'll sleep on the floor if

I need to—and reimburse you for half the cost when I get home."

Bob had known this was coming as soon as Janet had uttered the word bear. He was looking forward to the privacy and space to spread out. It was getting odd, but he gave Hannah credit for camping by herself last night and hiking alone for much of the day. He was more relaxed hiking alone, free to stop and start as he pleased, to take a photo or take a piss.

"Hannah, what did that bear experience have in common with our encounter?"

"They were both at campgrounds."

Bob nodded. "Yes, where campers tend to get lax with their food storage. There's a reason we have to lug around those heavy and bulky bear canisters. What else?"

Hannah paused and shrugged her shoulders, then said, "No one was hurt."

"Exactly. They weren't interested in the people, just the food. When everyone got up and made a lot of noise, they wandered off. People get into trouble with bears when they surprise them or get near their cubs."

"Alright. I understand. I'll work on it. But, for tonight, I could really use a soft, clean bed."

"OK. The cabin has bunk beds. You can use the top bunk. Getting down from there in the middle of the night would probably end my hike. I can't promise that I won't snore though." Bob winked.

* * *

The contents of Bob's resupply bucket were spread all over the floor of the cabin. Hannah had not yet opened hers. Instead, she was inspecting her now clean feet. She winced as she squeezed her pinky toe.

"Blisters?" asked Bob.

Hannah nodded. "One on the bottom of each pinky toe. My feet were so dirty, I didn't really notice the blisters until now. They're still pretty small." She grabbed her first aid kit and took out a couple of small bandages.

"Have you ever tried Leukotape?

"What's that?"

"I call it miracle tape. Cathy used it all the time. Here, take a look." Bob tossed a plastic bag to her. "Really flexible and durable, with a strong adhesive. Stays on for days."

"Thanks. Can I use some? These bandages will probably come off by noon."

"You can keep the whole bag." Bob picked up a similar bag. "I packed more in my resupply bucket. Plus, I have some wrapped around one of my hiking poles." He pointed to his hiking poles near the door.

"Thanks. You're so prepared. I feel like an idiot."

"I have Cathy to thank for that tip."

"She sounds so wonderful. Sorry again for your loss." They both looked blankly at the mess on the floor. "I wish I had someone special like that. I thought I had, but then he was gone–just like that." She snapped her fingers.

"Why did he go to Qatar?"

"His name is Zach, and he was an architect. Some consulting firm dangled a bunch of money that he couldn't resist. They have so much construction over there. I have to admit that they build some cool skyscrapers over there. But I had been accepted by Stanford for graduate school in electrical engineering. We didn't even talk about it before he made his decision."

"Sorry Hannah. But you're a smart, courageous, and attractive young lady. You'll find someone before long."

"Thanks, but I don't think it will happen on this trail. I'll be a stinky, dirty mess again by tomorrow night."

* * *

Dear Cathy,

I generally record these notes on my phone at night, but I'm recording this one the following morning from the trail. Hannah stayed in my cabin last night after hearing about bears in Red's campground. I know. I know. She's a big girl and should be able to take care of herself. But every time I see her struggling, I think of your trip. Perhaps helping her is my way of making up for not being there to help you. Maybe if I had been with you, we could have finished the trail together. I don't want her to miss out on Mt. Whitney like you did.

I also thought of you a lot last night. You were here when we had our last conversation by phone. You asked me to join you here, and I refused. How selfish I was. How right you were. If I had only listened. The plant would have survived with or without me; you didn't. It may seem foolish and selfish to hike this trail with you now in spirit. But I have to do this. I hope it helps you somehow, but I need to do so to make peace with you and myself.

My legs feel good, and I no longer have symptoms of altitude sickness. However, I am not sleeping well. I've been exhausted from hiking and comfortable in my tent, so I should fall asleep immediately. But even in a real bed at Red's last night, I struggled. My mind is preoccupied with planning for the next day and wondering what could go wrong. Kind of like work, actually. At some point, total exhaustion should force the issue, or so I hope.

Love, Bob

10

Lost and Found

2021

July 20 -Red's Meadow Resort

Cathy let her backpack slide off her back onto one of the picnic tables between the grill and general store at Red's Meadow Resort. The table wobbled and caused a sip or two of beer to slosh out of the can in front of the lone hiker sitting there.

"Oh, I'm sorry. This table isn't as sturdy as it looks." Cathy carefully set her backpack on the bench and sat next to it.

"It's OK. I did the same thing to the person sitting here before. I'm Anthony." His hands held a messy double cheeseburger, so he just nodded.

"I'm Cathy." She pointed to his beer can. "Did you get that at the store or the restaurant?"

His mouth was full, so he nodded toward the store.

Cathy stood up, smiled at Anthony, and walked to the store. She returned five minutes later with two cans of beer resting on the top of her resupply bucket. She set the bucket on the ground and handed a can to Anthony.

"Thanks. You didn't have to do that."

"I know how much you've been looking forward to every sip, and I cost you a couple."

She popped the top on hers and took a drink while it was at its coldest and fizziest. Mountain stream water was nearly as cold, but didn't have the fizz–or the alcohol. After a few more sips, she turned to unbuckle the top of her backpack so she could remove her dirty clothes. But something was missing. Where's Marty? She rotated the pack on the bench and checked all the pockets. Perhaps she had been lazy and placed him in one of those at the last photo op.

"Oh no. Marty's gone!" Cathy said, then looked under the table. She asked Anthony, "Did anyone mess with my pack while I was gone?"

"No ma'am. I was here the whole time. Who's Marty?"

"It's a stuffed animal, a marmot, actually. I strap him to my pack and take photos with him. He was a gift from my husband, so he's kind of special." Her eyes darted around, looking for Marty on the ground around the table and along the path to the store.

"Do you remember putting him back at the last stop?"

"I don't know. It's become such a routine. The last time I remember taking his photo was at the waterfalls along Shadow Creek."

Cathy tugged on the strap that normally held him in place. "This strap is a little loose. He must have fallen off while I was hiking."

"How far back were those falls?"

She thought about the long, dry descent through the forest and shook her head. "Maybe ten miles."

Anthony pursed his lips and squinted his eyes. "Ooh."

"I've already done sixteen miles today. I can't go back and look for him." She placed her forehead on her hands with her elbows resting on the table.

"Don't worry too much just yet. Maybe somebody picked him up and will put him in a hiker bucket. I'll keep an eye out for him tomorrow. Give me your email address so I can get in touch with you if I find him."

"OK. But if another NOBO or a wild animal picks him up, I'll never get him back."

Three hikers had just arrived and were creating quite a buzz. Cathy had tuned out everyone but Anthony, so she didn't notice them. Anthony stood up and yelled, "Over here!"

Cathy looked up at him. "What are you talking about?"

"That hiker was asking if anyone lost a marmot."

She looked around and nearly everyone was laughing. Of course, no one lost a marmot; they are impossible to catch. Then she saw the approaching hiker with Marty in his hand. She ran over to him and grabbed Marty.

"Oh. Thank you! Where did you find him?"

"Sitting on the trail about three miles back."

"Thank you so much! I thought he was gone for good."

"You're welcome, ma'am. I guess that's no ordinary stuffed animal."

"It's a long story. Why is everyone calling me ma'am?"

The hiker and his two partners looked at each other and shrugged.

"Oh, never mind. My name is Cathy. What is yours?"

"I'm Joseph, and my buddies are Chet and Danny." They acknowledged her with a quick nod.

"Just three of you?"

Joseph nodded.

"Have a seat at the table over there. Three ice cold beers are coming up." She walked toward the store, hugging Marty against her face, mumbling, "Bad marmot. What were you thinking?"

* * *

Cathy stared at her phone as it tried to connect to cellular service. She heard cell service at Red's was hit and miss. When two bars appeared, she smiled and dialed Bob.

"Hi Bob!"

"Hi Cathy. It's so good to hear your voice. Are you at Red's now?"

"Yep. Right on schedule."

"How's it going?"

"Well, it's hard. Much harder than I expected, but the hike is going as planned. No gear failures or trouble with wild animals. Though I had another kind of animal scare today."

"Animal scare?"

"Yeah, Marty was a bad marmot today. I was enjoying a beer after I arrived here, and I noticed he wasn't on top of my backpack. He must have come free while I was hiking."

"What did you do?"

"There wasn't much I could do. I was exhausted after sixteen miles, so I couldn't go looking for him."

"Sixteen miles. Wow! I don't blame you."

"Yeah. I'm beat. Call it luck or trail magic, but a hiker picked him up and brought him to Red's. He showed up twenty minutes after I did."

"Great. Glad that worked out. He has so much more of the trail to see."

"Speaking of scenery. It's been wonderful, and it should get even better. I camped at Thousand Island Lake last night. I had a hard time leaving this morning after such a beautiful sunrise."

"So, what are you struggling with?"

"Uh. Nothing specific, really. Just so many chores and things to keep track of. Plus, I haven't been eating enough—though I'm about to make up for that with a double cheeseburger and a milkshake."

"Most people aren't hungry those first few days, but your hiker hunger should kick in soon."

"Bob."

"Yeah?"

"Will you please reconsider coming out here? Even if just for part of the trail, it would mean so much to me. I don't know if I can finish without you." Cathy sniffled. She held the phone farther from her face so Bob wouldn't notice.

"Oh, Cathy. Of course you can finish. You must be the most prepared person out there."

"But that only gets me so far. It's really hard."

"I don't know. The plant restart has become more complicated than originally thought."

"Hell with that. I need your help! The Piute Pass junction is about four days away, and Bishop Pass is another day or two after that. You should be able to get a walk-up permit for one person."

"OK, OK. Let me check with my team in the morning, as well as the flights and permits. I'll try my best, but can't promise anything. I'll send a message to your satellite device with the plan. OK?"

"Thanks, but please don't let work get in the way. I really want to finish this trail, and I need your help."

"Sure. I promise."

"Thanks. I need to get my laundry going and do some carbo-loading. I'll keep sending you messages every day, except tonight, of course."

"Alright. Have a good night at Red's and be careful on the trail. Try to do a short day tomorrow. Sixteen miles is enough to make most people second-guess themselves."

11

Fetch

2022

Day 4

August 8 - Red's Meadow to Lake Virginia

Bob checked his watch for the fifth time, and it was finally past five o'clock. Early at home, but not on the trail. The hard walls and soft bed of the cabin did nothing to help him sleep better. He couldn't blame Hannah, because she had barely moved all night. He was still tired, but he knew he wouldn't be able to get back to sleep. If Hannah wasn't in the room, he would have left his bed earlier and might be hiking with his headlamp by now. He felt silly donning his headlamp indoors, but he didn't want to wake Hannah with the harsh overhead light. However, as soon as he began shuffling through his bear canister, he heard a soft greeting, "Good Morning."

"Sorry to wake you, but I couldn't sleep. Might as well start early."

"No problem. It's your cabin, after all." She yawned and stretched her arms up to the ceiling, touching it with her fingernails. "I slept like a rock last night and was about to get up anyway. Aren't you eating breakfast at the grill?"

"You weren't the one keeping me up; I'm just a worrywart. I think I'll eat some of my leftover food for breakfast. Otherwise, I'll end up throwing it in the hiker buckets."

Hannah was surprised and paused. "I'm gonna wait. This will be the last chance for a fresh meal for about ten days."

"I have extra coffee. Why don't I make you a cup while I'm fixing mine? The grill doesn't open for almost two hours."

"Sounds great. Maybe I'll have a little snack too. Hiker hunger is kicking in." She climbed down from the top bunk. The tiny steps made it difficult, and she bumped her head on the ceiling while trying to put her first foot on the ladder.

"Where are you planning to camp tonight?" asked Hannah.

"I'm gonna try to make it to Lake Virginia. I'll be slow today after the long day yesterday, so I'm sure you'll zoom by me at some point."

"Don't be so sure about that. I hiked farther than you did yesterday. If I make it that far, I'll look for you."

* * *

Mark tapped Jessica on the shoulder, placed his index finger over his lips, and pointed to the left. She looked up and quietly gasped at a doe staring at them while her two fawns tore their breakfast from the ground. How fitting for a campsite near Deer Creek. She placed her Pop-Tart on her lap and slipped the phone out of her pocket. The fawns looked for the source of the noise, but resumed nibbling when their mother did not move. Mark sensed motion off to his right. Brock stood by his tent with his arm cocked and a rock in his hand.

"Brock, stop it." said Mark, but it was too late. The rock landed six feet from the doe. All three deer hopped out of sight within seconds. Jessica ran to Brock and slapped his shoulders repeatedly, yelling, "Why? Why? Why? You're such a jerk! Those deer weren't bothering anybody. They were just having breakfast like us."

"They're just deer!" he yelled back.

Jessica stood her ground and now waved a finger at her brother. "I hope a bear jumps on your tent tonight." She stormed back to where she had been sitting.

Linda, who had followed Jessica over to Brock, said, "What's gotten into you? That was just mean."

Brock ducked inside his tent. Linda walked over to Jessica and put her arm around her. She looked at Mark. "I don't think your plan is working."

Mark had hoped this adventure would bring back the old Brock. It now appeared that more than a stroll through the mountains was needed. Being around Brock so much during the last couple of days highlighted how much Brock had changed. In junior high, Brock had wonderful friends and was a well-behaved teenager. Due to redistricting by the school board, he lost touch with many of them. Brock made new friends and adjusted his behaviors to gain their acceptance. Unfortunately, those behaviors led to declining grades and a couple of suspensions at school, one for fighting, another for trying to cheat on an exam. The more Mark and Linda intervened, the closer he got to his troublemaking friends.

Mark now wondered whether this trip had been a mistake. Linda thought so from the beginning. He was not as prepared as he should have been. But he was proud of Jessica. She was determined to make this trip a success—and he liked the way she stood up to Brock. Maybe she would be the one to get through to Brock.

After Brock sulked in his tent for ten minutes, he packed up and headed down the trail without saying a word. Mark knew he wouldn't listen to anyone in such a state, so he watched Brock walk away and started packing his own gear. The next water source was at Duck Creek, five miles away. Brock hadn't refilled his water bottles in his rush to get away, so he would be desperate for water by then. They should be able to catch up with him there.

* * *

As Mark expected, they caught up with Brock at Duck Creek. He leaned against a rock, with his head back and face covered with his hat.

"Hey Brock. Are you OK?" asked Linda.

Brock sat up, and his hat fell to the ground. "Yeah, I'm fine. I drank a lot of water and ate a snack, so it's hard to get moving again."

"Good. Why don't you wait for us to eat a quick snack, then we can all leave together?" said Mark.

Brock shrugged his shoulders. "OK"

Ten minutes later, Brock led them up the steep trail leaving the creek. Mark followed, with Linda and Jessica beginning to fall behind already. Mark saw a group of five ahead, all dressed in green pants and brown long sleeve shirts. They also wore hard hats of varying colors. Not your typical backpacking outfits. Two of them were swinging picks to loosen dirt on the trail. Another was prying rocks out of the ground. The other two were sawing a fallen log off to the side of the trail. Buckets, sledgehammers, and heavy iron stakes lay to the side, along with five day packs. They all looked up as Brock walked around them without pausing.

Mark stopped on the trail before he reached them. "Hey Brock, hold up."

Brock stopped. "Why?"

"Please. Hold on a minute," said Mark.

All five of the trail workers appeared to be just a bit older than Brock. Three men and two women. One of the women looked at Mark. "We'll be out of your way in a minute. Let me finish getting this rock out of the ground first." The two who were chipping away at the trail had already moved to the side.

"Take your time. You're working harder than we are."

Linda took off her pack, and Jessica stepped up to Mark's side.

Mark said, "Looks like you're putting in some steps here. Good idea."

"Yeah. The water runs straight down this part of the trail when it rains, so we'll be diverting it to the side as well."

Mark nodded. "We appreciate you making things easier for us. The trail is a little rough in spots, but overall, it's in fantastic condition."

"Thanks for that. A lot of people take the trail for granted. It doesn't take care of itself."

The entire crew turned around when Brock asked, "How long do you work out here? Just for the weekend?"

The trail workers smiled at each other, and two of them snickered. "We're out here all summer."

Brock raised his eyebrows. "All summer! You're kidding, right?"

Another of the crew replied, "Nope. Work all day, walk to camp, rest, and repeat."

Brock shook his head. "I don't know how you do it. I can barely get through each day just walking."

"It's tough all right, but look where we get to work." She pointed to the peaks above Duck Creek.

Linda opened her pack and shuffled things around. Jessica smiled during the entire exchange.

One of the young men said, "We get a day off every once in a while to explore wonderful new places." He looked at Mark. "And it means a lot when hikers like yourself recognize our work."

Brock said, "I think you're all crazy, but thanks for making our hiking easier. It's hard enough already, even when the trail is perfect."

Linda stepped past Mark and Jessica and handed the closest worker a couple of bags of Peanut M&M's. "We only have two, but maybe you can share. Thanks, again."

"You're welcome, and thanks for these. The toll has been paid, so you can pass now." He smiled and waved them through. Mark looked at Brock; he was smiling too.

* * *

Bob arrived at Duck Creek by mid-afternoon. He had just completed one of the longest stretches on the trail without a water source, so his first priority was to drink a bottle of water. He squatted on a large rock on the shore to fill his water bag. The current nearly ripped it out of his hand, and his heart skipped a beat. If he lost or punctured the bag, he would have to use one of his water bottles for dirty water. Contingency plans were just as important on the trail as they were at the plant.

While relaxing on the shore, he observed the log bridge over the creek. The bridge over Deer Creek had been wide and flat, with little risk of falling off. However, this bridge was so narrow that his hiking poles would not provide much stability. No one else was around; if he fell, he could be in trouble. Surely someone would arrive soon. He enjoyed a pack of cheese crackers with his ice cold water while he waited.

About twenty minutes later, a solo NOBO hiker rushed down the trail. Bob stood and donned his pack, leaving the waist belt unbuckled, but he wasn't fast enough to beat the NOBO hiker across the bridge. The other hiker nodded and continued at his blistering pace.

"Excuse me."

The other hiker stopped and turned around. "Yes." He seemed irritated that Bob had interrupted his pace.

"I came from that way. The next water source is five miles away, so you might want to fill up here."

"Oh really. I've become so spoiled by all the water near the trail, I didn't even check the map this morning. Thanks!" He walked back to the creek and removed his pack. He used a different approach to filtering water–attaching the filter to the top of his bottle; the water was cleaned as he drank it.

"Where are you stopping tonight?" Bob asked.

"I'm trying to make it to Red's before the grill closes. That's why I rushed by you. Sorry about that. I'm glad you stopped me."

"Well, just think of hamburgers and milkshakes when your legs start screaming." The hiker grinned and nodded.

"What about you?"

"Trying to make it to Lake Virginia."

"Great choice. I passed by quickly, but it looked like a nice place to spend the night."

Bob noticed he was finished filling his bottles. "Nice talking to you. I better be moving on." Bob walked slowly across the bridge before the other hiker left, bringing his rear foot even with the front one before moving forward. He stabbed the bridge in front of him with the tips of his hiking poles and leaned forward slightly to help with his balance. Once on solid ground, he turned and saw the other hiker had already started down the trail.

* * *

As Bob approached Lake Virginia, a dog greeted him and placed a short, fat stick at his feet. He had never owned a dog, but he knew what that meant. *Please, sir. Can you throw this stick for me?* Far from the welcome he expected at a lake ten miles from the nearest trailhead. Pets were not allowed on much of the trail, so taking a dog on the entire thru-hike was not practical. The dog's fur was rusty brown, except for a white chin and a white patch around one of his eyes. He alternated between wagging his tail vigorously and staring at Bob with a tilted head and cocked ear. Bob looked for the owner and saw a man with jeans and a cowboy hat tending to two mules in the shade of a small cluster of trees.

Bob picked up the slimy stick and looked at the man who must be the dog's owner. The man nodded and pinched the lip of his hat with his thumb and index finger. As Bob cocked his arm, the dog turned around, laid his front legs flat on the ground, and raised his rear end like a sprinter ready to explode from the blocks. He turned his head back toward Bob. *Why haven't you thrown it yet?* When Bob tossed the stick, the dog left Bob's feet in a cloud of dust. The stick was back at his feet before the dust settled. The dog went straight back to the starting position. He must be proud of himself for hooking another hiker.

The man tending the donkeys walked over to Bob. "Good afternoon. You're the fifth best friend Rusty has made since noon. I'll give you two more throws. He'll wear his feet raw on the rocks if you let him, then I'll have to carry him out." Bob raised his eyebrows and nodded. He hadn't even thought of that. Dogs in the city didn't have such problems.

His two throws took less than a minute, then Bob rubbed Rusty's head and began walking around the right side of the lake, where his map showed several campsites. Rusty grabbed the stick and trotted a few steps up the trail, waiting for the next hiker.

Lake Virginia lived up to the hype. The lake hadn't seemed so appealing to him in photos–the surrounding peaks were not tall or unique and the water was crystal clear but not an exotic color. However, there was something about the 360-degree view a camera could not capture. He spun around and whispered, "Wow." Unlike many other lakes on the trail that were confined by massive mountain peaks, this one had a wide-open feel to it. A large meadow led to the lake on one side, and a tree-covered ridge rose only a couple hundred feet on the other. At the far end of the lake, the blue water was separated from the blue sky by only a sliver of white and green created by the distant mountains, giving the appearance of an infinity pool.

He set up camp near the back side of the lake under some trees, about two hundred feet from the water. Because of his early start, he had time to rinse his body and wash his clothes, then allow the sun to warm himself and dry his clothes. He was amazed how fast the filth and stink returned after a shower and laundry. The sun warmed his front; the rock he leaned against warmed his back. If he had a foam sleeping pad to get more comfortable, he was sure he could take a much needed nap. His sleep system consisted of an inflatable air pad and a down-filled sleeping bag. It kept him comfortable and warm during the cold nights, but the air pad wasn't as versatile as the thin foam ones used by some hikers.

He must have dozed off for a few minutes because a familiar but annoying voice startled him.

"Hey, I know you."

"Hi Nick. You must have put in big miles today." Nick was even dirtier than when Bob had last seen him at Garnet Lake. Couldn't he bother to take a shower and wash his clothes at Red's? Actually, his clothes were beyond the help of a washer and dryer. Perhaps he should have gone into Mammoth for some new ones.

"Same as you. Are you camping here?" Nick pointed to a flat, sandy spot ten feet away and only twenty feet from the shoreline.

"No, but it's not even close to one hundred feet from the water."

"Who cares? Looks like others have camped there. Great view, huh?"

Bob had warmed up from his swim and wanted to leave before Nick finished his camp chores and started mooching and ranting again. He had no excuse to ask for a handout tonight, having been at Red's Meadow yesterday.

"Enjoy the campsite. I'm camped up in the trees. I need to do some camp chores."

"You should have taken this spot. Oh well, your loss is my gain."

Bob shook his head as he walked away, carrying his now dry hiking clothes.

After changing back into his hiking clothes in his tent, a couple of his camp neighbors from fifty feet away walked up to him.

"Hi there. I'm Mark, and this is Jessica." Mark wrapped his arm around a girl who appeared to be his daughter.

"Hello, I'm Bob."

Mark and Jessica held two water bags and four one liter bottles between them. "We were going to sit by the lake and eat dinner. Do you want to join us?"

Bob looked at Nick, who had just finished setting up his tent.

"Well, I'd love to join you. But how about we eat over by your tent?" Bob pointed to Nick. "You see the guy down there? He can be a real pain in the butt, mooching for food and complaining about everything."

"Oh. Thanks for the warning. We'll see you in a bit." Mark and Jessica headed toward the lake, veering far from Nick.

Bob had forgotten to filter water while at the lake earlier, so he grabbed his water filtering gear and walked toward Mark and Jessica at the lake. About halfway there, a park ranger approached him.

"Hello, sir."

"Oh, come on. Please don't call me sir. Do you know how old that makes me feel?" Bob smiled. The ranger was young enough to be his son.

The ranger chuckled. "Sorry. It's a habit. Are you with that guy?" He pointed to Nick.

"No, I'm not. I'm camping up in the trees over there." Bob pointed toward his tent.

"OK, no worries for you then, but I need to talk to him about his campsite selection."

"I tried to warn him, but he didn't want to hear it."

"Thanks for trying. Hopefully, this uniform carries a little more weight."

"Good luck." Bob wanted to hear this, so he walked to the water, veering closer to Nick and the approaching ranger.

"Excuse me. Is this your tent?" the ranger asked Nick.

Nick said, "Yeah. Is there a problem?"

"Yes, I'm afraid so. Campsites are supposed to be at least 100 feet from water and trails. Your tent is thirty feet from the lake, at best."

"But people have camped here before. It's not hurting anything or anyone," Nick declared, waving his arms.

"It may seem so to you, but if everyone feels that way, the lake will degrade over time. Please move your tent. I saw several empty sites back in the trees less than 300 feet from here."

"Come on. I just finished setting it up. It will take me another hour to move everything."

"Sorry, that's what you agreed to when you signed your permit."

"You've got to be kidding. This is ridiculous. There are so many rules out here. You take all the fun out of it. Don't you have anything better to do, like search for lost hikers or pick up trash?" Nick yelled.

"Sir." The ranger's tone had changed from friendly, to patient, to firm. "If you don't move now, I will cancel your permit and ask you to leave the wilderness."

Nick threw his water bottle on the ground, then yanked the tent stakes out of the sand.

Bob's water bag was full, and he passed the ranger as he backed away to give Nick some space. The ranger said, "Sorry to create a scene, but this is my job. I'll hang around to make sure he moves his tent to an appropriate location."

Bob said, "Thanks. I understand. You're just doing your job. Like I said, I tried to warn him."

Bob grabbed his dinner and cooking kit from his campsite and walked over to Mark's.

Mark introduced him to Linda and Brock, then asked, "What was all the yelling about?"

"That guy's tent was too close to the water, so the ranger asked him to move. He wasn't happy about it."

Brock said, "What's wrong with that campsite? Looks perfect to me, great view, easy access to water."

Bob continued to watch Brock after he finished speaking. Was he another Nick? What were the odds? Everyone else on the trail seemed so nice and laid back. "The regulations say you need to camp at least 100 feet from water and the trail. Otherwise, it causes erosion and makes it more likely for waste to get in the water."

"Everything's got to be just right out here. No music, no tents close to the water, bear canisters, and on and on. Kind of takes the fun out of it."

Mark squirmed. "Enough about our rude neighbor. So, Bob, where are you from and what do you do?"

"I'm from Houston, Texas, and I retired late last year. I was a safety manager at a chemical plant. What about you?"

Mark said, "We had a much easier time getting here. We're from Sacramento. We started at Red's two days ago. Linda and Jessica are exiting at Bishop Pass, and Brock and I at Kearsarge Pass. We aren't up for the whole JMT yet."

"To tell you the truth. I'm not sure I am either. I started at Tuolumne, and I'm already worn out. I'm having a hard time sleeping. My wife tried to hike it solo last year and didn't finish. It's hard not having the extra support during the tough spells."

Mark turned off his stove. "Alright, everyone. Bring over your dinner bags and I'll add the water. Bob, I should have enough for you, so don't fill your pot just yet."

"Great."

While their meals were rehydrating in their insulated food cozies, Nick finished packing up and moved into the trees. The ranger followed at a distance.

* * *

Dear Cathy,

It seems like we just talked since I recorded last night's message this morning. Lake Virginia has been a pleasant surprise. I wonder what you thought of it. As wonderful as the evening has been, it would be so much better with you here. Jumping in the lake together, taking a nap together, and watching the sunset together. I imagine that you felt the same while you sat on the beach alone.

I added several hikers to my trail family today. The first was a dog, though I suspect he has dozens of trail friends. We played fetch until his owner intervened. What a life for a dog! Water everywhere, an unlimited supply of sticks, marmots to chase, and an endless selection of trees to pee on. He would have loved to meet Marty, but I don't think Marty would have survived the encounter with all of his stuffing intact.

I am camped near a family of four. The son, Brock, seems a little angry, but a nice family overall. Jessica, the young daughter, appears to be the only one who really wants to be out here. I can't imagine being in the shoes of Mark, the father, trying to look after himself and three others. I'm having a hard enough time taking care of myself.

I took my first lake bath. What a way to wake up every nerve in your body! But twenty minutes later, I dozed off leaning against a warm boulder. I hope that means I will sleep well tonight. It is seven o'clock as I record this, and you may notice the pauses as my mind keeps switching off. Time to zip up the sleeping bag and make up for some lost sleep.

Love, Bob

12

Fresh Fish

2021

July 21 - Lake Virginia

Cathy sat on her foam pad on the rocky beach at Lake Virginia, replacing the salt she had lost during the day with an electrolyte drink and roasted nuts. The sun warmed her back, but a slight breeze cooled her face. The small ripples on the water flickered in the sun and were occasionally disrupted by hungry fish.

A man with a fishing pole resting on his shoulder approached her. "It's going to be a beautiful sunset, isn't it?" He glanced at her, then looked at the ridge across the lake.

Cathy looked at him and shielded her eyes. "Yes, indeed."

"Have you seen any fish jumping?"

"I wouldn't call it jumping, but I've seen quite a few breaking up the ripples on the surface."

"Mind if I try my luck near here? My name is Brett, by the way."

"I'm Cathy. Go right ahead."

Brett walked forty feet down the shoreline and another five feet into the shallow water. He flicked the line back and forth until the artificial fly settled on the water just right. He yanked the pole back within seconds, and the tip bent over as he reeled in the line.

"That was quick," said Cathy.

Brett continued reeling as he replied, "Yeah, I've heard the fishing here is excellent."

When the line was almost vertical, he lifted the pole, and a six-inch fish flopped in the air. Its golden skin nearly matched the color the setting sun created on the granite peaks to her left. As Brett reached to grab the fish, it spit out the fly and fell into the water.

"Oh no. So close."

"That's OK. He was too small to eat anyway," Brett said, preparing to throw out the line again. "I've also heard there are some big ones in here."

His next attempt snagged a larger one, about fifteen-inches this time. The hook held until the fish was in his hands. "That's what I'm talking about!" He walked onto the beach. "Can you take a picture of me with this beauty?"

"Sure. Where's your phone or camera?"

Brett nodded to a log lying ten feet away.

Cathy picked up the phone. "It's locked."

"Oh yeah. The passcode is 123987."

Cathy took a couple of pictures of Brett holding the fish in two hands with the lake in the background. He couldn't have had a bigger smile. The gold fish had eight dark circles, about an inch in diameter, down its side. The top of its body and tail were speckled with black dots. Its mouth and gills opened and closed, begging to be thrown back in the water where it could breathe.

"Now that's a keeper." He pulled a stringer out of his pocket, threaded it through the mouth and gill, and put the fish in the water.

"You're going to eat it?"

"Absolutely. A great way to break up my boring backpacking dinners. Can't get any fresher than this."

He held the pole out toward her. "Do you want to try it?"

"I don't know. Looks kind of complicated to me. I've only fished with a normal rod and reel with a bobber."

"It can be tricky sometimes, but you saw how easy it was here. Give it a try."

"OK. I guess it can't hurt."

He handed her the pole and showed her how to hold it. "Don't worry about all the flicking back and forth. Just toss the fly out there. These guys appear to be starving."

Cathy did as he instructed. The water splashed, and the fly disappeared. "There you go. Reel it in, and I'll grab it." After he grabbed the fish and brought it to her, he said, "Looks a little bigger than mine. Nice job."

"Wow. Such a beautiful fish."

"What kind of fish do you think it is?"

"A golden trout?"

Brett smiled and nodded. "You got it. Would you like some fresh fish for dinner? If not, I'm going to throw it back."

Cathy was torn between releasing the beautiful creature and the unique opportunity for a fresh meal on the trail. Her next fresh meal would be over a week from now, and even then, it wouldn't be as fresh as this. "Sure. That would be wonderful."

An hour later, Cathy savored her last bite. She had done the same with the first couple of bites, but her hunger took over, and she devoured the rest. She rehydrated mashed potatoes for a side dish and shared them with Brett. Usually, she put bacon bits or beef jerky in the potatoes to liven them up, but that was unnecessary tonight.

"What a delicious meal. Now I see why you carry the pole and that heavy pan."

"I carry a little less food because of it, but it's the thing I enjoy most about the trail, so it's all worthwhile to me. My only regret tonight is that I only got to fish for ten minutes. I may fish again in the morning."

"Thanks for letting me try it. That's something I never would have done otherwise. I'll never forget the experience."

Message from Cathy: *Sorry for the late message. At Lake Virginia. Had a better dinner than you for a change. Fresh fish. And I caught it too!*

13

Double Trouble

2022

Day 5

August 9 - Lake Virginia to Pocket Meadow

Mark laid awake in his tent, mustering the courage to leave his toasty sleeping bag. Putting cold and stinky hiking clothes on his warm skin was one of his least favorite parts of the day. He heard, "Move! Move! Now!" coming from the girls' tent. He opened the zipper to peek outside. Jessica stumbled out of the tent and ran into the trees with a plastic bag in her hand. Mark left his tent in his sleeping clothes and walked over to Linda's tent.

"What was that all about?" He spoke softly so he wouldn't disturb Brock or Bob.

Linda rubbed her eyes and yawned. "Guess she needed to go to the bathroom in a hurry. A bit of a rude awakening."

Go to the bathroom? Bathroom on the trail meant squatting over a six-inch-deep hole behind a tree. Flushing meant covering your waste with dirt and rocks and stuffing the used toilet paper in a plastic bag. Given how fast

Jessica was moving, she'd have to dig the hole after the fact and push in the waste with a stick.

Linda emerged from her tent a few minutes later with her puffy jacket and wool cap. She pulled the gloves out of her coat pocket and covered her hands.

Mark walked back to his tent to grab his jacket and hat. He began to heat water for coffee and breakfast. About ten minutes later, Jessica hobbled out of the trees, hunched over, one hand over her lower abdomen. Her face was as pale as the granite being reflected on the lake.

Linda rushed over and put her arm around her. "What's the matter, honey? Are you sick?"

"Kind of. I had loose poo last night after dinner. I never have to go then. This morning, it came on so fast. Sorry about waking you that way."

Linda helped Jessica sit next to Mark, and she sat on the other side. "Did you throw up as well?"

Jessica shook her head.

"You didn't drink any water without filtering it, did you?"

"No, Mom. You've warned me enough already." She leaned forward with both hands over her stomach.

Mark said, "Sorry you don't feel good, Jess. Hopefully, it's just your body reacting to the different foods you've been eating. Do you think you can eat breakfast?"

Jessica shook her head. "I'll just have water for now. Maybe I'll eat some crackers later." Linda fetched her water bottle from their tent.

Brock stuck his head out of his tent. "What's all the noise about? Did you see a bear?"

"No. But I wish one would come to knock some sense into you." Jessica's voice trembled.

Brock walked over in his sleeping clothes and camp shoes. "What's up, sis'?"

"Oh, it's nothing, just a little stomach trouble. Mom, do we have any medicine for this?"

Linda touched her forehead with her fingers. "Oh, you must mean

Imodium. No, sorry. I didn't think of that. Mark, did you bring any?"

He shook his head.

Mark nibbled on a granola bar as he prepared coffee for Linda and himself. Brock pulled Pop-Tarts out of his bear canister. Jessica sipped water from her bottle.

"Do you think you can hike today?" asked Mark. "We can stay here if you want."

Jessica nodded, still grimacing. "Let's just go a little slower. It shouldn't be any worse than sitting here all day."

Mark patted her knee. "OK, I'll let you set the pace. Brock, you can go ahead of us if you want. Wait for us at Fish Creek, and we'll regroup there."

Brock perked up and replied, "Or maybe we should turn around so we can get to a doctor quicker?"

Mark stared at Brock, trying to assess his true motivation. "There's another exit point at Lake Edison, which is closer than returning to Red's. VVR runs a ferry to their place. We could get a ride into town from there." VVR, or Vermillion Valley Resort, was another popular resupply location for JMT hikers. If there was a room available, they could rest there while Jessica recuperated.

"Hold on, Mark," said Linda. "Jessica, are you sure you want to continue? It's mostly downhill back to Red's. We could be in Mammoth tomorrow and get you some medicine."

Mark looked back and forth between Brock and Linda. He didn't expect Linda to support Brock. Perhaps she felt guilty about not packing Imodium. He wondered what else he had forgotten.

Jessica didn't hesitate. "No, I don't want to quit. Let's give it another day."

Linda scooted closer and gave her a hug. Jessica leaned her head against Linda's shoulder. "I can't believe I forgot that medicine."

Mark said, "Don't be too hard on yourself. I didn't think of it either."

"Well, if there's any doubt, we should try to catch the ferry to VVR this afternoon," said Brock.

"Jess, we'll each take a thing or two from your pack to make it easier for you. I'll carry some of your food. Brock, why don't you carry her sleeping pad. Linda, maybe you can take her electronics bag."

Brock saw Linda nodding and said, "OK. I guess."

Linda looked at Jessica. "Let me get changed, then why don't you lie down while your dad and I break down camp."

* * *

Bob sat on a rock near the shore, staring at the mountainside reflected on the still surface of Lake Virginia. When he leaned forward and looked down at the water, he saw his long stubble and greasy face contrasting the serenity in his eyes. Unlike yesterday afternoon, the rock was chilling his bottom rather than soothing his back. Only the roar of his stove disturbed the silence. Soon, the birds would join in.

He shut off the gas to the stove and poured the steaming water into his cup containing dehydrated coffee and powdered milk. Both of his hands held the insulated cup. He leaned his face over the wisps of steam rising from the coffee to soothe his dry sinuses. Early morning was one of his favorite times of the day. It was so quiet. He didn't have to squint in the harsh light, and his legs were fresh. The caffeine would soon give him the boost he needed to pack up and start hiking.

With the stove shut off, he now heard noise from Mark's camp. Instead of the noise ramping up as they all got up, it seemed as if everyone was involved. He walked up the hill to check if they needed any help.

"Good morning. Is everything OK over here?"

Mark turned around. "Good morning. Yeah, just a little tummy ache. Hey, do you have some Imodium you can spare? Jessica's idiot father forgot to bring any."

"I sure do. I haven't been able to sleep, but my stomach has been fine. You don't have any sleeping pills, do you?" Bob said with a big grin, and then added, "Just kidding. I need to be alert enough to fend off the rodent raiders that come in the night."

Jessica was listening and perked up. Bob didn't know whether it was due to the mention of the medicine or the rodent raiders. "Thanks, sir. Dad said if I'm not better by the morning, we're taking the ferry to VVR."

"We wouldn't want that to happen. Call me Bob. Sir makes me feel too old." Bob grinned.

"OK, Bob. I don't want this trip to end early because of me."

"Well, I don't want that either. I'll be right back."

Jessica walked over to the tent. "Mom, guess what? Bob has some medicine for me."

"Great, honey."

* * *

Bob loosened up his legs on a flat section of trail before a 1,000-foot descent over two miles to Tully Hole. A wall of mountains lay beyond the bright green meadow, which resembled a golf course from far above. A dark, wide stream carved the meadow in two. The initial descent was in the sun via long switchbacks with sharp turns. The shade along Fish Creek provided an opportunity to cool down and for his aching knees to recover. At his age, Bob preferred the huffing and puffing of climbing to knee-jarring descents.

At last, he reached the long cascade of water down Fish Creek. When viewing the cascade from the footbridge, it almost appeared that the boulders in the creek were rolling down toward the bridge. The valley below was aptly named Cascade Valley. He stepped off the bridge and sat in the shade. He wasn't hungry or out of breath, but his quivering legs needed rest before regaining all the elevation he had just lost to get to Squaw Lake.

About fifteen minutes later, Brock arrived.

"Hi Brock. Stop and take a break. This waterfall is the best one so far."

Brock took his pack off and sat next to Bob.

"Yeah, that's pretty cool. I like the way the water kind of rolls down the hill." Bob thought he detected a small grin.

"Is the rest of the family far behind?"

"I don't think so. They were about five or six switchbacks behind me."

"Good, sounds like Jessica must be doing OK."

Bob opened his backpack and removed Marty.

Brock smirked. "You're carrying a stuffed animal all the way to Mt. Whitney?"

"Long story, but could you take a photo for me?"

Brock hopped up. "Sure."

Instead of hopping, Bob used his arms to push himself into a squatting position and slowly rose. He hadn't hopped in years. He took Marty on the bridge and handed Brock his phone. Bob placed Marty on the handrail on the upstream side of the bridge and posed for Brock with the cascading water appearing to crash on their heads. As Bob reached back to grab Marty, he knocked him over the side. He turned around, looked down, then crossed the bridge and looked down the other side. "Oh no! Marty!"

Brock pointed at the white water on the right side. "There he is."

"Where? I don't see him."

"Look! The water flipped him up on that boulder near the shore."

"Where?"

"Stand behind me and follow my finger."

"Oh, I see him."

Bob ran off the bridge and climbed over the boulders next to the creek. Marty was resting on a boulder four feet into the stream. White water rushed around each side, threatening to carry Marty away. Bob looked at the nearby rocks to find a way to retrieve Marty. He saw a rock halfway between Marty and the shore. It looked pretty stable, but he froze.

Brock arrived at Bob's side. "Bob, what are you waiting for?"

Bob didn't reply or even look at Brock. He just stared at the water.

Brock put one foot on the rock between the shore and Marty. When it didn't move, he brought his other foot to the same rock and reached for Marty on the boulder.

"Brock, be careful!" someone yelled from the bridge.

Brock lost his balance while turning around and started waving his arms. Bob reached out, and Brock grabbed his hand before jumping to the shore.

Brock handed the drenched marmot to Bob, who sat down on the rock on which he had been standing. "Oh Marty. I almost lost you again!"

Brock sat down next to Bob. "Bob, what's the matter? It's just a stuffed animal."

"No, you don't understand. He's very special. My wife took him on the trail last year. And now she's gone. I have to take care of him."

"Oh, sorry. I didn't know. Let's get away from the creek where we can hear."

Brock stood up and pulled Bob up, then they climbed the creek bank. Linda and Mark greeted them at the top.

Linda said, "Brock, what were you thinking? That current is dangerous."

"Not really. I just stepped on a rock like we do on other water crossings."

"I can't thank you enough. I couldn't have done that. I am scared to death of rushing water."

"Come on. It wasn't a big deal," said Brock.

"You don't understand…" Bob walked to the log where Jessica was sitting and sat down. His legs were even weaker now. Mark, Linda, and Brock followed, and Brock sat next to Bob.

"As I was telling Brock, I gave this marmot to my wife, Cathy, to accompany her on the JMT last year when I backed out of the trip. His name is Marty. Well, she passed away on the trail, and Marty helps me keep her memory alive." Bob paused when he felt a tear run down his face. "After her death, I vowed to bring him along and take his picture at her favorite spots." Bob wiped his eyes with his sleeves. "First, a real marmot tried to run off with him, and now this. He'll never make it to the end at this rate." Bob wrung out some of the water from Marty. "Well, looks like you get to ride outside of the pack again!"

Bob patted Brock on the back.

"Bob, I didn't know. I saw you rush down there and thought you would just go out and get him. But then you froze. So I just stepped out and grabbed him before the water washed him away."

"Well, anyway, it means a lot to me. Thanks again."

"Nice job, Brock," said Mark.

Bob looked up at Mark. "As they say, *the trail provides*. Not three hours after I gave Jessica some medicine, Brock rescues Marty."

Jessica said, "I think they call that trail magic."

* * *

Squaw Lake appeared out of nowhere after a short but steep climb in the sun. Mark's family had pulled away from Bob, despite Jessica's ailment. The two 15+ mile days in a row were taking their toll. This lake had a different vibe than Bob's previous favorites. It was hard to describe, but wild, quiet, isolated, and simple came to mind. He would likely see more like it as he entered the higher elevations of the trail. The lake was circular and much smaller than Garnet Lake. Granite walls rose from the water's edge for 180 degrees, making him feel like he faced an altar from the back row of a massive cathedral. At first glance, he thought the perfect U-shaped trough across the lake was Silver Pass. However, a few minutes later, he saw some hikers descending on a trail far to his right. Good thing. He didn't think he could climb the wall of rock across the lake.

Bob walked through a small meadow to the shoreline. He placed his backpack near a slab of rock from which he would enjoy an early lunch while soaking his feet. With the cool wind in his face and the ripples of water hitting the sandy shoreline, he was oblivious to the trail behind him. He managed to eat his peanut butter and jelly tortilla without squirting the contents out of the ends. When only a bite of tortilla remained, he shared a few pinches with the lone trout swimming in circles in front of him. He alternated his feet between the frigid lake water and the warm rock on which he sat. They would be too numb to complain on the climb to Silver Pass.

As he walked back toward the trail, he spotted Hannah ahead on the top of the next ridge. She must have passed while he was mesmerized by the view in front of him while eating lunch. He passed several lakes with Native American-themed names: Squaw, Chief, Papoose, and the longest name on the trail, Lake of the Lone Indian. He made a mental note to look up the history of this naming convention when he got home.

Some passes on the trail were clearly visible and teased hikers from far away. However, the trail to Silver Pass meandered so much that Bob couldn't spot the pass until he was nearly on top of it. It wasn't as broad as Donohue Pass, but he still could not see both sides from one spot. Silver Pass Lake came into view as he descended. Despite the unimaginative name, he had heard this was a popular campsite, especially for NOBOs preparing to climb Silver Pass first thing in the morning. While he was tempted to set up camp there, he needed to hike farther so he could arrive at Marie Lake early the following day. While planning the hike, Bob acknowledged that it was pointless to select all his campsites ahead of time. Too many variables could disrupt the best laid plans: weather, occupied tent sites, fatigue, injury, food supply, etc. However, he selected a few targets, like Marie Lake, to plan around. Marie Lake was one that Cathy anticipated the most, and the last major one she visited on her hike.

The trail was flat and straight as he walked by Silver Pass Lake. Hannah waved both arms from the shoreline. An equally beautiful spot for lunch. He had dawdled enough already today, so he waved back and kept walking. He figured she would pass him during the afternoon.

* * *

Mark and his family set up camp under large trees alongside Pocket Meadow, which was much bigger than the name implied. The small creek winding through the meadow was filled with trout in search of insects landing on the surface. VVR's ferry landing was two miles ahead. Jessica was feeling better, but she still wasn't drinking or eating enough. Unlike himself, she had few reserves to begin with. While Jessica had nibbled on cheese crackers at lunch, Brock had lobbied for picking up the pace to catch the afternoon ferry to VVR instead of setting up camp. Mark overruled him since he thought Jessica might hurt herself if she pushed the pace in such a weak state.

Mark sat down on a large rock against which Jessica had been leaning as he set up her tent. She usually did more than her fair share of camp chores, but he insisted that she rest instead. She didn't resist the suggestion like she often did. He brought her a bottle of freshly filtered water to encourage her to drink. She took a few sips and tried to hand it back, but Mark pushed it back toward her. "Keep working on it. You need to rehydrate and eat if we are going to continue the hike."

Brock was lying in his tent with the flap tied up to let in the breeze. It sounded like he was watching a video, but this time, the volume was unobtrusive. A sign of progress?

Bob veered off the trail toward them. He was close to six feet tall, but fifty pounds lighter than Mark. Mark tried to imagine how much easier this hike would be if he didn't have to lug those extra pounds up the passes. A few locks of white hair dangled under Bob's hat, which had a wide brim and a long flap covering his neck. Together with his long-sleeved shirt, long nylon pants, and sun gloves, Bob was well-protected from the intense mountain sun. He probably only used a couple of dabs of sunscreen a day for his nose and cheeks.

"Hi Bob. Had enough fun for the day? Plenty of room here if you want to stop."

Bob stopped and leaned his poles against a tree. "Yes, if you don't mind."

"No problem."

Mark noticed a tall, young woman had followed Bob off the trail.

"You have a tail."

Bob turned around. "Hi Hannah."

"Hi Bob."

"Mark, this is Hannah. We hiked together the first couple of days after a traumatic bear encounter at Tuolumne Meadows."

Hannah nodded. "Hi. Nice to meet you. Looks like you have a crowd. Maybe I should move on."

Mark said, "Don't be silly. There is plenty of room here. We're all family anyway."

"Thanks. I started at Purple Lake, so it's been a long day. Silver Pass Lake would have been a nice place to camp, but it was a little early to stop."

"We were tempted to stop there as well," said Mark.

"Hey Mark," said Bob. "How is Jessica doing?"

"I'm right here, you know. And I'm feeling a little better. Hopefully, I'll be just fine in the morning."

Bob smiled. "Oops, didn't see you over there. Glad you're feeling better."

Mark said, "Why don't you two make camp, then we can eat dinner together?"

***

An hour later, while Mark was sorting through his bear canister, Jessica asked, "Do we have any instant mashed potatoes left? That might be a safe dinner to try tonight."

Mark reached into the bear canister, shuffled things around, and grabbed a bag of Idahoan instant potatoes like a magician pulling a rabbit out of his hat. Jessica smiled for the first time in two days.

Linda was sitting next to Jessica and put her arm around her. "You must be feeling better."

"Yeah. I don't think we'll need that ferry tomorrow."

Brock was also rummaging through his bear can. He looked up when he heard Jessica, then continued searching for his dinner. Mark had expected a rebuttal about catching the ferry or some sign of disappointment, but he got neither.

When they gathered to eat dinner, Bob sat next to Brock.

"Hannah, I didn't tell you about Marty's escapades today."

"Oh no. What now? Did he fall off a cliff or something while you were taking a picture?"

"Close–but into a creek. Remember the bridge over Fish Creek after the long downhill?"

Hannah nodded. "Oh no! Not there."

"Yep. And Brock here was the hero." Bob patted him on the back.

Brock lowered his head. "Come on. It wasn't a big deal."

"But, it was. Marty's a constant reminder of why I'm doing this hike. And it took courage for you to step out into that stream."

Hannah said, "Brock, he's serious. You should have seen him panic when a real marmot ran off with Marty near Thousand Island Lake."

"I'm glad I could help. I didn't know how important Marty was at the time. I just reacted."

Mark felt pride in his son for the first time in a year. Perhaps this wasn't a bad idea after all. He had expected the sheer beauty of the trail to trigger a change, but maybe the magic was in the shared experiences of fellow hikers overcoming the inevitable obstacles.

* * *

Bob woke up when he heard metal hitting metal. In the daytime, it might be a bear bell attached to the pack of a cautious hiker or a cooking pot banging on a trowel while hanging outside a backpack. But at night, it usually meant trouble. He also heard someone or something slapping tent fabric, and then Hannah saying, not yelling, "Go. Get away." Bob unzipped the flaps of his tent door and rainfly and turned on his headlamp. When he looked toward Hannah's tent, he saw a couple of marmots scurry off toward the creek. The tent fabric popped out as Hannah slapped it from the inside. "Stop it. Get out of here."

Bob scanned the area to see if a bear was also involved. Hannah's cooking pot, stove, and spoon were laying on the ground next to her bear canister. Some hikers put such things on top of their bear canisters so they would be alerted of attempted break-ins. Bob didn't do so because he didn't particularly want to know. He had a hard enough time sleeping. He just made sure his food and toiletries were stored properly and assumed the curious animals would investigate no matter what he did.

The slapping of the tent stopped. Hannah wasn't screaming or sobbing. She hadn't turned on her headlamp. Bob smiled and tried to return to sleep.

* * *

Dear Cathy,

I thought I really lost Marty this time. He took a dive off the Fish Creek bridge and ended up on a rock just a few feet from shore. I couldn't bring myself to step on a rock surrounded by rushing water to save him. I'm not afraid of bears or heights, but rushing water terrifies me. Fortunately, Brock has no such fears and saved Mary while I was frozen in place. This marmot must have a death wish. He broke free on your way to Red's, and I've almost lost him twice in the first week. He must want to live in the mountains with his brothers and sisters instead of Houston, but I need him too much to set him free.

I now have a trail family to help me out. Did you get any help from other hikers? Help you should have gotten from me. Perhaps they will help me finish this hike. And maybe I will make a difference in one of their hikes. Brock showed me today that he is not entirely selfish, and Jessica's determination reminds me of yours. She refuses to let a little stomach bug end their hike. I'm glad I was able to help her by sharing some of my Imodium, something I would have probably forgotten if I hadn't had your list.

I've set myself up well for a night at Marie Lake. I know it was one of your most anticipated sights on the trail, but I don't know what your experience was like there. What did you do? Did you get to camp there? Did it live up to your lofty expectations? I plan to arrive early so I can explore its jagged coastline and take another lake bath. And Selden Pass is one pass I am looking forward to so I can enjoy the view from above.

Love, Bob

14

Company

2021

July 22 - Silver Pass Lake

Cathy was pleased with her campsite at Silver Pass Lake. Being only 400 feet lower than Silver Pass, campsites with shade were limited, but she had claimed the last one. Many more campsites were available on the wide open east side of the lake. Her site sat thirty feet above the lake, allowing her to see the deep blue color over the glare on the surface. Mountains almost fully surrounded her, the only open direction being her path to the south in the morning. The mountain hovering over the lake was almost invisible in the glare now. She would see it better after sunset, but it would glow in the morning sun tomorrow.

Before dinner, she walked to the lake to get a closer look. The lake was a large oval, but the southern end was a bit more irregular, with small islands and peninsulas and a green marshy area surrounding the outlet stream. She went there first, walked out on a peninsula, and watched the trout dart away as they heard her footsteps. She heard splashing to the north. An older couple rushed to the shoreline after a quick rinse. Older couple–huh! They appeared to be about her age–who was she trying to fool? She walked down the shoreline to say hello and visit. She was lonely. If Bob were here, they could be the ones basking in the sun.

The couple didn't notice her approach with the breeze in their ears and their eyes closed while the sun dried their faces. They leaned back, catching as many of the sun's rays as possible. "Hi. How was the water?"

They both jumped and sat back up. "Oh, Hi. We didn't hear you coming."

Cathy covered her mouth with her hand. "Sorry about that."

"No, it's OK. The water was freezing, but we always feel refreshed after drying off," the man said.

"Are you going to try it?" his wife added. "My name is Rita, and this is Frederick." She tilted her head to her right.

"I'm Cathy. Mind if I sit with you?"

"No, please do. It's nice to have someone else to talk to." Rita grinned at her husband and patted the rock slab next to her.

Cathy sat next to Rita. "I think I'll pass on the bath today. Not sure there is enough sun left to dry off."

Frederick said, "Well, usually one of us says the same thing, then we remind ourselves how much better we always feel afterwards and go for it."

"It must be nice to have someone else to look after you—OK. You talked me into it."

Cathy took off her shirt and hiking pants, and gingerly walked into the water in her camp shoes and underwear until it was waist deep. She bent her knees and held her nose while she went underwater. She ran the fingers of her other hand through her hair to remove some of the grime and tangles. After raising her head above water, she scrubbed her face and arms with her hands, then rushed out of the water, as Rita and Frederick had earlier.

She shivered as she sat back down. Rita offered her camp towel so Cathy could wipe off some of the water. "The sun and rock will warm you up in no time."

"Thanks. I feel better already."

"Are you hiking solo?" asked Rita.

"Yeah." Cathy glanced at Rita, then stared at the shoreline. "My husband,

Bob, was supposed to be with me, but he canceled at the last minute due to a work conflict. I've been trying to convince him to retire for years now."

Frederick said, "Well, it's none of my business, but tell him it's the best thing I ever did. I feel better now than I did three years ago. Not easy to say when you're sixty-three."

"What a coincidence. That's how old he is, and me too."

"I don't know how you do this alone. The trail is gorgeous and you run into so many interesting people, but this is hard. Really hard! The climbing and the chores. Packing and unpacking. Eating and drinking enough. I couldn't do it without Rita."

"Same here," said Rita. "But plenty of people finish it solo. You'll probably be one of the strong ones who does."

"So far, so good. But there's a long way to go. Thanks for letting me invade your privacy. These conversations help when you're all alone."

"Like I said, we get tired of hearing the same things over and over." Rita winked at Cathy.

Rita was right. It only took twenty minutes for her skin and underwear to dry enough to put her hiking clothes back on. Her legs were refreshed and her mind was clear. Her skin didn't stick when she bent her elbows. She was grateful to Rita for nudging her into the water. And she would certainly tell Bob about Frederick's recommendation. Maybe he needed to hear it from someone other than her; he had tuned her out on that subject. If only she could find a couple like Rita and Frederick to hike with every day. Unfortunately for her, they were heading NOBO. It was hard to find people whose hiking pace and resupply strategies matched up, and more importantly, had compatible personalities.

Frederick groaned as he stood up, then pulled Rita up. "Thanks for stopping by. We're going back to camp to eat dinner now. We wish you the best going south."

"Thank you. You gave me the boost I needed. Good night."

Five minutes after she arrived back at her tent, her satellite device chirped. She removed it from her backpack and saw she had an incoming message:

Message from Bob: *Sorry, I can't make Bishop Pass in time, but I will meet you in Independence for your zero day, and finish the hike with you. Love, Bob.*

Like many thru-hikers, Cathy was leaving the JMT over Kearsarge Pass in eight days to pick up her resupply in the town of Independence. She had reserved a room at the Mt. Williamson Inn and Basecamp. They would spoil her with a soft mattress and an opportunity to clean up. She had hoped Bob would meet her at the Bishop Pass junction a few days earlier, but at least he was trying. If she could make it through the next eight days, he would be there to support her when she needed it most–those last five days when they would have to climb Forester Pass at over 13,000 feet and Mt. Whitney at 14,505 feet.

Message from Cathy: *Thanks. Can't wait to see you. Met a couple our age at Silver Pass Lake, Rita and Frederick. Frederick says you'll love retirement:)*

15

Fireworks

2022

Day 6

August 10 - Pocket Meadow to Marie Lake

Mark was jolted awake by slapping on his tent. He heard a whisper. "Dad, it's me."

"Jessica, is that you?"

"Of course, it's me. Who else would be calling you Dad?"

"What's the matter? Are you sick again?"

"No, I'm feeling better. We can keep hiking!" She wasn't whispering anymore. Her energy had the same effect on him as those first sips of coffee. He opened his tent flap and rainfly. There was just enough light to see a smiling face topped with tangled hair.

"That's great, honey. Try to be quiet since we have neighbors today."

Jessica put her hand over her mouth. "Oops, sorry."

"Why don't you get dressed, and I'll start working on breakfast and coffee. You are hungry, aren't you?"

He was delighted she was feeling better, but wanted to see how she handled breakfast. Was she really better or did she just want to start hiking before the diarrhea returned, trying to get past the easy escape via Lake Edison?

"Do you want me to fix you some oatmeal?"

Jessica paused. "Umm. Do we have any Pop-Tarts left? I don't want to push it." Mark grinned.

"I'll check our bear canister. If not, Brock might have some."

Jessica walked back to her tent. Linda had dressed while Jessica was gone and left the tent so Jessica could do the same.

Linda wasn't smiling, but Mark smiled at her. "What's the matter? Couldn't sleep with that bundle of energy by your side?"

"She climbed over me to get out of the tent. I got a knee to the stomach. But I'm glad she's feeling better."

As the water for Mark's coffee came to a boil, he heard two zippers, one right after the other. Jessica ducked out of her tent wearing her hiking clothes and a wide grin. Brock stumbled out of his tent, still wearing his sleeping clothes. One of his feet was missing a sandal. There was no way he could have slept through all the noise. Once the first person in camp left their tent, all but the soundest sleepers followed.

Brock smiled too. "Are we getting ready to head to the ferry landing? What can I do to help?"

Jessica beat her dad to the punch. "No! We're going to keep hiking. I'm much better this morning."

Brock's smile disappeared. "That was a quick recovery. Don't you think we ought to play it safe and take the ferry back to civilization? Just in case you get worse again."

"No way. If we tried to quit every time things got tough, we'd never finish." Jessica spoke faster with each word.

Mark tried to defuse the building tension. "Hey Brock, do you have any Pop-Tarts left? Jessica thinks it would be the safest breakfast for her this morning."

"Oh, so maybe not so much better after all. But yeah, I have two packs left. One for today, one for tomorrow."

"Can you please give one to your sister?"

Brock looked back and forth between Mark and Jessica, like a bear trapped between two hikers on a trail with steep slopes on both sides. "I guess," he muttered. He removed a pack of Pop-Tarts from his bear canister and tossed them to Jessica.

"Thanks, Brock," said Mark. "Don't worry, we have plenty of extra snacks to replace them."

Bob walked up with his pack on and hiking poles in hand. Mark said, "Good morning. Sorry about all the noise, but it looks like we didn't wake you."

"Nope. Couldn't sleep, so might as well hike." Bob noticed Jessica eating Pop-Tarts. "Look who's feeling better this morning."

"Yes. Thanks again for the medicine."

"So you're not taking the ferry to VVR after all?"

"Nope," Jessica declared.

Mark said, "Hold on, let's see how you handle breakfast."

Jessica put her hands on her hips and scowled at her father.

Bob walked toward Mark. "Where are you headed today?"

"Not sure. It depends on how Jessica feels."

"Have a great hike. I wouldn't be surprised if you pass me up. Slow and steady is my game. I'm planning to camp at Marie Lake. It was one of Cathy's most anticipated stops on the trail."

Linda said, "Enjoy your time there. I don't know how you do it. Coming out here after what happened last year."

Bob looked down at the dirt he was moving around with the tip of his hiking pole. "I had to. The guilt was killing me."

Linda walked over and put her hand on his shoulder. "Well, I hope you find the peace you are looking for. We appreciate what you have done for us."

* * *

Bob walked along the trail through a flat green strip on the right side of Marie Lake. The lake was filled with so many peninsulas and islets that Bob wondered if it was several lakes instead of one. Very little climbing remained to Selden Pass, which was clearly visible straight ahead. He could afford to overextend himself this afternoon exploring the vast shoreline. The grade rose to his right with outcrops of granite and dense clumps of small trees. He was beginning to worry about finding a legal campsite when he heard a high-pitched voice hollering his name. Jessica waved her thin arms so hard she appeared to be doing jumping jacks. Bob climbed up to the rock where she stood.

"We saved a spot for you," said Jessica.

Bob sighed. "Thanks. I didn't know if I would find a spot with all the grass and rock surrounding the lake."

"Turn around and look at our view. Not bad, huh?" Jessica held an arm out toward the lake.

Bob dropped his pack and his poles and turned around. "Oh yeah. This is why we wipe ourselves out day after day."

"Have you seen Hannah? She flew by me just you like y'all did."

Jessica nodded and pointed to a clump of trees to the north. "Yeah, we got here about the same time. She knew you wanted a spot here too, so she found her own place to leave us more room."

"You two are the best trail friends ever. I'm going to set up camp, then go exploring."

After Bob set up camp, he began to refill his empty backpack. His exploration of the lake required more stuff than his hands could carry. He packed his water filtering gear and a few snacks to enjoy on the shoreline. He added his pack towel and sleeping clothes in case he got wet, either intentionally or deliberately. His camp shoes were still hanging from a clip on the outside of the pack. Finally, he pulled a colorful rock from a ditty bag and stashed it in one of the hip belt pockets.

He hadn't noticed Jessica and Brock watching, so he stood up quickly when Jessica said, "You've been carrying a rock all this time?"

"Yeah. Seems silly, doesn't it, when we're surrounded by rocks. But this one is special." He removed it from the pocket and handed it to Jessica. It was a rounded granite rock painted on one side. Brock leaned over to look, and Jessica gave it to him.

"Is that a painting of this lake?" asked Brock.

"It sure is. Remember the story I told you about my wife?" Brock nodded. "Well, I had several rocks painted with her favorite scenes, whether or not she made it to them. I left the last one at Thousand Island Lake."

Jessica said, "Cool! We didn't get to see that lake, but it looks just as beautiful as this one in the pictures I've seen."

Brock handed the rock back to Bob.

"Can we go exploring with you?" asked Jessica.

"Jessica, Bob may need some time alone."

"Oh, I get it. Sorry. Maybe we can go off on our own."

"Thanks, Brock. You're right. Perhaps Hannah will go with you."

Brock and Jessica walked toward their parents. Mark and Linda nodded to them, and they headed toward Hannah's tent. Linda gave him a little wave. Mark yelled, "Have fun, Bob!"

Oh, Marty. He almost forgot. Bob ran to his tent to retrieve the little marmot. "Put your smile on, Marty. We'll be taking lots of pictures."

Bob walked to the nearest shoreline. As he did at Squaw Lake, he submerged his aching feet in the water while he filtered and drank water. He drank the first bottle a little too quickly and gave himself brain freeze. He filtered more water and placed the full water bag and bottles in the shade so the water wouldn't warm up in the sun. He surveyed the surrounding shorelines. Where should he explore first? Where should he leave the rock? To his left, a thin peninsula almost crossed the lake, nearly dividing it into two. A large island sat in the middle of the lake near the peninsula. He wondered how deep the water was between the two. Could he walk across? He had imagined standing on islands at both Thousand Island and Garnet Lakes, but they were much too far from shore. Here was his chance. He would be surrounded by the water of his favorite lake and get a much needed bath in the process. There was only one way to find out.

He walked down the peninsula to where the island was the closest, about fifty feet away. The bottom of the lake was not visible through the crystal clear water, meaning it was much too deep to walk across. He continued to the end of the peninsula, where the opposite shoreline was a mere eight feet away. The bottom was visible, but he wasn't sure how deep it was. Maybe waist deep? Unlike the many creeks and rivers he had crossed, the water was still. As long as the water wasn't more than waist deep, he should be able to cross safely. He was a good swimmer, but his experience was in the warm waters of the Southeast. Swimming in cold mountain lakes was much riskier. He knew how much it hurt his feet, but he couldn't predict how his body would react when entirely submerged. Muscles might cramp or the shock may cause him to inhale water. In either case, he could drown.

Bob removed his shirt, shoes, and socks, and placed them in his pack. After putting on his camp shoes, he stepped into the water, holding his pack above his head. His feet, already numb from soaking earlier, barely felt the first few steps. He inhaled deeply as the water reached his thighs and gritted his teeth when it covered his shorts. He was halfway now; he should be able to make it. Another step brought the water a few inches higher. Oh no! He lifted his pack higher and felt around with his feet for a larger rock to step on. Only three more steps should do it. After the next step, the water was back below his waist, and he took two quick steps to the shoreline.

He let out the breath he didn't realize he was holding. That wasn't bad. After setting his pack down, he walked back into the water and rubbed his hands all over his body while squatting. He then dipped his head underwater so he could rinse off his stiff hair and greasy face. When he was back on shore, he stood with his arms stretched high and surprised himself with a scream. "Ahhhhhhh." Before he laid down to dry and relax, he rinsed his dirty clothes in a plastic bag several times each. He wrung out what water he could and laid them on the warm rocks to dry with him.

Once he and his clothes were dry and he had taken a photo of Marty looking back over the lake, he headed south along the grassy shoreline. Another peninsula approached the large island from this side. But once again, he only saw deep water in between. *Where should I place Cathy's rock?* He had initially planned to leave this one on Selden Pass, where Cathy could look down on the lake from above. But the pass received a lot of traffic, and unless he scrambled up the mountainside, it might be discovered and taken as a souvenir. Perhaps the island would be a better home. She would be surrounded by the lake on all sides. Hikers braver than himself might venture through the deep water to get there, but they would be unlikely to discover the rock. The island was large and flat, so he figured he could lob it over there without it bouncing into the water. He found a similar rock at his side and took a practice throw. Perfect. It bounced three times and came to rest near the center. *OK, Cathy, here you go.* He kissed the painted picture and repeated the toss with a similar result. He raised his arms in quiet celebration. *Enjoy the view, Cathy! You'll be surrounded by beauty forever.*

Instead of turning back and repeating the water crossing, he continued clockwise around the lake. The southern shoreline was marshy in spots due to the small streams feeding the lake during snowmelt. Soon, he was back to where he had started and he retrieved his water bag and bottles. His exploration in the hot sun left him parched. The water was cool but not frigid, so he gulped three quarters of a bottle without fear of another headache.

Brock, Jessica, and Hannah were sitting by the lake tossing pebbles into the water. Brock said, "Did you throw the rock on that island?"

"Yep," Bob said, staring at the island, looking for a few square inches of blue paint.

"Nice choice," Brock said as he nodded.

"Did you three go exploring as well?"

"We climbed a little way toward the pass for a view from above," said Jessica.

"That's a climb I don't mind repeating," said Hannah.

Bob stood up without his typical moans and groans. He felt years younger. "Well, it's time to go back to camp and boil some of this water. I want to finish dinner early so I can enjoy what must be a splendid sunset."

* * *

Mark sat with his arm around Linda, watching Bob, Jessica, and Hannah squint at the bright yellow tips on the mountains across the lake. Hannah wrapped her hands around a mug of green tea. Everyone else was sipping hot chocolate prepared by Mark. The flames on the mountain tops were extinguished when the sun dipped farther, and the face of the mountain slowly changed to orange. Next would be red, then purple. A grand fireworks show in super slow motion–without all the noise. Mark's camera was capturing a time lapse on a tripod. Suddenly, the show was accompanied by noise, not deafening booms and bangs, but music blaring from Brock's tent. Mark began to stand up, but Bob rose faster and motioned for him to sit down. Mark shrugged his shoulders and raised his eyebrows as Bob walked to Brock's tent.

Bob crouched down and ducked his head behind the tent flap. A few minutes later, Mark almost fell off of the nearly empty bear canister he was sitting on as Brock followed Bob back to their front row seats. Bob pointed to the east. "Enjoy the show. Better than any fireworks show you will see between Houston and Sacramento."

When the color of the mountains to the east was replaced by reflected white moonlight, they all rose as if the credits for the show were scrolling down the mountain.

* * *

Dear Cathy,

What a day! It was ALL good today. You know how usually there's some 'suck' every day that you just accept or go home, like searching an hour for a campsite or clouds building over a pass you're approaching. There was none of that today, or at least I was in such bliss that I didn't notice.

You were so right about Marie Lake. It is the most beautiful place on the trail so far. I didn't think it was possible, but my high expectations were surpassed. I hope that yours were as well. Thousand dollar cameras cannot capture the full beauty, and the best vocabulary can't describe the experience of exploring the lake from all sides. I wish we could have enjoyed it together. Mark's family and Hannah enjoyed the sunset with me. It was no substitute for the experience we would have had together, but at least they kept me from breaking down as the colors of the rainbow ran down the mountain. I hope you like where I placed your rock. You'll be surrounded by blue water and mountains forever.

My clothes and I are clean, or at least as much as can be on the trail. My legs and mind are refreshed. My pack is light. And my wonderful trail family, or 'tramily', is all together. Jessica seems to be over her stomach ailment. Even Brock has been a pleasure to be around lately. Unfortunately, I don't think I will be able to keep up with them much longer. I prefer to hike alone during the day, but the company and support at camp are helpful.

Tomorrow will be a long day, but I hope to arrive at MTR to resupply. I hope I sent some delightful surprises in my bucket. I mailed it so long ago, I can't remember.

Love, Bob

16

Out of Touch

2021

July 23 - Bear Creek Junction

Cathy set up camp where Bear Creek intersected the JMT. Technically, she hadn't crossed a pass today, but she had climbed 2,000 feet up Bear Ridge early in the afternoon. Unlike the climbs to most passes, trees shaded a smooth, dirt trail. After crossing a broad ridge, still covered with trees, she had descended 1,000 feet to her campsite.

When she finished setting up her tent, Cathy removed the satellite device dangling from a clip on her pack to send Bob her daily message. The device was off. She always left it on while hiking so she would have fewer buttons to navigate in case of an emergency. The battery indicator had shown 75% last night when she sent her message. Had she somehow turned it off? She held down the power button. Nothing. She pressed the button again, longer and harder. Nothing. Maybe the battery ran down while she was hiking. She hooked it up to her power bank and set it aside for thirty minutes before trying again. Still nothing. The device didn't even show the charging status as it normally did while connected to a power supply. She decided to let it charge overnight and try again in the morning. Bob should know better than to be worried because of one missed message. Neither she nor the devices were perfect. If he really wanted to know how she was doing, he should be here.

17

Worry

2021

July 24 - Marie Lake

Before Cathy left her tent, she tried to turn on her satellite device again. Still no response. Perhaps it needed to be reset somehow, but she didn't have a copy of the user manual or access to the internet. She tried pushing a couple of buttons at once, but the potential combinations were endless, and she gave up. Bob would just have to wait until she got to MTR, which had a computer for rent so hikers could check and send emails. She would send Bob an email telling him she was OK, but not to expect updates every day. Her main regrets were losing the ability to send an SOS message in case of emergency and to check on updates from Bob on their reunion in Independence. She feared he would find yet another excuse to abandon her, and now she would be unable to keep the pressure on.

* * *

Cathy ate lunch while admiring Marie Lake from the rocks above the trail to the right. Many vloggers described Thousand Island Lake and Rae Lakes as their favorites. She hadn't seen Rae Lakes in person yet, but Marie Lake was her favorite so far. She couldn't describe exactly why, and photos couldn't fully capture it. The blue water, dwarfed trees, grassy meadows, and white granite were somehow in perfect proportion. Selden Pass was visible to her right. Only the promise of a splendid view from the pass could pull her away from here—and staying on schedule to meet Bob in Independence.

Leaving the trail for resupply in Independence created a bit of a dilemma for thru-hikers since lodging options were limited in the small town. Hikers could either make a reservation and stick to their itinerary or risk having to return to the trail immediately after picking up their resupply. The trail provided many challenges for even the best planned itineraries. Thunderstorms might keep them from crossing a pass as planned. They might sleep in after an awful night of sleep. Or they might be tempted to set up camp at an unexpectedly beautiful lake at noon. But no, she couldn't afford to do that. She was already half a day behind schedule, so she needed to hike another eight miles to MTR today. As much as she regretted moving on, she knew other wonders awaited her. She had thought Thousand Island Lake was the pinnacle of the trail a week ago, but Marie Lake had proved her wrong. The bar kept rising as she marched south. Muir Pass, Rae Lakes, the Woods Creek suspension bridge, Forester Pass, and Mt. Whitney were still to come. She couldn't spend a night at each of them.

The climb to Selden Pass seemed easy with all the breaks for photos. Instead of packing away Marty each time, she stuffed him in her pants pocket for easy access. Though she was still full and hydrated, she took another break on top to admire the lake from above. A man about her age joined her from the other side. He dropped his hiking poles and yelled, "Wow!" as he saw the lake for the first time.

"I know. I just came from there, and I'm kicking myself for leaving. I keep telling myself better sights are ahead, but it's still hard."

"Well, that's true, but this may be the best. I'm camping there tonight."

Cathy was close to climbing back down the pass to the lake to join him. It seemed crazy, but she couldn't shake off the idea. She needed to head down the south side of the pass before she succumbed. Perhaps Heart Lake and Sally Keyes Lakes would distract her enough to keep moving south.

* * *

Bob rolled over when his phone chirped. He looked at the clock on his nightstand yet again: 12:11 AM. *Finally! That must be Cathy's message.* It usually arrived in the early evening when Cathy arrived at her campsite. From the accompanying link, he could see exactly where she was camped and compare her location to her itinerary. He unlocked his phone and went to his messages. *Oh no!* It was just work, the source of most of his texts. Nothing urgent, but still no word from Cathy. She had told him not to worry about a missed message or two. The devices weren't perfect; sometimes the message just didn't go through, especially when camping under heavy tree cover. She carried the device mostly for the SOS function, which sent a message to emergency response organizations with the single push of a button. The daily updates were more of a convenience and for peace of mind–until they didn't come.

He knew he should try to calm down and go back to sleep, but it was just like waiting for an update on an injured person in the hospital. There was nothing he could do, but he couldn't get it out of his mind. Now he'd probably have to wait until this evening to know if the missing message was just an anomaly or a sign of trouble.

Bob was starting to regret backing out of the trip. The crisis he had anticipated at work had not materialized. There was a lot of unscheduled work to plan, but his team was doing well. Cathy had been right about that; he really didn't have to be at work. And now she had no one to help her with the challenges on the trail. He hoped this missing message wasn't the first sign of something serious. *If only you can make it to Kearsarge Pass, I'll be there for you. I'm so sorry. You were right all along.*

18

Change of Plans

2022

Day 7

August 11 - Marie Lake to Muir Trail Ranch

Bob woke up early but energized after his most restful night of sleep on the trail. His exploration of Marie Lake and the beautiful sunset distracted him from his nightly worries. He was now fueled up and packed up. Mark was enjoying his coffee and oatmeal as Bob prepared to leave. Jessica left her tent to join him.

"Morning, Jessica. How are you feeling?" asked Bob, delaying his departure for a few minutes.

"Back to normal. Ready to go."

"Great. I'm feeling good this morning myself." Bob grabbed his hiking poles. "I'll see you up the trail."

Though Selden Pass rose to almost 11,000 feet, Bob never became winded because of all the breaks he took to admire the lake and its surroundings from different perspectives. He took more photos on the climb than he did during the entire hike yesterday. He was almost disappointed when he reached the top of the pass. After a quick peek down the south side, he returned to the north side to perch on a boulder and enjoy the view while sipping some water. It was a bit early for a snack.

He looked at the large island in the lake and second guessed his choice for Cathy's rock. The view from the pass was more spectacular than he imagined. He wouldn't mind staring at this forever. He looked at Marty who was strapped to the top of his pack. *Did you enjoy the climb, buddy?* He would return Marty to his spot inside the pack shortly. Or should he leave Marty here? He could be with his own kind instead of stuck in a pack all day. Then Bob noticed how worn he had become from his near-death experiences and countless photos. He wouldn't last long up here in the summer thunderstorms and brutal winters, not to mention the other marmots and curious hikers. *Sorry Marty, you're stuck with me.*

He noticed movement below. Brock and Jessica already? When they reached the top, Bob said, "Was I really that slow or are you on a mission to get to MTR?"

Brock said, "Sorry, Bob. You're really that slow. Every time I looked up, you were taking a picture."

"I know, but this is as good as it gets. Just relishing what I've been missing all those years."

The rest of the trail family arrived.

"Brock and Jessica were just telling me how old and slow I am." Bob winked at them.

"I think they're right. But you always seem to catch up with us by the end of the day. As they say, hike your own hike," said Hannah.

"I thought I might at least make it to the first snack break before you caught me. I'll wait until you go by so you don't need to pass me on the trail."

Unlike the other passes on the trail, Selden Pass had a few trees to provide shade and color. As Bob descended the south side of the pass, he walked through a tunnel created by trees on the left and a rock face on the right. The descent wound through a lush landscape fed by mountain springs, reminding him of the south side of Donohue Pass. He soon reached Heart Lake. He wasn't able to make out the V at the top of the heart until he reached the tip at the southern end of the lake. The shape would be obvious from above. The first of the two Sally Keyes Lakes was straight ahead. He expected it to resemble Marie Lake, but there was no comparison. Sitting on his couch in Texas watching vlogs, Sally Keyes Lakes looked like a wonderful place to spend a weekend. After Marie Lake, it was almost ordinary. Going SOBO, the views generally became grander as he went. He felt sorry for the NOBO hikers. Though they had a few spectacular views to look forward to, the rest of the trail might become a letdown, just as their bodies were wearing down.

* * *

A sign pointing to Florence Lake appeared next to a side trail dipping off to the right. Someone had etched MTR into the blank space on the sign to clarify that this was also the way to MTR. The spur trail was not as well constructed and maintained as the JMT. He slowed his pace to navigate the steep trail filled with ruts and tree roots.

Muir Trail Ranch had a mixed reputation among backpackers. On one hand, it was a functional ranch where guests could hike or ride nearby trails, then feast on home-cooked meals and relieve their aching muscles in a spring-fed hot tub. The ranch's rustic cabins had to be reserved well in advance. Since MTR didn't typically provide single night rentals and backpacking itineraries were so uncertain, most thru-hikers did not stay in the cabins. However, the ranch also provided resupply services to thru-hikers. Its convenience was surpassed only by Red's Meadow. MTR earned its mixed reputation by keeping its ranch and resupply areas segregated as much as possible, trying to protect its guests from the dirty and smelly hikers. Hikers expecting to be the center of attention, as they were at VVR, were disappointed. Those expecting just what was advertised, pickup of a resupply bucket and an opportunity to buy a few essentials, were delighted with the service.

Bob arrived at MTR at noon to a bustle of activity around a rustic, thirty-foot-wide building with a large porch. On the left side of the porch was a counter where hikers requested their resupply buckets or purchased from a limited selection of supplies. Homemade tables and benches were scattered in front of the building under large trees.

Unfortunately, Mark's family was the center of attention. Mark and Brock appeared to be arguing, both using liberal arm gestures. Linda and Jessica sat at a picnic table, Jessica with her hands covering her face and Linda looking away from everyone else. The other backpackers were dividing their attention between the theatrics and the complicated task of sorting their leftovers and new food. Backpackers are notorious for over-packing food, and only so much could fit in a bear canister.

"Hey guys. What's up? I could hear you before I could see you," said Bob.

Brock was the first to reply. "MTR screwed up. They only have one of our resupply buckets. All the food Dad and I packed is gone. How could they mess up something so simple?"

Bob thought to himself that getting the buckets to the ranch was not so simple. If they survived the trip to the Lakeshore Post Office via the USPS, they still had a truck ride to a storage facility, a boat trip across Florence Lake, and a horseback ride to the storeroom at MTR. MTR insisted on the use of plastic buckets to fend off attacks by rodents and bears.

Mark added, "What do you want me to do about it, Brock?"

Bob said, "Did you ask about the hiker buckets? Or maybe they have some unclaimed buckets? I remember reading that hikers who cancel their plans can donate the contents of their buckets to other hikers or the communities along the Sierra. Heck, I can even give you a day or two of food."

"If yours is even here!" Brock said, flinging an arm in the air.

Bob paused. He had received confirmation that his bucket had arrived at the Post Office, but not that it was actually at the ranch. Because of limited storage, they brought the buckets to the ranch a few days before hikers were expected to arrive. He may have received an email confirmation after he left, but he wouldn't see it until he arrived in Independence. If his bucket didn't make it, he could probably scrounge up enough food, but what about Cathy's rocks? He had packed them in his bucket to reduce the weight of his pack for the first leg of the hike. They would be impossible to replace out here.

"Let me check while I'm getting my bucket. We should be able to work out something." Mark walked to the faucet marked for drinking water, and Brock sat against the nearest tree.

Bob removed his pack and set it next to the table where Jessica and Linda were trying to remain invisible. He opened the top of his pack and removed his electronics bag so he could charge his phone and power bank while he tended to his resupply and helped find a solution for Mark's family. "You two are quiet. How are you doing?"

Jessica shrugged her shoulders, and Linda shook her head. "And he was doing so much better…"

Bob walked to the service counter, behind which was a rack containing small backpacking essentials such as duct tape, water filters, first aid supplies, and sunscreen. Bob thought they were missing a golden opportunity by not carrying food, especially for situations like Mark now faced.

"Hi. I'd like to claim my resupply bucket." Bob handed the attendant the claim ticket emailed to him when he paid his fee. The service wasn't cheap, but the options were limited and the convenience was worth it. While waiting, Bob plugged in his electronics to the tangled mess of power strips and charging cords. He noticed Hannah sorting through her new goodies at a table under a tarp and waved. He began to worry when the attendant didn't return within a couple of minutes. *Had Brock's prognostication been right?* A few minutes later, he relaxed as the attendant opened the other door on the porch and dropped his bucket on the patio with a thump.

"Do you need any supplies from the store?"

Bob shook his head, then pointed toward Mark. "Hey, I understand my friends are missing one of their buckets."

The attendant looked at Mark, filling his water bottle, and then Brock. "Yeah, I'm sorry about that. I don't know what happened. Our records show we received it here. Maybe we gave it to someone else by mistake or sent the wrong one back across the lake due to a cancellation."

Bob asked, "Do you have any buckets from hikers that canceled their plans?"

The attendant pointed to Brock and spoke more quickly. "You know, the older kid threw a fit and disturbed everyone else here, so I wasn't too interested in helping them out. Heck, our guests in the back probably heard everything. But I've calmed down a little since then. Let me check our records. In any case, they can pick from the hiker buckets on the porch. People leave all kinds of food and supplies when they realize they packed too much."

"Thanks. I'd appreciate it." Bob held out his fist. "By the way, what's your name?"

"Oh, sorry. Terry," he said as he bumped Bob's fist and walked inside the building to service a solo hiker who had just arrived.

Bob peeked in the hiker buckets, then waddled over to Mark's table carrying his heavy bucket between his legs. He took a seat at the wobbly table, jolting Mark, Jessica, and Linda out of their funk. "I asked the attendant to check for buckets that might have been donated. Did you see the hiker buckets?" Bob pointed back to the porch. Two hikers were depositing handfuls of surplus food.

Mark said, "No. Brock and I got into it immediately. He never wanted to come on this trip and sees every setback as an opportunity to leave early."

Mark and Jessica followed Bob to the porch. Linda walked over to Brock.

As they passed the two hikers leaving the porch, Bob smiled. "Sent too much food, huh? I know how you feel. I have almost two days of leftovers from Red's. Would have been nice not to carry those three extra pounds."

The male hiker grinned and shook his head. "Yep. I hope the extra helps someone else."

"My buddies here are missing a bucket, so I'm pretty sure you just did."

Mark added, "Thanks. You may have saved our hike."

They skipped over the buckets containing gear and clothes and found the ones dedicated to food. Jessica reached into one of them and grabbed six commercial freeze-dried dinners. Mark reached into another bucket, grabbed two packs of tortillas, handed them to Bob, and reached in again for some fish packets and a small jar of peanut butter. Looking at the number of snack bars and packets of oatmeal in another bucket, Mark said, "You know, I believe we'll be alright. Maybe not everyone's favorites, but a lot of the basics."

Jessica took the tortillas from Bob and headed to their table to drop off a load. She returned and grabbed an assortment of bars, oatmeal, cheese crackers, and cookies.

The attendant returned to the porch. "Sorry, we don't have any unclaimed buckets, but I see you found the hiker buckets. You can take what you need, but not what you don't."

Bob saw a box of Pop-Tarts and grabbed it. All three of them walked to their table and emptied their arms.

"Hey, did you get all that from the hiker buckets?" Bob recognized the voice. He took a deep breath before he turned around. "Hi Nick. Yes, we did. There was a mixup with one of Mark's buckets."

"I need about five more days of food to get to Onion Valley. Can you spare some of those dinners?" The Kearsarge Pass trail began at the Onion Valley trailhead, which was thirteen miles west of the town of Independence.

"Didn't you send your own bucket?" Bob replied.

"No, I just figured I would raid the hiker buckets."

Mark replied this time. "Sorry, Nick. We won't be able to finish without all of this."

"That sucks! It's not fair to hog all the extra food." Nick walked to the porch, mumbling something about selfish hikers.

Mark looked at Bob, who said, "I warned you at Lake Virginia. Hey, why don't y'all sort out what you have and what you need while I go through my bucket. I'm sure I'll find a few things to contribute to the cause."

Brock and Linda walked over. "Dad, the Piute Pass trail is only a few miles south of here. We only need two days of food to make it to the trailhead." From the trailhead, they could catch a bus or hitch a ride to Bishop.

Mark pointed to the table. "We pulled about three days of food from the hiker buckets. We had another day or two of food leftover, and Bob says he has a day or two of extra food. If we keep checking the hiker buckets, I'm sure we'll find enough to make it to Onion Valley."

"Yeah, but is it food I like?" He picked up a pack of oatmeal. "I hate this stuff." Brock's voice was rising. "Did you find any Pop-Tarts? And almond M&M's?"

Bob picked up the single box of Pop-Tarts he took from the bucket. "I only saw this one, so I grabbed it for you."

Mark said, "Brock, why don't you check if they have anything else you like? Linda, can you see if they have any of the toiletries we need?"

Linda replied, "Yeah, we need more toilet paper, toothpaste…" She walked toward the porch.

Brock huffed, then calmed down enough to say, "When will you realize this trip wasn't meant to be? Who knows what will be next? A lightning strike, a bear attack…"

"I'm still waiting for a bear to get you," said Jessica.

Brock took off toward Linda.

Hannah arrived and dumped an armful on the table. No one had to ask her; she couldn't avoid getting the gist of the conversation. "I'll never eat all this. If you don't want any of it, just put it in the hiker bucket."

"Thanks Hannah." Jessica grabbed a plastic bag of Oreos. "You're getting rid of these? I love them."

"They were one of my favorites too. I'll ask you how you feel about them after you've been eating them five straight days."

* * *

Once their electronics were charged, Mark, Linda, and Bob followed the short spur trail to the camping area near MTR. Brock and Jessica had gone ahead to scout out tent sites. Bob could hear the South Fork of the San Joaquin River on the right, occasionally glimpsing the white water through the trees. He walked into the trees to investigate potential sites and soon saw a sign indicating *No Camping Here.* When the trees thinned, tents were packed even more closely than at Tuolumne Meadows backpacker's campground.

Brock yelled, "Dad! Over here."

Brock and Jessica stood at the top of a rocky knob waving their arms. Bob and the others trudged up the short, steep slope to find the best view of the river yet. However, there was only enough space for the three tents Mark and his family used. Mark said, "This is kind of small. Bob, why don't you take it?"

Bob noticed Brock glaring at Mark. Mark started to say something, but Bob held up his hand. "No, you stay here. The area on the other side of the trail is even more crowded. It will be easier for me to find a single spot."

He started to leave. "Hey Bob." When he turned back, Brock continued. "Thanks for helping us out earlier. I can't believe how much hikers help each other out. Except for you and Hannah, they don't even know us."

"You're welcome. This hike is tough. They're just paying it forward or returning a favor they received earlier." Linda smiled at Bob.

Bob descended the short slope and wandered among the campers in a well-worn area across the trail. The river was not visible from here, and he couldn't even hear it. Tent stakes were being pounded with rocks, and stoves were roaring. Families and friends laughed about the struggles that had nearly brought them to tears earlier in the day. The size of the crowd shocked him after days of dispersed camping. He saw a tent resembling Hannah's in the back corner. Two others were within fifty feet. The backpack sitting in the open vestibule resembled Hannah's.

"Excuse me. Can you please help me?" Bob said.

Hannah sat up and smiled at him.

"Can I share this campsite with you? I promise I'll be quiet, but I can't speak for all your other neighbors."

Hannah opened the zipper and stuck her head out of the tent. "I don't know, mister. I've heard about an irritating hiker about your age whom I should watch out for."

Bob watched her fight off the giggles, but she quickly gave in.

"Of course. This camping area is a madhouse, isn't it?"

"Yep. Looks like another sleepless night." Bob shook his head and started setting up camp twenty feet from Hannah's tent. If another bear visited camp tonight, at least he would be close by. He hadn't heard this was an area frequented by bears, but he thought it might be with everyone struggling to fit all their new food in their bear canisters. Visiting bears would hardly be able to walk through the campground without bumping into tents or tripping on guy lines.

After setting up camp, Bob walked back down the trail and turned left to find the river. Hannah had gone back in her tent to finish her nap. His quick rinse yesterday had been so invigorating, he decided to try it again. The hike today had been easy, but the sorting of his resupply and the drama created by the missing bucket had worn his nerves. He stared at a lone camper sitting on an ultralight chair in the *No Camping* zone. Was he blind or just disrespectful? Something Nick would do.

Thick trees lined both banks of the river. Rounded rocks the size of baseballs to basketballs filled the shallow, fifty-foot-wide river. The water rushing over and around the rocks was frothy white. A hot-tub-shaped structure made of rounded river rocks sat against the river bank. How creative! Small depressions around the edges allowed fresh water to flow through the tub.

Bob piled his filthy clothes on the shore. As he stepped into the tub, the cold water reminded him this was no hot tub, despite its appearance. Blayney Hot Springs was across the river if he still had energy after laundry and dinner. He dipped his head underwater and rubbed some of the grime off his body before sitting on the top of the rock pile, leaving his feet and knees in the water for therapeutic soaking. While taking his legs in and out of the water, he washed his socks, underwear, and even his hiking shirt and pants.

Unfortunately, he still had chores in camp, so he dressed in his sleeping clothes and walked toward the trail, trying to hold his pile of wet clothes away from his only dry clothes. Brock and Jessica walked down the trail toward him. He pointed through the trees to the left of the lone tent. "Hey, if you head for the river that way, you'll find a tub made of rocks right along the bank. Great way to enjoy the water without fighting the current."

Jessica opened her mouth and took a quick breath. "Thanks, Bob. Brock, let's go!" She jogged toward the river. Brock trotted after her. Bob thought he heard another "Thanks, Bob!" over the noise of the rushing water.

Bob took short, choppy steps up to Mark's campsite to find some sun to dry his clothes. "Mark, do you mind if I spread these clothes on the rocks? I found a campsite by Hannah, but it's in the shade."

Mark held his arm out toward a boulder. "Sure. It's the least I can do after avoiding the conflict over the tent site." Bob spread out his hiking pants and shirt on the warm boulder and hung his socks and underwear in a small tree a few feet away. "I'll be back in an hour or two."

"You're welcome to eat with us," Mark said.

"Sounds good."

* * *

Instead of hauling their cooking gear and bear canisters up to Mark's campsite, Bob and Hannah boiled water at their campsite and carried only their rehydrating dinners and water bottles.

"Hi Hannah. Glad you came," Linda said.

"Hannah, come see this view. It's hard to see the river from anywhere else." Bob set his dinner down and waved her across the site. Hannah followed. "Nice. I wish this site was larger. It's so crowded where we are."

Brock and Jessica were already eating their dinners. "Bob, that tub on the river was so cool. You should see what Brock did to it." Bob lowered his head and squinted his eyes. What was Jessica trying to tell him? Did Brock destroy that work of art?

"I just rearranged some rocks on top so more water flows through. Someone did a lot of work to build that thing. Thanks for showing us where it was."

In contrast to a few hours ago, Mark and Linda smiled at each other.

"No problem. I just stumbled upon it. I didn't expect you to be doing some home improvement. Maybe you should look into engineering."

"Hey, I only moved a few rocks around."

"Wait until you see Muir Hut in a couple of days. Now that's some remarkable construction work at 12,000 feet."

120

Jessica put her dinner cozy on the ground. She rubbed her eyes.

"What's the matter, Jess?" said Linda.

"You and I have to leave the trail before we get there."

Linda put her arm around Jessica. "Oh, honey. You'll get another chance someday. Remember, we didn't want to bite off too much this first time."

"But Dad and Brock get to go. It's not fair. I've proved I can handle this." Tears ran down her cheeks.

Brock stood up, looked at Mark, and moved his head toward the viewpoint Bob and Hannah were enjoying earlier. Mark followed him. They weren't yelling, but appeared to be debating something important. Mark came back, tapped Linda on the shoulder, and they both walked back to Brock. Hannah took Linda's place next to Jessica and whispered to her. Jessica nodded as her tears stopped falling. After a little more discussion, Linda nodded her head, and they all returned to where they were eating.

Hannah went back to her original seat, and Brock sat next to Jessica. "Hey kiddo—"

She slapped Brock's shoulder. "Don't call me that. I'm not a kid!"

"Sorry, Sorry. But we found a way for you to visit the hut."

Jessica sat up straight and opened her eyes wide. She looked at her mom and dad, then back at Brock. "How? I have to leave the trail with Mom tomorrow."

"Nope. Change of plans. I'm hiking out with Mom, so you and Dad can continue."

Jessica slapped him on the shoulder again, harder this time. "No way. Stop kidding me. It's not funny." She looked at her mom and dad, both smiling and nodding, then jumped up. She gave Brock as good a hug as she could without spilling food on his lap. "Thanks so much! Why?"

"You want it more than I do. I never wanted to come out here, and I'd still rather not be out here. It's not my thing. But I get it now. You'll enjoy the second half more than me, so go for it."

"Best trail magic ever!" yelled Jessica.

* * *

Bob laid in his tent and put away the map. Tomorrow, he should be able to make it to Evolution Lake, another iconic sight on the trail about five miles shy of Muir Pass. He was exhausted again and hoped he could fall asleep quickly despite the noise from his dozens of neighbors. While he and Hannah were away, a group of three guys had set up their tents twenty feet from his tent. He couldn't blame them, since he had trouble finding a spot as well. However, they were not using their soft camp voices like most of the other campers and sounded like they may have sent adult beverages in their resupply buckets.

"If we hike twenty miles tomorrow, we can camp in the Muir Hut. Wouldn't that be cool."

Another voice challenged the plan. "I read somewhere you couldn't camp inside. It's meant to be an emergency shelter from bad weather."

"Screw that. We can camp wherever we want. What's it going to hurt? Nothing is up there. No stream. No meadow. Nothing! Sounds like a great campsite to me." This voice was the loudest and also the most slurred.

"Just telling you what I read. I'm sure they don't want it to get trashed."

"I can't imagine any rangers going up there at night anyway. Who's gonna stop us?"

The third voice chimed in, "Sounds good to me. Let's do it."

* * *

Dear Cathy,

I made it to another big milestone, MTR. No problems with my resupply, but Mark's family had to scramble to replace the contents of one of their buckets. I now have your four other rocks to leave along the trail.

Lots of trail magic today, but the best came from Brock. Jessica was supposed to hike out with her mother via Piute Pass tomorrow, but Brock knew she wanted to continue more than him, so he switched spots. And I don't think he's just trying to get off the trail. I think he's starting to get it now. Jessica is so excited.

Me and my clothes are kind of clean and my bear canister is full, so I am as ready as I can be for the second half of the trail. This is harder than I imagined. I feel weaker almost every day. Last night was the only good night of sleep I've had on the trail. And now I'm approaching the point where your hike ended. I don't know how I'm going to get past it. Please help me. Please forgive me. That's the only way I'll be able to make it.

Love, Bob

19

Surprise

2021

July 24 - Muir Trail Ranch

Cathy arrived at MTR fifteen minutes before their 5 PM closing time. She faced a difficult decision–grab her bucket now and rush to sort through it or come back at 8 AM tomorrow. If she waited until tomorrow, she wouldn't start hiking until 10 AM or later. Though she was exhausted, she chose to deal with her resupply now. If only Bob were here—he could have gone ahead to get a head start on the sorting—or they might not have fallen behind schedule in the first place.

Cathy gave the attendant at the counter her claim ticket and threw her bag of trash into the trash can. They would put away the trash can and hiker buckets at closing time, so the squirrels and bears wouldn't get accustomed to easy food. Then she began charging her power bank and phone with the now empty power strip. She didn't even bother looking in the hiker buckets; she knew she had packed too much food and didn't want to complicate the sorting. The attendant brought her bucket to the picnic table where she had collapsed. What a nice young man. He must have pitied her. She'd gladly accepted the hospitality, no matter what his motivation.

When Cathy plugged in her phone and power bank, she remembered her dead satellite device. Her pleasant stay at Marie Lake and the rush to MTR had caused her to forget all about it.

"Excuse me. Don't you have a computer to rent for checking and sending emails?"

"Yeah, but we just had a power outage. By the time I get the computer and Wi-Fi back up, it will be well past 5 o'clock. It should be up and running in the morning."

"Oh no. My satellite device isn't working, and I wanted to update my husband. I can wait for it."

"Sorry, but I need to help out over at the ranch. Maybe someone at the campground will let you use their device."

"OK. I'll give that a try."

Cathy thought about Bob's bucket. She had not notified MTR that he wouldn't be picking it up, just in case he changed his mind. She could claim it now and pick the best out of each bucket, but she no longer had any patience or energy for that. Plus, it would continue to remind her of his betrayal.

"Oh, sorry. One more thing. My husband, Bob, couldn't make the trip. You can give his bucket to hikers in need if you want."

"Thanks. I'll take care of that tomorrow."

To keep things simple, she took all her leftovers to the hiker buckets. On the way back, she filled her water bottle with the pre-filtered water MTR provided–not as cold as she was accustomed to, but she didn't need to find a creek and filter the water. Now that she had disposed of her trash and leftover food, she could take her time sorting her resupply and packing her bear canister.

She opened her bucket and removed the bubble wrap filling the empty space at the top. *Oh, Bob. You've outdone yourself!* A small bag of chips and two packaged cakes sat on top. They were much too fragile to carry in a bear can. And a can of wine. He must have snuck these in before taking the buckets to the post office. That's the kind of support she needed every day.

How did he know she'd need such a boost right now? She ate the chips first, which caused her to drink more of the water she desperately needed. Next, she popped the tab on her can of Merlot and sipped it in between bites of the moist cakes. What a great decision to claim her bucket this afternoon.

Time to get back to work. She dumped the rest of the contents on the table. Fortunately, she had repackaged most things at home when she had more time and energy. She poked holes in a few of the packages that had bloated at the higher elevation so they would be easier to squeeze into the bear can. Next she began the game of bear can tetris by placing snack bars and fish packets vertically around the side and filling the void with her bags of dinners. She kept the bulkiest dinner, macaroni and cheese, out for dinner tonight. She continued to match available spaces to the items left until it was full–maybe a little overfull–then put her toothpaste and sunscreen on top. She stood up and pushed down on the contents. After rocking the lid back and forth and making a few crunching noises, she secured the lid.

After finishing her wine and dinner at the picnic table, she walked off in search of a campsite. Her legs nearly gave out when she saw the camping area. Where did all these people come from? There were more people here than she had seen the last three days on the trail. She set up her tent in the largest spot still available, but only had about forty feet of space on each side. She took her shoes off and laid on top of her sleeping bag. The inflatable air pad and pillow would have to wait until she caught her second wind.

Her mind kept working, even though her body was resting. She should be walking to the river to take a sorely needed bath, one she skipped at Marie Lake. She should be washing her clothes. She could be meeting some of her neighbors. But all she could do was lay there–and think. *I'm only halfway, and I'm tired, dirty, and lonely. How will I make another ten to twelve days? Bob will meet me in about a week, but I don't know if I can even make it that far. Maybe I should leave via the Bishop Pass trail. It's another day of hiking, but I hear it is beautiful. I could catch a shuttle to the town of Bishop from there.*

She woke up an hour later. She never took naps and attributed it to the wine. But she felt so much better. Perhaps her confidence would be restored by a full night of sleep, and she would be able to finish after all.

20

Sorry

2022

Day 8

August 12 - Muir Trail Ranch to Le Conte Canyon

Bob awoke when his entire body twitched. He was disoriented after being yanked out of his deepest sleep in days. The roof of the tent was bright. Zippers were opening and closing and stoves were roaring. It was all coming back to him now. His watch confirmed his fear; it was after 8 AM. He had checked his watch every sixty to ninety minutes for most of the night. At first, the noisy conversations of trail families catching up on their adventures kept him awake. Just as he fell asleep, the wind battered his tent and thunder chased his neighbors into their tents. The first flash of lightning had him seeing stars. Then, large drops of water pounded his tent. Shortly thereafter, he heard a few shouts–probably from a drenched backpacker with a poorly pitched tent. He used his headlamp to check for water on his tent floor or ponding around the tent.

He almost left his tent at 5:30 AM, but knew he needed more sleep.

Ironically, his best sleep came as the noise of waking hikers increased. He'd take any sleep he could get at this point. This wasn't a sprint. Too many sleepless nights would end his hike early.

He dressed quickly and stepped out of the tent. Cold rainwater dripped off the rainfly onto his back. Hannah was packing up. "Good morning. Did you sleep well?" she asked.

"Not really. I was awake most of the night with all the noise and the storm, but then I kind of overslept. If I break down camp in a hurry, can we hike together?"

Hannah stopped packing and stared at him for a few awkward seconds. "Bob, relax. Muir Hut isn't going anywhere. Take your time. Enjoy a relaxing breakfast. Let your tent dry a little."

Bob didn't respond. Finally, she said, "Sure. I'll wait for you." Following her own advice, she took her tent out of the mesh pocket of her pack and spread it over a small tree at the edge of the camping area. "Let me know when you're ready to take your tent down and I'll help you. It will be a little messy."

After he and Hannah shook out his rainfly and placed it on another tree, Bob made enough coffee for two. Hannah usually drank tea, but she didn't hesitate to accept the cup of coffee. Bob savored his instant coffee as his oatmeal mix soaked up hot water. The mix contained instant oatmeal, dried cranberries, pecans, brown sugar, and powdered milk, the kind of breakfast that stuck to his bones for hours.

With such a late start, he wouldn't reach Muir Pass today. The hut on top of Muir Pass was Cathy's most anticipated sight on the trail, but she didn't make it that far. He needed plenty of time to explore it for the both of them.

Bob and Hannah strolled out of camp just after ten. He committed to hiking at his normal pace, not trying to make up the lost time. The rocky knob where Mark's family had camped was empty. His shoulders drooped even further when he realized he may never see them again.

* * *

Mark's family had rejoined the JMT a mile ago. Two spur trails leave the JMT for MTR, one north and one south of the ranch. All but thru-hiking purists missed the two miles of the JMT in between, if they were stopping at MTR. The South Fork of the San Joaquin river grew fiercer on their right, carving its way through a tortuous canyon instead of rippling over a flat, rocky channel.

A trail sign by a bridge marked the turnoff for the Piute Pass trail and entry into Kings Canyon National Park. He and Jessica would not leave the park until they crossed over Kearsarge Pass on their exit.

Mark stopped, turned around, and said, "This is it." Time to part ways with Linda and Brock. Brock's surprise last night had forced them to pack differently this morning to ensure that Mark and Jessica had the right food and equipment to be comfortable and safe on their own. The father/son trip was turning into a father/daughter trip, but he couldn't be happier. Brock's behaviors were beginning to resemble those he remembered fondly from three years ago. Jessica was beaming with her new opportunity. They dropped their packs right after they crossed the bridge to take one last break together.

"Brock, don't push your mother too hard on the way out. It's about 16 miles to the trailhead, so it's going to take two days."

"Don't worry. We'll be careful."

Jessica sat next to Brock and put her arm around him. "Thank you so much. I can't believe I get to see Muir Pass and Rae Lakes now. You're not the same brother who threw rocks at those deer."

Brock leaned closer to her. "You're welcome. I know how much this means to you."

Mark said, "I'm so proud of you, son. What caused the change?"

"I don't know. It's hard to pick one thing. Watching everyone help each other when they run into trouble made me realize how selfish I've been. I got used to blaming others when things didn't go my way, but it's hard to do so when everyone else is trying to help you. If I had to pick one thing, it started when I saved Marty at Fish Creek. I didn't think about it. I just stepped on that rock and grabbed him. But then I saw how much it meant to Bob. I was proud of myself for a change. And then yesterday, with the food—anyway, thanks for making me come. I needed something like this."

"Maybe next year you and I can do the whole thing?" said Mark.

"Don't push it," said Linda.

Mark stood up. "OK, Jess. Ready to finish this thing?"

Jessica popped up, and Linda rose slowly. Linda appeared to be fighting back tears. She gave Jessica an extended hug, using the word careful at least three times. She let go and faced Mark. "Please take care of my little girl."

"Don't worry, she'll be taking care of me instead."

Jessica smiled and nodded.

"And send two messages a day, when you start and finish hiking every day."

"Yes, Mother. Can we go now?"

* * *

The roar of Evolution Creek drowned out Bob's huffing and puffing as he crested the first part of the climb to Evolution Valley. Evolution Valley, and Evolution Basin above it, were two of the most popular sections of the JMT. The thunderous waterfall straight ahead had enticed enough hikers off the main trail to create a well-worn social trail. How could anybody ignore the source of the noise?

When he broke through the trees, he saw nothing but white falling over 100 feet. The water made a loud slapping noise as it pounded the rocks below. The bottom of the fall wasn't visible from the end of the path, or at least as close as he was willing to get to the end. He scrambled on the rocks and ledges upstream to explore the impressive cascade of water from pool to pool. He took photo after photo, but resisted the urge to remove Marty from the sanctuary of his backpack. One little stumble and Marty would be pummeled and lost forever. Not even Brock could save him here.

He heard someone call, "Hey Bob!" If she hadn't yelled, he wouldn't have heard it. Hannah sat under a tree watching the waterfalls. He didn't think he would see her again after she opened a gap between them on the last climb.

But the falls had captured her in their web as well. *Thank you, trail!*

When he got closer, she said, "I could sit here all day–though I may never hear again," still yelling.

He sat next to her and grabbed a snack bar out of his hip belt pocket. They sat in silence. Words couldn't describe the beauty and power. They would tire of yelling anyway. Their faces said all they needed to know right now.

Even though it was too early to stop for the day, Bob scanned the surroundings for potential campsites out of curiosity. The trickle of a nearby stream sometimes helped him sleep, but he wondered if he could even sleep next to this incessant roar. He concluded the terrain was too steep and rocky to camp anywhere close.

When he returned to the main trail, his ears were ringing. He couldn't hear his footsteps or the chirping of the birds. He could still hear the water tumbling down the creek, but he no longer felt the vibrations from the water pounding the rocks. He and Hannah walked in silence until they could hear their footsteps again.

* * *

While they were at camp earlier in the day, Bob had asked Hannah to wait for him for a reason, but he didn't tell her why. She had looked puzzled, but didn't pry. When they reached the Evolution Creek crossing, Hannah sat on the rocky beach and began taking her shoes off. Bob took off his pack and sat next to her.

"Hold on, Hannah."

"What? Looks like we need to take our shoes off for this one."

"You might be wondering why I asked you to hike with me today."

"Yeah, but it's no big deal. You hiked with me from Tuolumne Meadows when I needed some company."

"But it is a big deal. This is the place."

Hannah looked at him as if he was losing his mind. She was probably getting tired of his cryptic comments. "What place?"

"This is where Cathy died." Bob stared at the water rushing by. The current was noticeable, but he didn't see the raging rapids he imagined.

"Oh, sorry. I didn't know." She stopped untying her shoes and patted him on the back. Tears fell from his eyes, soon to be carried away by the stream.

"She was alone when she crossed. She must have fallen and hit her head on a rock. I'll never really know." He felt a tickle under his nose, sniffled, and wiped it with his sleeve. "Her backpack probably kept her head underwater, and no one was around to keep her from drowning." He was sobbing now. "I should—been there. She could have held on—could have pulled her out—the water."

Hannah put her arm around him, and he leaned into her. "I'm sorry, Bob. Don't blame yourself. If you had known something like that was going to happen, you would have been there."

"But—I should have known—She tried to warn me—getting worn down. I could have joined her at Red's."

Between her tight embrace and his running nose, he struggled to breathe, just like he did climbing to Evolution Falls.

Bob unzipped a hip belt pocket on his pack and pulled out a rock similar in shape to the thousands between them and the other side of the creek. But this one was painted–a peaceful stream winding through the forest, then exiting into a vast meadow. He handed it to Hannah.

"It's beautiful." Hannah handed the rock back to him. "What can I do to help?"

"Just wait for me. I need you to help me cross the creek afterwards."

Hannah opened her mouth and leaned her head back. "Oh. Lyell Creek. Now I understand why you asked me to wait. Why didn't you say something?"

"I don't know. We had just met. I didn't want to ruin the excitement of beginning the hike."

Hannah squeezed him again and took her arm back. "I'll stay right here. Let me know if you need anything else."

Bob stood up and looked around. Hannah tied her shoelaces.

Unlike at Marie Lake, where he had many choices, he didn't see an obvious resting place for Cathy's rock. If he left it in the stream, the water would eventually carry it away. He spun around to examine the surrounding area. He saw many campsites, so the resting place could not be too obvious. The forest floor was mostly flat, but about 200 feet from the trail, a pile of boulders rose from the floor of the forest. He walked over and circled the pile, then climbed to the top boulder. With all the campers in the area, he imagined many would do the same. It would be too obvious on top of the boulder, but he could bury it somewhere in the surrounding rock pile. He removed several rocks on the side facing the creek, placed Cathy's rock down, and piled the other rocks back on top. That would have to do.

He heard voices behind him. *Oh no. Not him again!* Nick and Hannah were looking his way. Nick started walking toward him, but Hannah ran in front of him and turned around. She pointed her finger in his face as she spoke. Bob couldn't quite understand the words, but Nick backed away.

Bob returned his attention to Cathy's new memorial.

Cathy,

I'm so sorry! I don't expect you to forgive me. I made a mistake, several of them actually. Otherwise, you and I would be crossing this stream together or scratching another hike off your bucket list. The best I can do is help you finish the hike through myself. This trek is hard—really hard—just like you said it was. But my memories of you keep me going. Please stay with me—all the way to Mt. Whitney. Tomorrow will be special in another way, a better way. I'll take you to Muir Hut. You came so close. Rest in peace.

Bob hugged the boulder on top of the pile. Tears rolled down his cheeks when he closed his eyes. The granite absorbed them as they fell on the boulder. He couldn't bear to face Nick in this condition. But he heard no more voices, so he turned back toward the creek. Hannah sat alone on the rocky beach. Nick was gone. *Well done, Hannah.*

Bob walked back to Hannah's side and sat down. Her arm was around him before he reached the ground. Tears still blurred his vision, and he sniffled. "I saw what you did. Thank you!" He wiped his eyes. "It's time to move on."

"Are you sure?"

Bob nodded. "I told her I would finish the hike for her. I can't do that if I don't cross this creek. Everything I see from here on will be new to her."

They both replaced their shoes with camp sandals. Hannah stood up and offered Bob a hand.

"You picked a lovely spot for the rock."

"Thanks. Can you follow me across?"

"Of course."

He stuffed a shoe in each side pocket of his pack and put it on without closing the buckles. Hannah watched and did the same. She didn't look puzzled as she had at Lyell Fork when he asked her to unbuckle her straps. He started across, moving each foot forward six inches at a time. After ten steps, he turned around and saw Hannah had just started. His focus on balance overshadowed the pain in his freezing feet. He planted each hiking pole firmly before moving the next foot. The water climbed to the middle of his shin before receding. The water level must be much lower than when Cathy tried to cross last year. He was three-quarters of the way across now. His next foot sank six inches farther than he expected. He leaned to the right, and his pack swung, but he used his hiking poles to stop the momentum. The following step was only a few inches deep. And then it was over. He was safely across. Hannah rushed across behind him. They both sat on some tree roots where the creek had eroded the soil underneath, a great bench to dry off their feet and put on their socks and shoes.

"Thanks. I don't think I would have made it across without you."

"Yes, you would. You were focused and ready. Nice job."

"Hey, the hike to Evolution Lake will be steep. I'm not sure I can make it that far. Feel free to go ahead now. I won't be very good company anyway."

"Thanks. I may do that. I really wanted to camp at Evolution Lake tonight. I hope I don't run into Nick again."

"You can handle him. I saw it first hand."

He grinned at her for the first time all day.

* * *

Fortunately, the trail following Evolution Creek was mostly flat. Bob was just going through the motions. He was physically and emotionally drained. Despite the massive meadows on the right and the beautiful walls of Evolution Valley, he focused on only two things: his next footfalls and the Hermit at the end of the valley. Unlike most of the mountains along the trail, the Hermit was a massive pyramid standing alone. It reminded him of a volcano, but he suspected it was just a dome of solid granite. He would camp near its base since he didn't have the energy for the steep climb to Evolution Lake. He would tackle that with fresher legs, and hopefully a rested mind, in the morning.

He noticed the sign for the McClure Meadow ranger station, but didn't bother walking up the hill to check for notices or the weather forecast. The trail began to climb, so Bob stopped and dropped his pack on the first clear spot to the right. The Hermit hovered over him now, providing some welcome shade. Some hikers might be intimidated by it or feel claustrophobic, but he welcomed the sight. He needed someone looking over him tonight. Hannah, Mark, and Jessica were probably at Evolution Lake. Good for them. They deserved the experience. If he slept well, he would leave early and attempt to catch them before Muir Pass. He would love to see their faces when they first saw the hut. They might resemble how Cathy would have reacted.

* * *

Mark and Jessica set up camp at the top of a small hill on the north end of Evolution Lake. Jessica was making the most of her new opportunity to finish the hike. She had pulled Mark along all day by taking fewer and fewer breaks for him to catch up. Fortunately, much of the hike had been flat, but the last couple of miles were straight up. He lost sight of her several times, but couldn't spare the breath to protest. However, it was all worth it. Evolution Lake was a favorite of many hikers. Mark placed it at number two so far; Jessica refused to pick one over the others.

Nick had surprised them earlier while they were setting up their tents. "Oh, you two again. Where are your wife and son?"

"They left the trail at the Piute Pass trail as planned." Nick scanned the area while Mark replied. His eyes fixed on a small, flat spot fifty feet away. "Is anyone using that spot?"

"Yeah. Bob is meeting us up here."

"Oh, great. Him, again. Alright, I'm getting out of here. I can tell when I'm not wanted." He walked down the hill.

They sat on their bear canisters facing the lake. The jagged peaks on their left were named after biologists who contributed to the field of evolution: Darwin and Mendel, among others. The granite was nearly white now, segmented into rectangular blocks and slabs by black stains and fractures. Trees were small and sparse, but they added some much needed contrast. Grass surrounded the outlet stream. This was his favorite setting on the trail: white granite, blue water, and green shrubs and grasses. The basin above would be even starker, just blue and white.

Several solo hikers and small groups had set up tents closer to the lake. It was too late in the day for SOBOs to contemplate crossing Muir Pass. NOBOs were exhausted from the climb and descent and couldn't bear to leave the beauty of the basin. A tall, solo hiker wandered off the trail looking for a campsite.

"That looks like Hannah," said Mark.

"Where?" Jessica sat up straight and blocked the glare with her hand.

Mark pointed toward the outlet of the lake.

"Yeah, it is." Jessica stood up and waved her hands while yelling, "Hannah!"

Mark put his fingers in his ears when she called a second time.

Hannah looked their way and walked up the hill.

"Please tell me there's a spot up here. I'm beat."

"Yep. One left." Jessica pointed to the side.

"May I?"

"Sure. If Bob hasn't shown up yet, I doubt he will," said Mark.

"He and I left MTR late and hiked together for a while. He didn't think he would make it this far, so he told me to go ahead."

After Hannah deposited her pack on her spot, she returned with her bear can and a bottle of water for a quick break before making camp.

"Bob had an emotional day. Did you know his wife died at the Evolution Creek crossing?"

"No. We knew she died on the trail, but not how and where. Poor guy," said Mark.

"What happened to her?" asked Jessica.

"She fell and drowned. Must have hit her head on a rock, and no one was around to help."

Mark and Jessica both looked at the ground and were silent for a minute.

"We should wait for him in the morning," said Jessica.

"Great idea," said Hannah. "Have you seen Nick today? I had to chase him away from Bob at the creek and was afraid I would catch up with him again."

"Oh, we took care of him already," Mark said. Jessica and Hannah grinned at each other.

* * *

Dear Cathy,

Today was the hardest day of the trip. Yes, I didn't sleep well again and I hiked twelve miles, but it was more of an emotional struggle than a physical one. I passed the point where your hike ended. I didn't know if I could pass through it alone, so I asked Hannah to hike out from MTR with me. She kept creeping ahead of me, but I caught up with her at Evolution Falls. I imagine that you stopped there to admire the power and beauty of the water as Hannah and I did.

I hid your most special rock in a big rock pile overlooking the creek so no one would ever mess with it. The guilt was unbearable. I couldn't help but picture your body, face down in the creek—still except for your hair flowing downstream. It was like a nightmare. I kept reaching for you, but my arm was never quite long enough. It took forever for you to fall. I would have never made it across without Hannah. She urged me on and followed me across to ensure my wobbly legs would make it.

But now that I'm across, the trail will be new to both you and I. I'm excited to show you the wonderful sights ahead, the sights you looked forward to so much: Muir Pass, Rae Lakes, Mt. Whitney ... I'm sorry I didn't share many views with you today. I was in a daze, marching toward the Hermit, one step at a time. But tomorrow is another day, a better day, the beautiful climb by lake after beautiful lake toward the Muir Hut. I will share every bit with you. You deserve it.

I just realized that Marty never made it out of the pack today. I'll make it up to him tomorrow. Maybe he can ride on top of the pack; I'll have to add secondary retention so he doesn't escape like he did on you.

Love, Bob

21

Loss

2021

July 25 - Evolution Creek

A wide, gurgling stream interrupted Cathy's brisk pace on the smooth trail through the forest. She looked for logs or stepping stones, which had given her dry passage on previous water crossings. None here. This must be the notorious Evolution Creek, in some years, the only water crossing on the JMT that required hikers to get their feet wet throughout the hiking season. Early in the summer and after heavy rainfall, the creek raged and caused some hikers to cross where it widened in an adjacent meadow. But it was late July. The rocks on the creek bottom caused ripples instead of rapids. The current appeared to be harmless from the shore. After 117 miles on the JMT and dozens of water crossings, she would finally have to get her feet wet to move forward.

But she was prepared. Wet shoes and socks could lead to blisters, so she had brought sandals to wear during such crossings and while washing off in the frigid lakes. She also wore them in camp to let her feet breathe and allow her shoes and socks to dry. Cathy removed her backpack and sat next to it on the rocky beach. She unhooked her sandals from a clip attached to her pack and replaced her shoes and socks. Her feet enjoyed the cool air after spending all morning sweating in her shoes. They would be shocked by the icy water during the first few steps, but their aching bones would be numbed and soothed by the time she reached the other side. She wiggled her toes to take advantage of their unexpected freedom. She stuffed her socks in her shoes, tied the shoelaces together, and hooked them to the clip on her pack, tugging on them to make sure they were secure. Watching her shoes float down the creek would be terrifying.

She stood up and buckled the waist belt and chest strap on her backpack. Bob would have wanted her to wait for company before crossing, just in case she ran into trouble. But if he hadn't abandoned her days before the trip, there would be no decision, no waiting. He would be her standby. She looked up the trail on both sides and saw no one. Based on how few hikers she had seen this morning, she might have to wait an hour before anyone arrived. She decided to forge ahead. After all, the water appeared to be less than a foot deep. How much trouble could she get into?

The first steps stung her feet and took her breath away. She stood still for a few seconds while her feet became numb and she regained her breath. The shallow water along the shoreline of a lake warmed in the sun, but the water in a stream was replaced every second by water just as cold. As she moved forward, her feet wobbled as they settled among the loose rocks on the bottom. She used her hiking poles to keep her balance, planting both poles before raising a foot. Her legs were surprisingly hard to move forward. Most hikers underestimated the power of flowing water on their legs. The water caught by her sandals as she lifted her feet burned her fatigued thighs. The current pushed her downstream with each step, so she angled slightly upstream to compensate, further increasing the load on her legs.

When she reached the middle of the creek, she abandoned any idea of pausing to soak her feet. This crossing was much more difficult than it appeared from shore. Her feet had already passed from their initial shock, through numbness, to a deep ache. The water was up to her knees now. Had she misjudged the depth? By how much? The water rose two more inches on her next step. Should she turn around and try another line? *One more step; maybe I just stepped into a small hole.* After her next step, the water was just below her knee. She sighed in relief.

She tried to pick up the pace, but her legs were tiring. The water was only about eight inches deep now. Her right foot came down on a large, round rock and slid down the side. Sharp pain jabbed her right ankle, so she lifted her right leg to relieve the pressure. Unfortunately, she had already shifted her weight to that side, and her heavy backpack was leaning that way. Her arms flailed and her hiking poles swung as she tried to regain her balance. She tried to stab the bottom of the creek with her poles, but she no longer had a grip on the handles. The water rushed toward her face. Her last sensation was the frigid water stinging her face, just as it had done to her feet minutes ago.

* * *

Bob was at the plant, but his mind was elsewhere. He checked for texts on his phone every thirty minutes in case the audible alerts were disabled somehow. One of his safety inspectors had even sent a text to test it. He checked his email just as often, both his work and personal addresses. He had not received a message from Cathy for two and a half days now. After his first sleepless night, he convinced himself that she had run out of juice in her power bank. During the second night, he considered that perhaps she had lost or damaged the device. But she should be at MTR by now, and they had a laptop hikers could rent by the minute to send emails. If her device wasn't working, surely she would have sent him an email. She wouldn't have left him worrying like this, even if she was still mad at him.

He logged in to Cathy's email account and found the email confirming receipt of their buckets by MTR. He replied to the email, asking if Cathy had claimed the bucket yet.

He should have gone with her. She even gave him a second chance at Red's Meadow. His team at the plant was doing an excellent job on their own. Sometimes he even felt like he was slowing them down. One of his inspectors told him he was crazy for staying behind. "I know you love us, but she's your wife, man! There's no way I could hike 200 miles by myself." He was right. She was right. He had abandoned all the values he espoused at work when he refused to go with her. *Please be safe, Cathy. Just make it to Independence. I'll be there to help you finish. I love you!*

* * *

When Bob got home, he went straight to the computer and checked Cathy's email. Nothing from MTR. He couldn't wait any longer. From their preparation for the trip, he remembered that the counties provided search and rescue services in California. He found a California map and saw that she had most likely been in Fresno County for the last couple of days.

"Fresno County Sheriff's Office. How can I help you?"

"Hi. My wife is hiking the John Muir Trail. I've been getting daily updates through her satellite device, but I haven't received one for a couple of days. I was wondering if you've received any calls for help?"

"What is your name, sir?"

"Bob. Bob Riley."

"Oh—hold on just a second."

Bob's stomach clenched. Why did she pause when she heard his name? Had she heard something?

A one minute wait seemed like ten.

"Hello, sir."

"Hi, I was calling to check on my wife hiking the JMT."

"My name is Officer Chadwick. What is your wife's name, Mr. Riley?"

"Cathy."

There was no immediate response. Bob thought the line might have been disconnected.

"Hello. Are you still there?" Bob asked.

"Uh. Yes sir. I'm still here. Where do you think she would be on the trail right now?"

"I'm not sure. I haven't heard from her in a couple of days, but I would

142

guess somewhere around MTR. I emailed them earlier today, but I haven't heard back yet."

"Sir, I'm afraid I have some bad news for you. Your wife was found in Evolution Creek this morning. Ummm. She has passed away."

Bob couldn't speak. In fact, he had stopped breathing. By the time he started breathing again, he was sobbing.

"Sir, I'm so sorry. We've been trying to find her contact information. Neither her phone or satellite device were working. I'm so sorry you had to find out this way."

"But—but—how could that be. She was experienced—what happened?"

"We don't know much. A couple of hikers found her face down in the water. They tried CPR, but she was already gone. She probably fell, hit her head on a rock, then drowned. The coroner might be able to figure out more."

"Oh my God! This can't be. She wouldn't fall."

"I'm sorry for your loss, Mr. Riley."

"Where—is she?

"We flew her out a few hours ago. She's in the county morgue in Fresno."

"Oh—Oh—No ..."

"Mr. Riley, can I call anybody to help you?"

"No ..."

Bob dropped his phone and laid on the floor in a fetal position. He felt as if he would sob forever. How could he have left her alone when she needed him most?

22

Guilt

2022

Day 9

August 13 - Le Conte Canyon to Muir Pass

Bob felt refreshed even though he left the tent before 5 AM. The combined physical and emotional exhaustion finally allowed him to sleep soundly. A bear could have batted around his bear canister for hours, and he wouldn't have heard it. He finished his morning chores in forty-five minutes versus the typical sixty to ninety, hoping he could catch up with Mark, Jessica, and Hannah before Muir Pass.

Evolution Lake came into view after he passed a marsh created by the outlet stream. When approaching these large lakes from below, he relished the first view where his eyes were at water level, as if he were standing in the lake with the water just below his nose. The water seemed to go on forever. But this time, three silhouettes interrupted his view across the lake, one topped with a pink hat. They had waited for him! Mark, Jessica, and Hannah sat in a row–their backpacks leaned against each other nearby. They were packed and ready to go. He paused so he could greet them with a dry face.

They didn't turn around as he approached, but Bob immediately understood why. The still water was disturbed only by the expanding ripples made by trout snatching insects from the surface. Jagged peaks lined the left of the lake. Smaller hills of granite on the right could easily be climbed by those with extra time and energy.

"Was breaking down camp so tiring that you needed a break already?" Bob said.

Mark and Hannah spun their heads around. Jessica stood up and jogged toward him. He braced so she wouldn't topple him over, but she stopped just in front of him.

"No. We were waiting for you."

Mark and Hannah approached him. "We know you had a rough day yesterday, but figured you wouldn't be far behind," Mark said.

Hannah added, "We wanted to experience Muir Pass with you. I know how special it is to you—and Cathy."

"Y'all are too kind. I must admit that I left a little early, hoping you would be waiting. Otherwise, I wouldn't have caught up with you. You've been waiting long enough. Let's go!" Bob knew their favor was not complete. He could only keep up with them if they slowed their pace. Jessica was the first to take off. After a few steps, she looked back at Bob, still standing. She waved him on. "Are you coming?"

Bob followed. Mark and Hannah lagged, allowing him and Jessica to set the pace. As they walked up and along the left side of Evolution Lake, Jessica stopped frequently for him to catch up. When his pace slowed, she waited for him, but began walking again before he could catch his breath. By the time they reached the inlet of the lake, they had compromised on a pace that allowed them to enjoy the views of the long series of lakes along the way, yet still make steady progress to the pass.

The crossing of Evolution Creek at the inlet of the lake was much wider than the one he struggled across yesterday. Large rocks with flat tops were staggered at a stride length apart all the way across. Unfortunately for Jessica, the stride length was that of a six-foot adult. He couldn't blame the trail crew. The rocks were massive, and he winced when imagining how they moved them into place. He felt sorry for Jessica as she overextended her short legs to reach rock after rock. He wanted to help, but he couldn't figure out how to do so without making it harder for both of them.

They all stopped when they sighted Sapphire Lake. Its name needed no explanation. The lakes were becoming bluer as they climbed, helped by the rising sun. The blue was so dark that it appeared to have dyed the rocks along the outlet stream black. The splashing water sparkled against the dark background as if it was carrying silver glitter.

Jessica stopped at the top of a rise in the trail, but she wasn't looking back to urge him along. He joined her and saw another wide expanse of blue water surrounded by white rock. The sun made the contrast even deeper–the white was blinding, the blue seemed fluorescent. The trees had given up a few hundred feet below, creating a moonscape interrupted only by the blue water. Without sunglasses, the sunlight reflecting off the surrounding granite and the ripples on the lake would have reduced their open eyes to slivers.

They stood on the north shoreline of the lake, not able to see the far end around a bend in the trail. This was Wanda Lake, named after one of John Muir's daughters, as was Helen Lake on the other side of Muir Pass. The trail followed the lake on the left, just feet from the water's edge. When he looked down at the edge of the lake, the clear water deepened at a forty-five-degree angle. Bob dipped his hand in the water to feel the coldest water yet on the trail. The sharp bank and frigid water, along with the anticipation of Muir Hut, kept everyone from taking a late morning dip to freshen up. However, Jessica surprised Bob by insisting on a water and snack break.

He and Jessica waited for Mark and Hannah before finding a place to settle. As they ate and drank, Jessica peered at a dip between the peaks in the distance. Bob followed her gaze. He was terrible at identifying passes from afar. Selden Pass was the only one so far which was clear from a distance. His map showed they were only two miles and 600 feet of elevation from the top. The climb had been steady and manageable so far, but he knew the last 500 feet would be straight up. They usually were.

"I can't see the hut, can you?" Jessica asked.

"I think so, but I'm not sure." Hannah said and then took a photo. She zoomed in on the picture with Jessica looking on. "There it is."

Jessica looked back at the pass. "I see it now. It still seems so far away. We've been climbing for hours."

"But what a beautiful climb it's been," said Hannah.

"Can we get moving again?" said Jessica.

Her dad said, "Yes ma'am."

* * *

Despite the increasing grade, Jessica accelerated as she approached Muir Pass. Bob picked up his own pace so he could reach the pass with her. The top of Muir Hut was now just above Jessica's head, a couple of switchbacks ahead of him. When she stopped for the final time to wait for him, he marched right past her.

"What are you waiting for?" he said, without looking back.

"Bob!"

A couple of minutes later, the entire hut was visible. Though it only filled a fraction of his field of vision, it was all he saw. He was finally here. He turned to watch Jessica's reaction. Instead of the bouncing girl he observed on other occasions, he saw a motionless young lady with a wide open mouth. Only her eyes moved, from top to bottom, left to right. Mark and Hannah arrived behind her. Finally, Jessica took a big breath. "Wow. This is awesome."

She turned toward her dad and hugged him. "Dad, thank you so much for letting me come this far."

Mark put his arm around her. "You have Brock to thank for that."

"Yeah, I know, but he's not here."

Hannah walked over to him. "What do you think? Is it everything you hoped it would be?"

"And then some. I can't believe I'm here."

The Muir Hut is a marvel of construction in the wilderness. The Sierra Club built the structure in 1930 in homage to John Muir and to provide shelter for hikers caught on the pass during storms. Except for the door, windows, and a few other accessories, it appeared to be constructed of local materials. Massive rectangular blocks of granite served as steps to reach the wooden door. Smaller granite blocks of varying sizes formed the circular structure about fifteen feet across. The blocks on the roof were similar, but they sloped toward the center, like on an igloo.

Only the incessant chirping of marmots and pikas disturbed the serenity. What were they trying to say? Maybe Marty could interpret? They must encounter people all the time without consequence, and predators were rare at this elevation.

Jessica dropped her pack and leaped up the steps which were half the height of her legs. Bob didn't know how she did it; his knees wouldn't allow such a feat. Mark followed her up the stairs. About halfway up, the door was split in two horizontally, such that the top half could open with the bottom still closed. Why they included this feature, he didn't know. It resembled a door at a concession stand, but no cold beers or popcorn were available here. Three small panes of glass with embedded steel wire let light into the hut, along with a larger window on the side.

Jessica pushed both portions of the door open, and she and Mark stepped in. Bob heard Jessica yell, "No!" He entered the hut but saw nothing until his eyes adjusted from the bright white rock outside. He heard something crunch under his feet. Broken glass littered the floor of the hut. He felt no pain, but looked at the bottom of his shoes to ensure none of the glass had punctured his soles. Mixed among the broken glass were empty snack bags and wrappers. He expected to see crumbs, but the marmots must have cleaned up before they arrived. Bob thought of the group camped next to him and Hannah two nights ago. Maybe they had a party up here after all. The guilt and the smell of day-old whiskey nearly made him sick. Why hadn't he said something?

Mark followed Jessica when she left the hut abruptly.

Hannah appeared by Bob's side. "What is Jessica—oh, I see. Why would anyone do this?"

"It was probably the loud group camping near us at MTR. They were scheming to sleep up here."

"Yeah, I heard them too. But I figured it was just drunk talk."

"We won't let this spoil our experience. Let's clean up this mess. It won't take long."

Hannah set her pack on the bench along the wall. They each grabbed a discarded plastic bag and began filling it with food wrappers and glass fragments. Bob figured the smaller ones he couldn't pick up would turn into sand over time, just like the granite did.

Once they were done, he collected all the bags, took them outside, and placed them under some rocks so they wouldn't blow away. Jessica sat with Mark on the lower step to the hut.

Bob stood in front of Mark and Jessica. "Jess, let's start over. This is how you were meant to find the hut." Mark urged her up from the step and held her hand as she reentered the hut. Bob followed them in, pretending he was just arriving. Hannah sat on the rock bench which surrounded the wall. Jessica let go of Mark's hand, walked to the center, and looked straight up. "Wow!" She swayed, so Mark held her shoulder, then looked up himself. When he swayed, he looked at Bob and mouthed, "Thank you."

Bob walked to the fireplace. The hearth was sealed with concrete, presumably to discourage camping at night and to reduce water infiltration. A brass plaque sat on the mantle, explaining the history of the hut and showing busts of John Muir and William Colby. As Mark and Jessica circled the hut, examining all its features, Bob moved to the center and looked up. Hannah joined him and put her hand on his shoulder to steady them both.

The granite blocks appeared to spiral as they closed in on the apex. How did they do that? Did they succeed on the first try? When he had tried to build an igloo during a rare winter vacation in Michigan, it caved in when he was half done. The three stones forming the top fit together perfectly; not even a pinhole of sunlight shone through.

"Hold on." Bob retrieved Marty for the first of many photos. He handed his camera to Hannah. "Can you take a photo of us with the ceiling in the background?" Bob held Marty and looked up. Hannah stooped to capture both of them admiring the craftsmanship. Next, he took a photo of Marty on the mantle, just under John Muir's bust. He stepped over to the side window which was about two feet on each side and made of the same type of glass used in the door. No hikers were approaching from the north; perhaps they would have the hut to themselves a while longer.

Bob followed Mark and Jessica outside. He grabbed his sunglasses out of habit, but found he didn't need them. A large gray cloud had eliminated most of the glare. That moved in quick. Good thing he had left camp early. He grabbed Mark's shoulder as he passed him and Jessica on the steps. "Wait here for a second."

He took their photo in front of the door. Jessica's smile had returned, and Mark grinned. Hannah stepped out of the door, so he took a photo of the three remaining members of his trail family. When they were down off the steps, Bob placed Marty on the top step for a solo photo.

"Hey, Bob."

Bob turned around and Hannah took a candid shot of him. He walked clockwise around the hut for a better view of the chimney. The top was a thin slab of rock resting on four vertical stones to reduce the amount of water entering the chimney. A few smaller rocks formed a decorative pyramid on top.

After they had all circled the hut, they took a lunch break.

"Bob, where are you going to place Cathy's rock this time?" asked Hannah.

He took the rock out of one of his hip belt pockets and handed it to Hannah. "Wow. It's beautiful. I wouldn't be able to part with it." She gave it to Mark.

"I can have others made. This one is Cathy's, not mine. I don't know where to put it. I can't leave it inside. Someone would find it. I guess I could climb up the slope behind the hut and put it there. Or—if I could climb on top of the hut, it could go in the chimney. It would be safe there, and she could be part of the hut forever. But that looks kind of dangerous, and I'm too old and stiff to get up there anyway."

Jessica now had the rock. She stood up and walked to the north side of the hut by the window. "Bob, I think I can get up there from here." He joined her, along with Mark and Hannah. Rocks leftover from construction were piled about halfway up the vertical wall. The rocks in the wall were placed unevenly, creating lots of footholds, especially for small shoes. The roof rose at a sixty-degree angle, and the footholds were even larger.

Bob shook his head. "Jessica, no! It's too dangerous!"

Jessica placed the rock in her pocket and climbed on top of the stack of rocks.

Mark yelled, "Jessica, stop! We'll find a better place."

Jessica turned around and stared at her dad. Mark held his hand out for the rock. Hannah walked next to Jessica and held her hand out until Jessica removed the rock from her pocket and put it in Hannah's hand. Hannah helped Jessica down and immediately replaced her on top of the rocks.

"Hannah, how is this any better? Please get down." Bob said.

Jessica stood at the base of the hut and stood on her toes.

"Please don't." pleaded Mark.

"Hannah, stop!" yelled Bob.

Hannah could easily reach good handholds on the roof with her long arms. Her first step was on the windowsill, and second was on a rock that protruded several inches farther than the surrounding ones. She scaled the roof in seconds on her hands and toes. She sat on the apex and cherished the view, ignoring their continuing pleas for her to return to solid ground. As she prepared to go down the other side to the chimney, Bob, Mark, and Jessica ran to the other side of the hut. When they arrived, Hannah was already standing on the small flat space where the chimney joined the roof. The opening of the chimney was at her waist. She looked down at Bob, then dropped the rock in the chimney. She smiled when she heard the echoes of the rock bouncing on the bottom.

"Bob, toss Marty up here."

"No way! Get down before you hurt yourself."

"But I'm already up here." She held out her hands, ready to catch Marty.

Bob shook his head and didn't budge.

Hannah climbed around the side of the roof on her hands and toes, back toward the rocks where she climbed up.

Jessica said, "Hannah, be careful."

Bob, Mark, and Jessica jogged back to the other side of the hut.

When Hannah attempted to step on the windowsill with her left foot, it slipped off, and she slid down the side. Her foot only fell a couple of feet, but she lost her balance and fell backwards. Her arms went back to brace her fall, but her head hit a rock anyway.

By the time she hit the rocks, Bob and Mark were at her side. Jessica watched with both hands covering her mouth. Hannah was motionless, and her eyes were closed. Bob looked up at Mark and saw the same panic-filled expression that must have been on his own face.

"Hannah? Can you hear me?" Mark said in a jittery voice.

Bob bent down to place his ear near her nose. "She's still breathing." He saw no blood where her head rested on the rock.

Bob tapped her shoulder. "Hannah?"

Jessica screamed, "Hannah! No!" Mark left to try to calm Jessica. Bob brushed the hair off of Hannah's forehead. He didn't think she had broken her neck or back, but was reluctant to move her. He shook her shoulder, and she grimaced. His tone changed from grave concern to cautious optimism as he said her name again. She opened her eyes and rubbed the top of her head with her hand. She tried to sit up, but Bob held her shoulder down.

"Where am I? Who are you?"

Bob continued to hold her shoulder. "You don't remember? We're at the hut on Muir Pass."

"Muir Pass? How did I get here? And who are all these people looking at me?"

Jessica started sobbing.

"Hannah, it's Bob. We're hiking the John Muir Trail. You fell while getting off the roof of the hut." Bob's tears fell on Hannah's shirt. "I'm so sorry. I should have never mentioned going up there."

"But why would I go up there?"

"It's a long story. Let's make sure you're OK first."

Jessica sat down next to Hannah and held her hand.

Bob continued, "Does your back or neck hurt?"

Hannah lifted her head before Bob could stop her and rubbed where it hit the rock. "No. I don't think so. Just my head." Bob was relieved to see no blood on her hand.

"Can you move your hands and feet? Do you have any numbness?"

Bob looked down at her feet, and she rolled both of her ankles. "They're OK. I'm so confused."

She tried to sit up again, and Bob acquiesced now that she had alleviated his concern over back and neck injuries. Jessica helped her up, and Bob checked the back of her head more closely. No blood, but a knot the size of a golf ball. His first aid training at the plant was coming in handy.

"Good girl. Are you dizzy at all?"

"No. I think I'm OK, but I still don't know who you are."

Bob lost his breath momentarily. "You may have a concussion. Your memory should come back soon. Let's get you back in the hut."

Hannah tried to stand up, but started leaning to the side immediately. "Whoa," she said as Bob helped her sit back down.

Jessica and Mark each grabbed an arm and helped Hannah up. They escorted her over the rocks to the door of the hut and helped her sit down on the bench along the wall. Bob grabbed the water bottle from her pack and brought it to her. She put it down at her side, but Bob held it near her mouth. "At least take a few sips. It will make you feel better."

"I feel like I might throw up."

Bob nodded to Mark and then the door. "Jessica, can you sit with Hannah?"

Instead of replying, Jessica sat next to Hannah and put her arm around her. Bob followed Mark outside.

Bob looked down and shook his head. "I shouldn't have—"

"Bob, stop it. It's not your fault. You can't protect everybody all the time." Mark patted his shoulder.

Bob looked up. "What do we do now?"

Mark said, "Let's give her a little time to rest. If she doesn't get better soon, we can call for help."

* * *

153

Jessica sat with Hannah while Mark and Bob checked in about every ten minutes. Hannah refused to eat anything despite their numerous requests. She remembered planning the hike and her father's objections, but still didn't remember who he, Mark, and Jessica were. After thirty minutes, Hannah said she needed to lie down and take a nap. Mark fetched her foam sleeping pad to lie on, and she placed her head on a fleece jacket bundled up on Jessica's lap. Bob asked each of the arriving hikers if they were a doctor. He was pleasantly surprised when one of the youngest visitors said she was a second-year medical student. She examined Hannah and agreed with Bob and Mark's suspicions that Hannah had a concussion. They discussed an evacuation by helicopter and agreed it was a likely outcome.

Bob removed the satellite device from his pack. He had never sent a message from it, much less an SOS message. With Cathy gone and no kids, no one was left at home to worry about his whereabouts. He looked at the SOS button and noticed that he needed to slide a switch to unlock it.

The clouds above him were becoming darker. "Hey Mark. I just pressed the SOS button. It looks like we'll be here a while. Can you go down and get more water before these clouds turn into a full-blown storm?"

"Sure, which side do you think is better?"

"I don't know, but I would head back down to Wanda Lake. We know where the water is down there. Helen Lake is on the other side, but I can't see it from here."

"OK." Mark took his pack inside the hut and unloaded the heavy and bulky gear. He put his water filter and all the empty water bottles and bags he could find in his pack and took off, nearly running.

"Be careful. We don't need another injury."

Mark didn't respond, but slowed his pace slightly.

Bob paired his satellite device with his phone so he could type messages more easily once he received a response. A few minutes later, he received an incoming message.

"What is your emergency?"

"We are on Muir Pass. My hiking partner hit her head, was unconscious briefly, and appears to have a concussion. She is nauseous and disoriented."

"How long was she unconscious? Is she bleeding? Any numbness or weakness in the limbs?"

Bob appreciated the grouped questions. If asked individually, this would take forever with the lag time. "Just a few minutes. No bleeding. No other symptoms, but she won't eat and just laid down for a nap."

"Thanks. Monitor her condition closely and encourage her to drink some water. Hold on while we check resources."

Minutes separated the first few exchanges, but he waited twenty minutes for the next reply. He walked inside to give Jessica an update, leaving his device outside so it had a full view of the sky. With all his experience in emergencies at the plant, he knew to be patient, but the waiting still distressed him. Finally, his device chirped.

"We are checking resources for a helicopter evacuation, but it may be delayed due to the weather. Stay tuned."

Bob's emotions swung from hope to despair in just those few words. Before he could reply, his device chirped again.

"The park ranger from Le Conte Ranger Station is on patrol just south of the pass. She is on her way to assist."

He was grateful for the help. The ranger would be better trained for emergencies in this unusual setting and would have better communication equipment.

He looked at the sky. More clouds. Darker clouds. On one hand, he wished they would just make a little noise, release their load, and move on. He knew the helicopter wouldn't fly after dark, especially over this terrain. They had the hut to protect themselves. In fact, its official name was the John Muir Memorial Shelter. But if it stormed now, Mark would be exposed to the violent weather for another sixty to ninety minutes. He feared they would all be spending the night in the hut.

* * *

Mark returned an hour later.

"That was quick." Bob looked at the sky. "And a good thing. We're about to get stormed on."

"I filled all the bags and bottles and left when I saw the skies getting worse. Six liters. I hope that's enough."

"Thanks. I've been in touch with the emergency responders. They plan to fly Hannah out, but can't come now because of the weather. By the time the storm moves on, I'm afraid it will be too dark to fly. Looks like we're spending the night up here."

"How's she doing?"

"About the same. She's been sleeping most of the time. I just woke her up, and she drank a few sips of water. I also told her we were arranging for a helicopter evacuation. Jessica has been with her the entire time."

"Doesn't surprise me. I'll go relieve her now."

"Oh. I forgot to tell you. A park ranger is coming to help with Hannah and the evacuation."

"Great." Mark walked inside the hut.

A few minutes later, Bob noticed the ranger approaching from the south side of the pass. A woman dressed in brown pants and a gray shirt approached Bob. *S. Curtis* was embroidered on a patch on her shirt. "Hello. Are you Bob?"

Bob shook her hand. "Yes."

"I'm Sally, the park ranger at Le Conte Ranger Station. I heard on the radio that we have a hiker who may need a helicopter evacuation?"

"Yes. Hannah is inside. Thanks for coming."

"No problem. It helps to have a ranger onsite to coordinate the evacuation." She patted the satellite radio attached to her shoulder.

Bob led Sally into the hut. Mark was now sitting with Hannah, and Jessica was filtering water. He tapped Hannah on the shoulder. "Hannah. Wake up. A park ranger has come to help you."

Hannah opened her eyes. "What?"

Sally squatted in front of Hannah. "Hi Hannah. My name is Sally. I'm a park ranger."

Mark stood up and Sally took his place on the bench.

"Hannah, do you know where you are?"

"Not really. Someone said I was in Muir Hut, but I don't know how I got here."

"How did you get hurt?"

"I don't know, but my head really hurts." She cupped her hands around her face.

"I'm going to look at your head." Hannah winced when Sally parted her hair to look for bleeding.

"Sorry, dear. Does anything else hurt beside your head? Your neck? Arms? Legs?"

"No."

"I'm going to check the rest of your body. Let me know if anything hurts."

Sally gently pressed on Hannah's neck and shoulders, then moved to her arms and legs, slowly moving the main joints. Hannah winced slightly when Sally tried to move her right wrist. Sally felt the area closely, apparently looking for obviously broken bones. She looked at Bob. "Did she try to brace her fall?"

"Yeah. That's probably why it is sore."

Sally nodded. "Hannah, do you remember my name?"

"No. Sorry."

Sally gently squeezed the top of her shoulder. "No need to be sorry. You must have hit your head pretty hard.

"Can you try to sit up now?"

"Sure." Hannah tried to sit up, but then grabbed the sides of her head with her hands and leaned to the side. "Ouch. My head really hurts." Bob grabbed her shoulders and helped her back down to the bench.

Sally said, "You're not ready to hike down the mountain. We're going to arrange for a helicopter to fly you out. But it might be a while before they get here since the weather is bad."

Bright light flashed through the window, followed five seconds later by a deafening bang.

Sally looked at Bob and Mark. "Can one of you set up a tent on the floor? The roof may look stout, but it leaks in heavy rain. We need to make sure Hannah stays comfortable and warm until the helicopter arrives." She looked at Jessica who was still filtering water. "Good call to fetch some water. It could be a long night."

Sally walked to the doorway and used her radio to update the emergency responders. Mark set up Hannah's tent and Bob helped Hannah into it. They tied the door flap open, and Mark sat outside the door.

Sally stepped inside and closed the door to the hut. "The search and rescue team said they would try to fly out first thing in the morning." She sat down next to Bob on the rock bench.

"Bob, how far did Hannah fall?"

"Not far, maybe four feet. She almost caught herself, but she still banged her head pretty hard. She was unconscious for a couple of minutes."

"How did she fall?"

Bob looked at Mark and Jessica, but didn't respond.

"Bob?"

"It's a long story, but she fell while getting down from the top of the hut. Her foot slipped off the windowsill, and she fell from there."

"What! Why do people feel they have to climb up there? She isn't the first and won't be the last."

"I know. It was a terrible idea, and nothing you can say will make me feel worse about it."

* * *

Everyone spent the next few hours protecting Hannah and themselves from the cold water leaking from the roof and counting the seconds between the flashes and booms. Using the rule of thumb of one mile for every five seconds, Bob figured most of the lightning bolts were a mile or more away, but the time gap was less than a second for two of them. What would they have done without the shelter? Sally told him the structure did not provide adequate protection from lightning, but they agreed they had no better alternative. Hannah was in no condition to move down the trail, even with assistance, and they would all be exposed to lightning and rain for hours making their way down to the tree line at a slowed pace. He felt more secure with a solid, yet leaky and ungrounded, roof over their heads.

The skies cleared several hours later, but the sun was already behind the mountains. Bob's heart regretted the delay in evacuation, but his experience told him an evacuation would extend into darkness even if the helicopter left now. Flying a helicopter in the dark over the mountains would just endanger more people.

Sally established a loose rotation to care for Hannah, but also to allow them to get some rest so they could descend the trail in the morning. She laid with Hannah in her tent and advised Mark and Jessica to take a nap on their sleeping pads. Bob moved around to avoid the worst water leaks and made tea for him and Sally. Instead of recording a verbal update to Cathy on his phone, Bob typed a note.

* * *

Dear Cathy,

Our visit to Muir Hut has gone from wonder to horror. Hannah fell and hit her head while climbing down from the roof of the hut. I was thinking out loud where to put your rock and mentioned the chimney. I never thought she would go up there, but shame on me for even mentioning such a dangerous stunt. She appears to have a concussion and doesn't remember any of us. All of us are distraught. Fortunately, a ranger was nearby and is helping to arrange for a helicopter evacuation. Sally is very well trained and a big help. I will keep you posted. I hope my next update is about Hannah's improving condition.

Love, Bob

* * *

A couple of hours later, Sally tried to wake Hannah. She tapped on her shoulder first, but Hannah didn't move. Next, she rubbed her finger on Hannah's cheek. Hannah turned her head, but didn't wake up. She only woke when Sally shook her shoulder more forcefully and spoke her name over and over. Bob squatted by the side of the tent when he heard Sally repeating Hannah's name.

"Hannah, can you hear me?" he said.

"What? Where am I?"

"You're in Muir Hut. A park ranger came to take care of you. Do you remember her name?"

"A park ranger? When did he come?"

Sally said, "Hannah. I'm going to help you sit up now. I'd like you to drink some water."

She helped Hannah sit up. Hannah covered her mouth with her hand, and Sally leaned to the side. Sally gave her a minute, then raised a water bottle to her lips. Only half of the water made it in her mouth, so Sally guided Hannah's hands to the bottle. "Here, you hold it." Hannah took several sips on her own.

"Good girl. Do you want anything to eat?" Bob said.

Hannah shook her head ever so slightly. "I don't feel good. My head hurts—really bad."

Sally said, "I can give you some Tylenol, but that's about it." Sally reached outside the tent, grabbed a pill bottle out of her bag, and handed a pill to Hannah. "There you go. Now, drink some more."

"Thanks."

Bob and Sally kept talking to Hannah and encouraging her to drink until her eyes kept closing. Sally lowered her to the sleeping pad.

Sally left the tent, and she and Bob sat on the bench. "She seems to be getting worse. I'll let the rescue team know so they can fly out as soon as possible."

Bob sat next to the tent and muttered, "Poor Hannah. We'll get you out of here. Hang on a few more hours."

Sally called for a shift change, but Bob refused to lie down.

"At least get some fresh air," Sally told Bob.

She nodded for Mark to come over and sit next to the tent door. Sally and Bob put on their jackets and stepped outside.

Bob sat on one of the steps to the hut. Sally sat next to him. He wiped the tears from his cheeks, hoping she wouldn't notice.

"Come on, Bob. She'll be alright."

"But how do you know? She's getting worse, and morning seems so far away. I understand why they can't fly, but it's still frustrating. What else can we do?"

"I can't give her any more medication. We just need to keep her comfortable and drinking and continue monitoring her condition."

"What a day. I just paid respects to my wife at Evolution Creek, and now Hannah …" Bob started sobbing. Sally put her arm around him.

"Wait a minute. Are you Bob Riley?"

"Yeah, why?"

"And Cathy was your wife?"

Bob nodded.

"Oh my gosh! I had no idea."

"What do you mean?" Bob looked her in the eyes.

"I responded to her accident while I was sitting in for my partner at McClure ranger station. He had to go to town for family business."

"No way."

"Oh, I'm so sorry. That was a terrible accident."

"It should have never happened. I should have been there to help her. I backed out of the trip, and she kept asking me to join her on the trail. If only I had listened."

"Oh Bob. It was nobody's fault."

Bob's head bounced up and down as he sobbed.

"Can you tell me more about what happened?"

"I don't think I know more than you do. She had been out of the water a few hours by the time I arrived. The young couple that tried to save her was still there. They did everything they could with CPR, but she wasn't coming back."

Sally continued. "But I saw her before the accident."

Bob's eyes opened wide. "What? Did you talk to her?"

Sally nodded. "I was covering some of my partner's territory up near Evolution Falls. She was sitting on a rock watching the white water pound the rocks below. Her hair was wet with the mist carried by the wind. She looked like she was in a trance."

"I was there yesterday. I know the feeling." Bob pictured himself sitting next to Cathy at Evolution Falls, instead of Hannah.

"I was hungry, so I sat next to her and had a snack. She was so happy. Neither one of us said much. Words couldn't compete with the falling water. She told me how tired she was, but she would do it all over again. She couldn't go slow enough to soak in all the beauty."

"She said all that? She seemed kind of depressed in her messages. And definitely mad at me."

Sally shook her head. "Oh Bob, she wasn't mad. She was happier than anyone I've seen on the trail. Happier than I was when I was offered this job."

Bob stopped sobbing. "Thanks for telling me all of this, Sally. You can't believe the guilt I feel. But I'm so glad to hear she was having a wonderful time—before she died."

"You're welcome."

23

Flying

2022

Day 10

August 14 - Muir Pass to Dusy Basin

Jessica yelled, "It's coming! It's coming!" She had appointed herself as lookout once Sally was notified the helicopter had departed. The clouds had returned, but they were high and white. According to Sally, more threatening weather was moving in from the west, but they had time to evacuate Hannah to the east. Hannah's condition had not improved. She stayed awake only long enough for them to coax her to drink a few sips of water. Bob cringed every time she asked, "Who are you?"

Sally had prepared them for the arrival of the helicopter. All their gear was packed. She and Mark had moved the larger rocks from a couple of relatively flat areas near the hut that the pilot might choose for landing and cleared the area of loose debris. Muir Pass was one of the few where such a landing was possible. On most other passes, Hannah would have to be hoisted up to the helicopter or helped down the pass by a rescue team, both of which involved risk of further injury. From the photos he had seen, Forester Pass barely had room for half a dozen people to stand, much less to land a helicopter. Sally had also asked Mark and Jessica to go down each side of the pass about 300 feet to keep other hikers at a safe distance when the helicopter made its final approach.

Bob wasn't happy with one aspect of Sally's preparation. When he asked about accompanying Hannah on the helicopter, Sally stared at him and didn't respond for a few seconds.

"Bob, I don't think that's going to work."

"Why not?"

"Flying helicopters over the mountains is dangerous. The pilot has to stay within his weight allowance to reduce the risk. He's only planned for Hannah."

"But she'll be so confused by all the strangers, and who knows when family or friends will show up?"

"Bob, they'll take good care of her. I'm sure someone will be with her soon. I gave the response team the phone number for Hannah's father."

Bob shook his head and looked down at the ground. He knew she was right, but it was still hard to accept. How often had he used similar arguments over the last thirty years? He'd jeopardize not only his safety but also that of the pilot, paramedics, and Hannah.

"OK. OK. I understand. Safety first."

"Normally they would take her to Fresno, but due to the weather, they're taking her to the hospital in Bishop. If you really want to be with her, you can take the Bishop Pass trail to South Lake. It joins the JMT in eight miles and is about another twelve miles from there. You'll be in Bishop by tomorrow afternoon."

"Oh really. Sounds good. Maybe I can make it by tonight."

"Whoa. It's all downhill to the junction, but the Bishop Pass trail is tough. Please don't try to do it in one day."

"OK. You're right. That would be a bit much."

"If I were you, I would keep moving south. We can arrange for you to be updated on her condition, but it's your call. Hike your own hike. I'm sure

Hannah doesn't want to be the cause of ending your hike."

Bob now sat with Hannah on the bench inside the hut. "Hannah, the helicopter is almost here." She didn't respond. Bob shook her shoulder and repeated her name. She turned her head toward him slowly.

"Hannah, wake up. The helicopter is here."

"Helicopter? Is that what all the noise is? I can't believe I'm causing this much trouble. Can I watch the helicopter?"

"It will be very noisy and make your headache even worse. Just stay here, and the paramedics will come to you."

"OK."

As the helicopter got closer, Bob felt as if someone was slapping his ears. Hannah raised her hands to cover her ears.

"It's so loud. It hurts. Make it stop!"

Ten minutes later, Sally led the paramedics through the door. Bob stood up and offered his hand to the first one. "Hi. I'm Bob. Thanks for coming." The first paramedic nodded and bent over in front of Hannah. The other sat next to her.

"Hi Hannah. My name is Tim, and my partner is Judith. We're going to check you out and give you a ride to the hospital. Have you flown in a helicopter before?"

"No. It's so noisy. It's not helping my headache."

Tim frowned. "Sorry about that. The weather is calm this morning, so the ride should be smooth. Sally said you bumped your head and are having a hard time remembering things?"

"Yes sir," Hannah replied.

"Do you feel any pain in your back or neck? Or any numbness in your arms or legs?"

"No, only my head. I've been a little nauseous too."

"Thanks. Can I look at your head?"

Hannah nodded slowly. Tim felt the lump on her head and parted her hair to check for bleeding. "Wow! You have quite a lump. I see why it hurts so much."

Bob and Sally watched Tim check her eyes, hands, and legs. When he was done, he nodded to Judith.

Judith said, "We're taking you to the helicopter now," then stood up.

Hannah tried to stand up, but Judith pushed down gently on her shoulder. "I'm sure you can, dear, but we need to be careful walking by the helicopter. It's safer if you're on the stretcher."

"OK, you're the boss."

Tim looked at Bob. "Can you bring her pack just beyond the stairs, and we'll come back for it?" He followed the paramedics down the steps with Hannah's pack, and Sally brought out the paramedics' bag.

The paramedics carried the stretcher to the helicopter, hunching over when they were near the spinning rotors. Hannah covered her ears and closed her eyes. Her hair flew in all directions. After loading her into the helicopter, Tim returned for his bag and Hannah's pack.

Bob asked, "Where are you taking her?"

"An ambulance will meet us at the Bishop airport and take her to the hospital in Bishop. From there, it's up to the doctors."

"Thanks again for your help."

Tim nodded, shook Sally's hand, and carried both bags to the helicopter. Shortly after the side door slid shut, the rotors increased speed, and the rear of the aircraft rose. The front lip of the rails tipped over a couple of rocks as the front of the helicopter moved forward slightly. The chopper rose straight up a couple hundred feet and wobbled before darting to the south. Mark, Jessica, and the four hikers they were holding back joined Bob and Sally, watching the helicopter fly out of sight.

Bob welcomed back the eerie quiet of the wilderness, even though it was now accompanied by a ringing in his ears. He was grateful that Sally entertained all the questions from the hikers who had just arrived. He focused now on getting to Bishop as soon as possible.

"So what's next, Bob? I'm surprised you didn't ride in with her," Mark said.

Bob frowned. "I wanted to, but Sally said it wasn't safe."

"Ooh—must be hard for a former safety manager to hear that." Mark grimaced and patted Bob on the shoulder.

"Yeah. Used my own words against me, but it was the right decision. I'm taking the Bishop Pass trail to the trailhead at South Lake. I should be able to get to the hospital by tomorrow afternoon."

Jessica raised her lower lip. "But Bob, you need to finish the hike."

Mark added, "They'll take good care of Hannah. She may even be out of the hospital by the time you get there."

"I know, but she's all alone and confused, and if it weren't for me, she wouldn't have been hurt."

Mark grabbed the top of both of his shoulders. "Come on, Bob. We discussed this last night. She's a big girl and made her own decisions."

"Promise me you'll return to the trail," Jessica pleaded.

"I'll try, Jessica. But this is all so much, and I'm exhausted. I need a break for many reasons."

Jessica said. "You've come so far. You can do it." After an awkward silence, she continued, "Let's go. I never thought I'd say this, but I've had enough of this pass."

When Bob entered the hut to grab his pack, Sally was holding the bags of trash he and Hannah had collected earlier. "Why do people do this? I'm not a garbage collector, but it seems to be the thing I do most. At least it isn't toilet paper this time."

"Oh that. I was just about to pick it up. There was an incident before Hannah got hurt. Pales in comparison to what happened afterwards."

"Tell me more."

Bob removed his phone from his pocket and scrolled through his photos. "Here, a picture will tell the story better than I can." He handed his phone to Sally. "When we arrived yesterday morning, this is what we found."

Sally shook her head. "Why would someone do this?"

"Exactly. We were all upset, especially Jessica. Hannah and I cleaned it up right away so we could enjoy the hut as we had planned. All the trash is in those bags."

"Did you see anyone leaving as you approached?"

"No. We were probably the first visitors of the day, so I suspect it happened overnight. I overheard a group of three guys at the MTR camping area talking about spending the night here. They were pretty drunk. And guess what we found—a lot of glass and a label for a bottle of whiskey."

"Ah ha. Can you describe them?"

"Can't miss them. Two of them were wearing neon yellow long sleeve hoodies."

Sally gritted her teeth. "Wait a minute. I ran into those guys on the way up here. They acted like it was a big burden when I asked to check their permit, but everything was in order, so I moved on."

"Don't feel bad. You couldn't have known."

"Yeah, I know. It's just so frustrating. Some people think we're out here just to check permits and clean up their mess, but at least you know there's a lot more to it. We have another chance, though. I'll notify the ranger at Bench Lake to keep an eye out for them and check their story out. They should be near there in the next day or two."

Bob held his hand out. "I'll take that trash down since I'll be leaving the trail soon anyway."

Sally brought it closer to her body. "No. I'll take it back to the station. My load is much lighter than yours."

"Well, I guess this is it. Thanks again for your support. I'll tell Hannah all about it when she remembers more."

"Hannah's fortunate you all were here to help. Despite the weather, she'll get the care she needs relatively quickly. She could have been alone, or another hiker might not have stayed with her once they saw she was conscious and not bleeding. You and Mark and Jessica may have saved her life."

Bob couldn't respond. He could only wonder if Cathy would still be with him if she had received the same help.

"What?" asked Sally.

"Oh, nothing. I guess the fatigue is hitting me now that Hannah is on her way to the hospital."

"I'm going to repeat myself. One rescue a week is about all I can handle. The first mile of the descent from Bishop Pass is rocky and treacherous. Please take your time to get down safely and try to enjoy the walk. It's beautiful."

"OK. I got it." Bob said softly in resignation. Jessica grinned, and Sally followed, providing a pleasant break in the tension before descending.

"Don't worry," said Jessica. "We'll keep an eye on him."

Sally gave her a hug, and Bob shook Sally's hand.

"I'll be checking permits on the way down and won't be able to keep up. Check back with me at the station if you return to the trail."

"What do you mean, 'if'? It's 'when' he returns, not 'if,'" said Jessica.

Bob swatted her shoulder and said, "Let's go!"

True to her word, Jessica led the way down the first switchback, followed by Bob, then Mark. Bob was being escorted down the mountain, like it or not. As difficult as it was to leave this special place, it was time to move on. Unlike many out and back day hikes where the highlight was a waterfall or lake at the end, followed by a rushed walk back to the car, more wonders awaited them down the trail.

*** *** ***

Much to Bob's delight, Helen Lake appeared within thirty minutes. The water Mark had collected before the storm had been enough to get them through the night and morning, but barely. They had skipped their hot morning drinks, and Bob had nibbled on dry snacks for breakfast versus his normal oatmeal. The lake resembled Wanda Lake, not quite as large, not quite as blue, but still magnificent. Bob and Mark stopped near the outlet to refill their water bottles, and Mark poured a liter and a half into his cooking pot–enough for all three of them. Back in a more peaceful setting, they enjoyed their warm drinks and more snacks.

After the short break, Bob followed Jessica down a steep, rocky descent with a large stream on his right, tumbling over ledges every few hundred feet. As on the other side of the pass, the rocks in the outlet stream were stained black. Unlike the other side, outcrops of black rock invaded the granite. He had to admit Jessica was being an excellent trailblazer, setting a reasonable and careful pace. Sally's warning on the trail condition was on the spot; he wouldn't want to descend any faster than being allowed by his escorts. Assisting Hannah down the trail in her condition would have been agonizingly slow and dangerous.

On the left, a deep trough was carved through a sheer, 1000-foot slope of talus behind an unnamed lake. The massive boulder that created it must now be at the bottom of the lake. He tried to imagine what it would have been like if he had been soaking his feet at the shoreline at the time. Not pretty. Some risks you could only avoid by staying home.

After several more miles, Jessica veered off the trail to the right. Was she setting him free after the worst of the descent? No, of course not. She was climbing into the jaws of the infamous rock monster, an enormous granite boulder with a horizontal crack about two-thirds of the way down. The small, jagged rocks laid on the lower lip by previous visitors made it resemble a hiker-gobbling monster. Bob and Mark both snapped photos of Jessica pretending to scream while lying in its mouth. Bob took Marty out of his pack and tossed him to her. She held him close to protect him from the jagged teeth of the monster while they took more photos. Jessica climbed away from the hungry monster, held Marty out to Bob, and asked for his phone. "Your turn."

"I'm too old for that. I'm so stiff, I may not escape like you did."

"Come on. You've hiked over a hundred miles. You can do this." She looked at her father for support, but Mark just grinned and shrugged his shoulders.

Bob satisfied his new taskmaster by leaning his head and torso in the gap and stretching out his arm with Marty, as if trying to rescue the unsuspecting marmot from the monster's jaws. Jessica giggled and snapped several photos.

They picked up the pace when the grade lessened and the trail surface improved. They passed Big Pete Meadow on the right, then turned to the right around another pyramid of granite called Languille Peak. They were now in the spectacular Le Conte Canyon and approaching the turnoff for the Bishop Pass trail. A wall of granite hovered over them to the right. Several waterfalls cascaded down the side, causing black stains on the white rock and feeding the already roaring Middle Fork of the Kings River. The views distracted Bob so much that Jessica pulled away and Mark nipped at his heels.

He caught up with Jessica about thirty minutes later, only because she was standing still on the trail with her pack off.

"Oh, this must be my turnoff. That was quick. And look, Sally's station is here too." A small sign marked *Ranger Station* pointed to the right. The cabin was barely visible through the trees.

Jessica said, "I'll miss you. Promise me you'll finish your hike once you know Hannah is OK." She backed up and waited for a response that Bob wasn't ready to give. It would be difficult to return to the trail. He was exhausted, both physically and emotionally. He was torn between lying to Jessica and easing her worries so she could enjoy the rest of her own hike.

"I'll try my best, Jessica. That's all I can promise."

Mark stepped around Jessica and shook his hand. "Thanks for everything, especially with Brock. I don't think my scheme would have worked without you. In fact, Jessica and I would probably be home right now."

"So, what's your plan from here? How many days do you have left?" Bob said.

"Four days, I think. We'll camp a few miles farther ahead, then tackle the Golden Staircase in the morning."

"OK, take care. It's still early, so I'm going to hike a few miles up this trail before setting up camp. But I promise I won't try to get over the pass today." He grinned at Jessica and Mark.

"Let's exchange the addresses of our satellite devices so we can stay in touch," said Mark.

* * *

The Bishop Pass trail rose steeply after leaving the JMT. Bob relished the challenge, as it took his mind off of the chaotic past twenty-four hours and put him closer to a reunion with Hannah. Giant juniper trees with fibrous tan bark seemed to mark the end of each switchback. A sheet of water flowed hundreds of feet down a smooth ramp of granite to his right.

Near the top of the initial climb, he found an excuse to take an extended break. A stout wooden bridge with no rails crossed a creek that fed the sheet of water he had seen earlier. On one side, water tumbled over a steep channel of boulders, reminiscent of the Fish Creek cascade. On the other side in the distance was the wall of mountains forming the far side of Le Conte Canyon. From the valley, the mountains hovered over hikers as they dared to walk and sleep below. From this higher perspective, he saw their jagged peaks more clearly. While many considered the Bishop Pass trail a side-trail to the JMT, the views were not second-rate.

The grade eased over the next half-mile and led to the flat and lush Dusy Basin. The trailhead was still ten miles ahead, with at least two more steep sections and a very long descent. He now understood why Sally insisted that he spread his exit over two days. The scenery was much like that surrounding his first campsite at Upper Lyell Canyon. Slow-flowing streams connected numerous ponds. Stunted pine trees and grasses filled the voids. Not a bad campsite to repeat. Before he forgot, he sent a message to Mark and Jessica.

Message from Bob: *Mark, Jessica: Stopped about three miles up the trail. Just as beautiful as the JMT.*

* * *

After ten miles of hiking, Jessica stopped walking and looked to the right. Mark wondered if she had finally spotted a bear. When he got closer, he saw a shaded campsite forty feet off the trail. Light green grass covered the wide open space between the campsite and the west wall of Le Conte Canyon. A handful of boulders dotted the meadow—only glaciers could have placed the massive rocks there. A wide stream looked dark and stagnant from here, but he knew the water must be flowing and clear. They both looked from the meadow to each other, nodded their heads, and stepped off the trail. Mark had been expecting Jessica to try to extend the day to lower

Palisade Lake at the top of the Golden Staircase–only seven miles ahead, but about 2000 feet higher. The emotional rollercoaster on Muir Pass and the sleepless night must have taken a toll on her as well. He set his pack down before she changed her mind. Perhaps a swim in the peaceful stream would calm their nerves so they could catch up on their sleep.

After setting up their tents, Mark and Jessica gathered their dirty clothes and strolled to the dark break in the grass. As Mark approached, he saw a few trout nearly motionless in the slowly moving water. These fish had it easy compared to those farther upstream where the water rushed through the narrow canyon. Unfortunately, the water was only about a foot deep. They followed the shoreline to find a suitable swimming hole where they could wash up without wallowing in the muddy bottom. The creek turned sharply around a large boulder, and the bottom dropped out of sight.

Jessica said, "You go first. I'll start washing clothes up ahead." When she passed the boulder and was no longer in sight, Mark stripped to his underwear and stepped into the water with his camp sandals on. The bottom looked smooth, but you never knew what was buried there. The gentle current and strong sun fooled him into expecting warm water, but the first step reminded him this water was snow not too long ago. His feet sank in the mud, making each step a struggle and nearly robbing him of his sandals. He stopped when the water approached the middle of his chest and cleaned himself with a small microfiber cloth. He finished by submerging his head and rubbing his hair. He stood up straight and yelled, "Woo!"

He heard a squeal from downstream. Jessica must have found her own swimming hole. "Doesn't it feel great?" he said.

"Yep. I'm glad we stopped early today."

"I'm going to start cooking dinner. Send a message to your mother telling her everything is OK, but we're running a day late."

"OK."

Message from Jessica: *Mom: At Grouse Meadow now. It's beautiful. We are doing fine, but running a little late.*

Message from Jessica: *Bob: Chilling at Grouse Meadow.*

* * *

Dear Cathy,

Hannah was evacuated by helicopter this morning, but it was a long night. None of us slept much between worrying about Hannah and dodging the leaks in the roof. You can't see daylight between the rocks on the roof, but water found a way through.

I am on my way back to civilization via the Bishop Pass trail since they wouldn't let me fly with Hannah. Sally tried to convince me it wasn't necessary, but to no avail. I was torn about what to do. Hannah still didn't have her memory when she left, and I cringed at the thought of her waking up alone with a foggy memory in a hospital bed. Plus, I feel somewhat responsible for her injury. But I have also promised you to complete the trail for the sake of both of us. I'm beginning to feel that the trail is conspiring to prevent us from doing so. What would you have done? I'm pretty sure you would do the same.

Perhaps the detour will help in the end. I'm exhausted in every conceivable way. I now appreciate the struggles you described to me over the phone. Words don't capture how difficult this is, just as my photos can't capture the beauty. I hope a night or two in town and an improving Hannah give me the boost I need to return. Without this break, I don't know if I would make it. Please keep encouraging me. I need it. We need it!

Love, Bob

24

Relief

2022

Day 11

August 15 - Dusy Basin to Bishop

Bob's alarm rang at 5 AM. He rarely set it on the trail, but he wanted to get to the hospital as soon as he could. By the time he ate breakfast and packed up, enough light would peek over the mountains so he could hike without his headlamp.

His legs and lungs welcomed the flat trail around the ponds and dwarfed trees. Hungry mosquitos were seeking breakfast, so he moved quickly. The mosquitos had driven him to eat in his tent last night for the first time on the trip. This practice increased the chances of encountering a bear, but he felt he had no choice. He was bitten a dozen times just while cleaning up afterwards. Those hiking the JMT in June and early July faced this battle nearly every morning and evening.

When the trail headed uphill again, he was fueled up and warmed up. Perhaps this was the final push to the pass? He must be making good time.

After thirty minutes of moderate climbing, he realized that a false summit had fooled him again. How often would he have to learn that lesson? He was now high above what must be upper Dusy Basin. The lakes below reminded him of Marie Lake. Perhaps he could make his way down to that basin another time, but for now, he was on a mission.

After another forty-five minutes of climbing, he arrived at the sign indicating Bishop Pass, 11,972 feet, but the view was anticlimactic. The pass sat in a bowl surrounded by high peaks to the north and south and lower hills to the east and west. His best view of Dusy Basin had come a half-hour ago, and he could see nothing of the upcoming descent. At least he wouldn't feel guilty about skipping the traditional pass break. Instead, he took a quick photo of Marty sitting on the sign, then continued on.

The initial descent from the pass was even more treacherous than the one from Muir Pass and much different from the smooth, gradual climb on the other side of the pass. He wound his way around small spires, carefully choosing each footfall on jagged rocks. When he finally had the nerve to look up, he saw the view he expected at the top of the pass, a chain of lakes cascading down the valley. The valley curved to his right, cutting off the view of the lowest lake. He sighed in relief when he saw the straight trail high above the lakes. He would be able to fly down the trail soon.

Despite his increasing speed on the smoother trail, the descent seemed to last forever. On a typical descent, most of the elevation was lost quickly, followed by a long, gradual descent into the valley. Here, the gradual descent was followed by another steep one to South Lake. Though his knees had recovered somewhat, he was no longer mentally prepared for such a challenge, similar to the feeling he had when cresting a false summit on a climb. He gritted his teeth and forged on. What choice did he have?

He arrived at the South Lake trailhead at noon. The parking lot was large and nearly full. Unfortunately, at this time of day, many more people were arriving than were leaving. Sally had told him there was a shuttle late in the afternoon, but he was hoping to get a ride from a departing hiker. After using the first enclosed toilet in over a week, he stepped outside and saw a couple about his age with backpacks. Their dirty clothes and tired faces indicated this was the end of their trip, rather than the beginning. Best to let them take care of their business before pursuing a ride to town.

When the man exited the restroom, Bob said, "Hi there. Are you section hiking the JMT?"

"Kind of. We just completed the North Lake-South Lake loop. Just over four days. A couple of those were on the JMT. How about you?"

"Long story. Trying to complete the whole JMT, but my hiking partner got hurt, so I need to get to Bishop to check on her. I'm Bob, by the way."

"Marvin." They nodded to each other rather than shaking hands. It was too obvious to both where they had just been.

Marvin's partner came to his side after exiting the other restroom. "And this is my wife, Gina. Honey, this is Bob. He's hiking the JMT."

Gina smiled at Bob. "Oh, you lucky guy. We may try that next year. This was a bit of a trial for us."

"Not as lucky as you think. I should be doing this with my wife. Not to be too morbid, but don't put it off. You never know how many opportunities you'll get."

"Thanks for the advice. Do you need a ride into town?" asked Marvin.

"That would be great. You can just drop me off at the hospital if it's not too far out of your way."

"No problem."

He had wondered if trail magic was real before the hike, but now he knew. He would never have pursued such a ride at home, but he had more options there. Here, where hiking and backpacking were so popular, many hikers were paying back a favor or paying one forward. When the Pacific Crest Trail hikers came through the High Sierra, former hikers and trail angels would shuttle hikers to and from town and sometimes provide food and drinks.

* * *

After three miles of smooth, slightly downhill hiking south along the Middle Fork of the San Joaquin River and four miles of slightly uphill hiking east

177

along Palisade Creek, the trail steepened gradually. To reach the source of the water in Palisade Creek, Mark and Jessica first had to scale the Golden Staircase. They wondered how a trail could climb the nearly vertical canyon wall in front of them. It rose over 1500 feet in two miles and was the last section of the JMT built over eighty years ago. It was essentially another pass. Mark wasn't sure whether the name referred to the narrow sections of switchbacks, which looked like steps built for a giant from afar, or the endless rock steps on the switchbacks they would be climbing themselves. He saw other hikers above resembling ants marching back and forth. In a few cases, one hiker appeared to be stepping on the head of another on a switchback below.

Mark used his hiking poles and arms to help his thighs lift his overweight self and backpack on the sections with large stone steps. As tough as this was for him, he pitied Jessica, whose legs were a foot shorter than his. But then again, she was always waiting for him to catch up a couple of switchbacks ahead. When he caught up with her, huffing and puffing, they gazed down the glacially carved valley from which they came. Mark couldn't linger as long as Jessica or they would be there until evening. They stood without speaking, hearing only the water rushing down the slope to the left, their heavy breathing, and the blood rushing by their ears on the way to their oxygen-starved brains.

After several steep, winding sections, the top of the Palisade Range peeked over the horizon. Lower and Upper Palisade Lakes must lay at the bottom of those mountains. But first, they had to make their way through grassy corridors between massive boulders. Mark was nearly out of water after the long climb in the sun. His shirt was drenched and beads of sweat dripped from his nose every minute or two. He was hoping to wait until the first lake to refill his water bottles and take a lunch break. But with the horizon continuing around every corner, he wondered if he should scramble down to the creek and refill now. No, he didn't like to take long breaks on climbs. It was too difficult to restart. Slow and steady, all the way to the top.

At last, Lower Palisade Lake appeared at the base of the peaks. The upper lake was not yet visible. It must be over the hump that the trail climbed on the left side of the lower lake. Jessica headed toward a series of boulders on the shoreline and set her pack against one. The shoreline in front of them was sandy, and the water was shallow. If they hadn't had such a refreshing bath in the creek yesterday afternoon, a short swim in the lake would be irresistible. A few puffy clouds had formed during the climb. Best that they eat their lunch and move on before the clouds turned into storms. First thing first, though–quench their thirst.

He and Jessica both drank a full bottle of water. They both squeezed peanut butter and honey on tortillas, then devoured them in minutes. They shared a bag of cheese crisps. That had satisfied Mark, but Jessica pulled the peanut M&M's out of their daily food bag to finish off her lunch. While she was eating dessert, Mark laid back on the grass and pulled his hat over his face.

In what felt like just a minute later, someone was shaking his shoulder.

"Dad. Let's go."

Mark had no idea where he was. "What? Where?" The bright sun that had caused him to cover his face was now behind a large gray cloud. A refreshing breeze cooled his face.

"We still have Mather Pass to get over."

"I don't know Jessica. This is such a relaxing spot. Plus, those clouds are starting to worry me. Remember the storm on Muir Pass?"

"But you had me tell Mom that we're a day behind schedule. The pass is right around the corner." She pointed to the mountains beyond the distant shoreline.

"Aren't you tired after last night?"

"Yeah, a little, but we can go to bed early tonight."

Mark's first attempt at sitting up failed. He rocked on his lower back a couple of times before successfully sitting up. "OK. But we're going to reevaluate at the upper lake. The weather is not looking good."

Jessica hopped up. She must have noticed him struggling to sit up because she offered a hand to pull him up. Jessica bolted ahead as if pushed by a gust of wind. Mark followed, wondering why he didn't get the same boost, though deep down, he knew why–about twenty-five years and a few extra pounds.

As they climbed high above the shoreline of Upper Palisade Lake, Mark noticed several potential campsites just off the trail to the right, overlooking the lake and Mather Pass. But Jessica was now several hundred feet ahead. She must not want to be a part of any reevaluation of the day's plan. By the time he could catch up with her, it would be too late to turn around. Mark admitted defeat and picked up the pace under the darkening clouds.

Jessica waited at the top of the final switchback. "Come on. You're so close." The dark clouds seemed to rest on her head. She held up her right hand as he approached and gave him a high five. "I knew we could do it."

Mark was too winded to reply. He didn't remove his pack, nor sit down. They couldn't linger. He grabbed his water bottle and swallowed mouthfuls between heavy breaths. "We can't—stay. Look—clouds—going to storm."

Fortunately, the trail surface was much better on the descent, and the slope was gentler. The wide-open Upper Basin dominated the view below. His spent body wouldn't make it to the shelter of taller trees beyond, so they would have to settle for camping at the first clump of stunted trees near a water source.

* * *

Marvin and Gina dropped Bob off at the hospital in Bishop. He thanked them profusely and gave them one last bit of encouragement to tackle the JMT the following summer. He withheld his doubts about continuing his own hike.

Bob walked through the lobby with his pack. Being so close to the Pacific Crest Trail, he didn't turn heads like he would have back in Houston. The receptionist confirmed that Hannah was still there and directed him to her room. Part of him was glad she was still here, but he hoped it didn't mean her condition had deteriorated.

He knocked and entered her room when he heard a faint, "Come in." Before the door closed behind him, Hannah greeted him. "Bob!" Her bed was inclined, and she held out her arms. Bob noticed the middle-aged man sitting in the corner, probably her father, and hesitated. "Come on, give me a hug."

Bob set down his pack, but Hannah's improved condition provided more relief than removing the thirty-plus pounds from his shoulders. He lowered himself into Hannah's embrace. When he rose, Hannah looked at her father. "Dad, this is Bob." She looked at Bob. "Bob, this is my father, Alex."

Alex and Bob met at the foot of the bed and shook hands.

"Hi. Alex Tracy." Bob started to smile, but stopped when Alex didn't.

The sudden relief and accumulated fatigue made him lightheaded, so he sat down quickly in the chair next to the bed. "Well, it looks like your memory has returned. That's great."

"It began last night and came flooding back this morning."

"Do you remember everything?"

"I think so. You don't know what you don't know, but I remember Jessica and Mark, Marty, what you told me about Cathy, and—climbing on the hut."

"About that," Bob heard from the corner. "I can't believe you asked Hannah to climb on top of that thing."

"Come on, Dad. I told you. It was my decision. Bob and Mark tried to stop me."

"No, Hannah. Your dad is right. I was irresponsible just bringing it up. I've been wracked with guilt ever since, but at least you're on the mend now. I'm sorry, Alex."

"Well, anyway, I appreciate your efforts to take care of her. You made the right decision by calling for help. Thank you."

Bob looked back at Hannah. "What have the doctors told you?"

"I have a concussion, a pretty nasty one. But they don't expect any longer-term effects. They were most concerned about my memory loss."

"That's good. Any idea when they'll discharge you?"

"Probably tomorrow morning."

"Wonderful." Bob's smile was just as wide as when he first saw Muir Hut.

"I can't believe you hiked all the way out just to check on me."

"I couldn't stand the thought of you alone and confused in the hospital. I didn't know your father would arrive so quickly."

"But I'm all better now. You wasted all that energy."

"Oh no. You can't imagine the burden I was carrying. You were feeling really bad and getting worse all night. I was scared."

Hannah raised her lower lip. "I guess I don't remember that part. Probably never will."

"That's a good thing."

"You're going back to the trail, right? I'll feel awful if I am the reason you abandoned your hike—and abandoned Cathy again."

Bob cringed. When he recovered, he said, "You sound just like someone else I know."

"Jessica?"

Bob nodded and Hannah raised her arms. "Yeah. Girl power."

Alex said. "Bob, can you show me this Marty character? Sounds like he's had some close calls as well."

Bob removed Marty from his pack and tossed him to Alex. "Oh. What is this?"

"Come on, Dad. He's a marmot. They're all over the trail. So cute. Toss him here." She held out her hands.

Hannah caught him and squeezed him against her face. "Bob, take a picture."

After catching up on his exit over the Bishop Pass trail and Mark and Jessica's plans, Hannah said, "Why don't you two go out to lunch and bring me back some real food? Hospital food just isn't going to satisfy my hiker hunger."

Bob didn't need to be sold on that idea. He looked at Alex who shrugged his shoulders and stood up. "Sure. Maybe Bob can tell me about your other escapades on the trail."

Hannah threw Marty at her father. He caught it and tossed it back to Bob.

"Any special requests?" Bob asked Hannah.

"How about pizza?"

"Pizza it is," said Alex. "But first, I'm going to drop your friend off at a hotel so he can clean up."

Bob stood up. "I was hoping you'd say that."

"Thanks, Dad."

* * *

Bob felt like he was punched in the gut as he entered the restaurant. He had set aside his hiker hunger and cravings in favor of focusing on Hannah, but now the smells of sizzling meat and garlic set them free again. His stomach was begging for food that wasn't prepared with boiling water.

After sitting down and opening their menus, Alex said, "Well, what will it be? Your choice."

"Let's keep it simple. I'll take a large double pepperoni."

Alex closed his menu. "Sounds good to me."

"Maybe you didn't understand. I said I'll take a large pepperoni. What will you have?" Bob grinned.

Alex picked his menu back up. "That must be the hiker hunger Hannah was talking about. I thought she was just exaggerating so she didn't have to eat hospital food."

"No, it's real. Believe me. Seriously though, I won't eat the whole thing, but we need plenty of leftovers for Hannah. What does she like?"

"She likes pepperoni, but she also has veggies on her pizza sometimes. I'll get a medium supreme. That should be enough, huh?"

Bob nodded, then whipped his head around as a waitress carried a large supreme to a nearby table. On the way back, she took their order. "And what will you have to drink?"

"I'll take the best IPA you have on tap." Bob looked over at Alex.

"Iced tea for me."

"Sorry, but—"

Alex held up his hand to Bob. "I get it. Maybe I'll join you tonight."

Bob grabbed his glass as soon as the waitress set it on the table. He closed his eyes as he swallowed the first sip. When he opened them, Alex was holding out his glass of iced tea. "Oops. Sorry." Bob was slow in adjusting back to town manners. "To a full and speedy recovery for Hannah."

Alex added, "Thanks for taking care of her out there," before they touched their glasses.

"I think she helped me more than I helped her. It's been a very emotional trip for me."

Alex lowered his head. "Yeah. She told me about your wife's horrible accident. I can't imagine how difficult this is. Heck, I can't even imagine myself carrying a heavy backpack up just one of those passes."

"You should be proud of your daughter. She's very determined. I have no doubt she would have finished if she hadn't been hurt."

Two pizzas appeared on the table. The discussion had been somber, but it had kept Bob's mind off the wait for his first town food in over a week. Bob remembered his town manners this time and looked at Alex. Alex grinned and held his hand out toward the pizza. "Go ahead. Hungry hikers first."

Bob grabbed a slice of pepperoni pizza, dragging strings of cheese all over his side of the table. After a couple of blows, he took a cautious bite. Burning the roof of his mouth would take away from the rest of the meal. He continued to blow after each bite so he could take bigger and bigger bites. Every time he looked up, Alex was staring at him. He was half done with his first piece before Alex grabbed a piece of supreme pizza.

Four pieces and another beer later, Bob threw his red-smeared napkin on the table. Alex had just finished his second piece. "What's the matter, big guy? Eyes bigger than your hiker belly?"

"Quite the contrary. I saw a German bakery on the way here. I'm saving room for something sweet, and I know Hannah has a sweet tooth too."

Alex chuckled. "Since she was a baby."

* * *

The storm came, but Mark and Jessica had set up their tents and eaten dinner. "Time to hunker down in our tents," said Mark. "Better send your mom a quick message."

Message from Jessica: *Mom: Got over Mather Pass today, but the rain is coming. Need to get in the tent now.*

Within five minutes, Mark's tent flapped madly in the wind, and heavy rain pelted the fabric. He obsessed over looking for leaks through the roof and floor of his tent. To his surprise, everything inside remained dry. He wondered if Jessica's tent was faring as well. Did she pull the guy lines tight enough? Would all the stakes hold? He was glad they had bought freestanding, double-wall tents with dedicated tent poles. It seemed like half the hikers on the JMT used single-wall tents supported by their hiking poles, stakes, and guylines. The single-wall tents were lighter and more compact, but tended to collect moisture inside and were less stable during high winds.

Mark yelled, "Jessica, are you alright?", but thunder drowned out his voice. He could barely hear himself. He tried again. No response. He opened his inner door flap. No wonder the noise is so loud. Hailstones the size of peas bounced on the ground. He kneeled at the edge of his tent and lifted the rain fly so he could see Jessica's tent. He dreaded the thought of seeing one side of her rain fly blown over the top of her tent. Nope! The tent shook, but no more than his. Before he zipped up the door flap, he held his hand out beyond the rainfly and caught a few hailstones to eat. Once he laid back down, he tried yelling again, with no response. She would never hear him over the raucous wind, rain, and thunder. Fortunately, the gap between the flashes of lightning and the crack of thunder stayed between four and six seconds. Her tent was in good shape. She was tough. If she needed help, she would let him know.

Forty-five minutes later, the hail turned to rain, then to drizzle. Only an occasional rumble of thunder remained. Mark's eyes were closed; he wasn't sleeping, just relaxing in the relative quiet. "Hey Dad. Are you OK?" He opened his eyes and grinned.

"Yes, Jessica. And you?"

"Yep. That was quite a storm."

So much for making up for lost sleep.

Message from Bob: *Mark: Made it to Bishop safely. Hannah is doing much better. She remembers me now, and you too. The pizza was great. Sorry, couldn't resist:)*

Message from Mark: *Bob: Whatever you do, don't climb the Golden Staircase and Mather Pass on the same day. Basically two passes. Relax at one of the Palisade Lakes instead.*

* * *

Dear Cathy:

What a relief! Hannah is much better. She remembers me, Mark, and Jessica now, and the doctors think she will fully recover. It turns out that I wasn't the only one feeling like I was responsible for her injury. Her father gave me a chilly reception, but Hannah keeps reminding us that it was her choice.

How can you eat half a large pizza and three fresh-baked cookies and still be hungry? It felt so good to put a dent in my hunger, even if just for a while. We snuck the leftovers into the hospital for Hannah. I think her hunger pains are worse than her headache at this point.

With all the concern over Hannah's injury, I never told you about our visit to the hut before she got hurt. Mark, Jessica, and Hannah waited for me at Evolution Lake so we could enjoy the hut together. I think Jessica was looking forward to seeing Muir Pass as much as you and I. Only the beauty of the approach made the anticipation bearable.

As hard as it was, we had to pause our tour when we saw the inside of the hut. Some idiots had made a mess of the place the night before. Why didn't I say something?

Hannah and I cleaned up the mess, then we pretended we had just arrived all over again. We enjoyed our time inspecting every detail, both inside and out. I still don't know how they built the roof. I wonder if they intended on the spiraling sensation the inside of the roof creates when you look up.

I mentioned the idea of putting your rock in the chimney while we were eating lunch, and you know what happened from there. Our best morning on the trail turned into a terrifying afternoon and evening in a heartbeat.

I hope you enjoyed your visit and didn't hang around after Hannah got hurt. I'm glad I was around to help her out, but you didn't need to endure that. I tried to show you the hut from all angles and perspectives. It's a special place, just as you imagined.

Let's not talk about returning to the trail tonight. You wouldn't like my answer. My belly feels better, but I am still exhausted. The sleepless night in Muir Hut may have put me over the edge. BUT, give me a night or two in a real bed, and I may be a new man. I suspect Hannah will drag me to the trailhead no matter what I say. You have a friend in her!

Love, Bob

25

Recovery

2022

Day 12

August 16 - Bishop

Bob heard banging. What was that? His tent didn't have a door. Maybe it was a bear trying to break into his bear canister. He rolled over, a move that should have thrown him off his narrow inflatable sleeping pad. Now someone was calling his name.

"Bob! Are you still there?"

He recognized the voice. Much stronger than it was at Muir Hut. Hannah! Oh, that's right. He was in Bishop, in a hotel. No wonder he had slept so well.

"Hold on. I'm coming." He looked at the clock on the nightstand: 9:15! He hadn't slept so late in—decades. But it felt so good, almost as satisfying as the pizza yesterday. Maybe he could be put back together again after all. Or perhaps the exhaustion would return as fast as the hunger had yesterday.

He slipped on his hiking pants and opened the door.

"Surprise!" Hannah held her arms out wide. Alex waited behind her, holding a bakery box with a tray of coffee cups sitting on top. Bob salivated instantly.

"Come in." He turned around. "Excuse the mess." He hadn't even tried to clean up his pack explosion from last night. He quickly grabbed everything off the table and two chairs and threw it on the bed. He pulled the table close to the bed and pulled the two chairs next to it.

"There." He grabbed the tray of coffees from Alex and set it on the table. Alex did the same with the box.

"I thought you'd be at the hospital first thing this morning. The doctor came by early and released me. We were hoping you had just slept in."

"I intended to come over, but I feel so much better after a full night of sleep."

Hannah smiled. "Great. Hopefully, I can do the same tonight without the nurses constantly checking on me."

Alex distributed the coffee cups and opened the box. "We brought a mix of breakfast croissants and pastries. I dare you two to finish all of these—minus this one." He grabbed a croissant.

"You still haven't learned your lesson, have you?" Hannah said.

The coffee started lifting the fog left by Bob's long night of sleep. He started with an apple fritter so the sugar would speed up the effect. He savored the first bite, but was half finished before Hannah grabbed a savory croissant. She took two large bites.

"What did the doctor say?"

When she stopped chewing, she sipped her coffee and said, "Just take it easy for a couple of weeks. He told me to stay off the trail, but I expected that."

"Sorry."

"What about you? What's your plan, now that you had a chance to sleep on it?" Hannah asked.

Bob smiled while he finished eating his fritter. "Can I wake up first?" He took a few sips of coffee and grabbed the last ham and cheese croissant.

"Are you two heading home today?"

Alex looked at Hannah. "I wanted to, but my daughter insists we stay another day to take you back to the trailhead."

Hannah grinned at her dad. "I figured you needed a full day in town first."

Bob raised his coffee cup toward her. "We can agree on that. I still have some laundry to do."

"And—" Hannah rolled her hand in front of Bob to elicit an answer to the burning question. He grabbed a cinnamon roll from the box and took a bite.

Bob chewed, and bit, and chewed, and sipped.

"Bob?" She gently slapped his forearm resting on the table.

"I don't know, Hannah. The last few days have been exhausting. Nothing like you've been through, but still very stressful. I'm not sure I can go back. I still have eight, nine, ten days of hiking left. Sure, I feel pretty good right now, but I'm afraid I'll be worn out again by the time I get back to the JMT. The Bishop Pass trail was tough."

"I wish you hadn't come off trail. It was sweet, but I was fine, and my dad got here quickly. It's all my fault. If I hadn't climbed up on the roof, or had come down when you asked me to …"

Tears welled in Hannah's eyes. She wiped them with her napkin, smearing sugar on her cheeks.

"Come on, Hannah. We've been through that."

Alex jumped in. "OK, you two. This is no one's fault. It happened. Everything is OK now. Move on."

"Well said, Alex," said Bob.

"Hannah, let's give Bob more time to think and rest. We can resume this discussion at dinner. In the meantime, you two still have a couple of pastries to finish." Alex raised his coffee cup, and they all banged the lids together. It wasn't the same without the clink.

* * *

Mark and Jessica arrived at the Woods Creek suspension bridge around three o'clock after a twelve-mile hike in the scorching sun. All afternoon, they had tried to summon some of the clouds they ran from yesterday. They had planned to camp here at one of the lowest points of the trail at 8,500 feet. Pinchot Pass had been much easier to climb than Mather Pass since the trail only dropped 2,000 feet before rising again. The descent along Woods Creek was one of the least scenic sections of the trail, but the bridge at the water crossing was an icon.

The bridge consisted of open steel grating hung from cables supported by wooden towers on each side. Smaller cables acted as guardrails and handrails to protect against trips and falls on the wobbly bridge. Coming from the north, hikers climbed steep metal steps to a landing, from which they stepped onto the first section of suspended grating. A sign indicated that only one hiker at a time was allowed on the bridge. Mark wondered if the rule was in place to prevent exceeding the weight limit of the bridge or to discourage hikers from trying to bounce each other off the bridge.

Neither he nor Jessica feared heights or water, so they smiled as they stood on the landing. However, Mark could see how those with such fears might struggle with the view of the water through the grating. Mark crossed first, taking a video of the bouncing surface ahead. He stopped in the middle to film the creek passing underneath. When he was three-quarters of the way across, the bouncing suddenly increased. He turned around and saw Jessica approaching him, making no attempt to step softly.

"Can't you read?" he said.

"Well, if you weren't so slow." She laughed so hard that her pack bounced on her shoulders.

She stepped off the bridge after he did and handed him her phone. "Here, take a video of me while I cross again." Jessica's smile reminded him of those from her carefree childhood, which he clung to after Brock's woes. He knew the smiles might come less often, but he hoped she took a different path than Brock. He wondered if Brock would be enjoying himself as much as Jessica if he were still with them.

"Sure. Go ahead. You may only get here once, so make the most of it. No one else is waiting for us to cross." Because of her small stature, she created much less movement than Mark did. On the way back, she exaggerated her steps to increase the bouncing motion. She paused in the middle to watch the water rush by.

The camping area was the busiest they had seen since MTR. It was one day's hike away from both Pinchot Pass and Rae Lakes, with little camping opportunities in between. The wide creek provided an excellent opportunity for washing off and drying in the sun. Plus, it was fun to sit and watch the various reactions of those crossing the bridge.

On a sign near the other end of the bridge, a ranger had posted some colorful and animated warnings about bears. *A fed bear is a dead bear.* A bear box was located across the trail, near many of the campsites. They saw the greatest variety of trees yet on the trail: aspens, firs, spruces, and several types of pines.

"We might finally see a bear tonight." Jessica hadn't lost her smile yet.

"I guess with so many people here, someone is bound to be careless with their food. Maybe we should move on."

"No way. This is such a cool place."

Mark hesitated. He saw at least a dozen campsites. Even if a bear didn't show up, it would be noisy.

Jessica continued, "Come on. We can wash up and relax."

Mark suspected that he may be paying for law school in the future. He was still feeling the effects of the rushed ascent of Mather Pass. "OK. You win, as usual, but we need to be extra careful with our food. Not just tonight, but even while washing up in the creek or using the bathroom."

"Yes, Dad." Jessica led them in search of a campsite.

An hour later, Mark sat on the rocky bank of the creek, just to the right of the bridge. He and Jessica had already rinsed off in the creek, and he had washed the dirtiest of their clothes. He wished he had a bag of nuts or cookies to snack on before dinner, but he hadn't felt comfortable leaving them on the bank while he was in the creek.

Jessica was back in the water for another rinse cycle. They had set up camp near a family of three with a ten-year-old girl. Desperate for a break from only adult companions, they instantly became friends. It hadn't taken much for Meredith to convince Jessica to enter the water again when she came down with her parents. Mark volunteered to watch both of them so

Meredith's parents could finish setting up camp. The splashing created by the water rushing around the rocks wasn't enough for Jessica and Meredith, so they playfully splashed each other.

Mark smiled. This hike had been hard, but so worthwhile. He was grateful for the trail magic allowing them to get this far: the extra food provided by others at MTR, Bob's gift of medicine for Jessica, and most importantly, the apparent return of the old Brock. He wished Linda was sitting next to him, though he wondered if she ever would have crossed the wobbly bridge. Perhaps another day.

Message from Mark: *Bob: Having a blast at the suspension bridge. But only stay here if you are up for the crowds and ready to chase bears.*

Message from Jessica: *Mom: The suspension bridge is cool. Made a new friend—not an adult for a change.*

* * *

Pizza, check! Baked goods, check! Only burgers and ice cream remained on Bob's town food list. During a visit to the local grocery store, Bob received a recommendation for a local brewery with excellent burgers. When he confirmed they served milkshakes as well, he was sold. And Alex could imbibe as well since it was within walking distance of their hotel. He still felt bad about downing a couple of beers in front of Alex yesterday while he sipped on iced tea. Per doctor's orders, Hannah would have to settle for a milkshake—or two.

Bob knew dinner wouldn't solely be a fond recollection of their favorite sights and the challenges they overcame; Hannah expected an answer. And if Bob didn't want to jeopardize the validity of his permit, he needed to get back on the trail tomorrow.

* * *

Dear Cathy:

I don't usually message you during the day, but I need your help. I don't know whether I can continue. I slept soundly last night, and after lots of carbs and caffeine for breakfast, I felt I could do anything. But three hours later, I was both hungry and sleepy again. My thighs burned as I walked to the grocery store. The toll the trail takes on my body and mind is steep, too much to be paid with a day and a half in town. But I promised you I would take you to Mt. Whitney. And unlike last time, I really intended to keep it.

I had a great trail family to help me through the first couple of weeks. Hannah helped me to pace myself and enjoy the journey. Brock saved Marty from drowning. Jessica's energy was contagious. And Brock showed me I could still make a difference, just like I did at the plant. But they won't be with me any more. I'll be alone, like you were.

Some of the best wonders of the trail still await: Rae Lakes, Forester Pass, the suspension bridge, Guitar Lake, and Mt. Whitney. But will they be enough? I won't be able to finish without you. Can I depend on you to help me through the rough spots?

Love, Bob

* * *

Six three-ounce glasses sat in cutouts on wooden boards in front of Alex and Bob. The beers ranged in color from gold, like the grass waving in the meadows following Muir Pass, to dark brown, like the slow flowing creek in

194

Dusy Basin. Hannah gave up on sucking her thick chocolate shake through a straw and now had a brown mustache after drinking from the glass. Bob's palate was out of practice. He struggled to distinguish the different hops and malts which the microbrewery used in crafting the variety of ales and stouts on his board. Most foods tasted the same on the trail after being confined in a resupply bucket and bear canister for weeks.

Hannah allowed him to finish two of the six samples before popping the question they all expected. "Well, Bob?"

"Well, what?" He held off his grin for two seconds before succumbing. Hannah tried to grab his plank of beers, but he slid it out of her reach.

"OK, might as well get this out of the way before the burgers come. I will try my best to finish. I'll get back on the trail tomorrow and—" Hannah put her elbows on the table and clapped her hands softly.

"As I was saying—reevaluate when I get to Onion Valley. I'm looking forward to the suspension bridge, Rae Lakes, and even Kearsarge Pass."

Hannah nodded her head. "Make sense. That was always going to be your final resupply."

Alex held up one of his tiny glasses, Bob selected the next one in his lineup, and they both clinked their tiny beer glasses against Hannah's twenty-four ounce milkshake. Bob and Alex lost a sip or two, but Bob was surprised his glass survived at all. They stopped laughing and their eyes grew wide when the burgers appeared on the table. They all asked for glasses of water so they could continue to savor their drinks instead of using them to wash down their burgers and fries. Alex was finally getting the concept of hiker hunger and had ordered an extra serving of fries for Hannah and Bob to share.

When they were down to nibbling their last fries, Bob said, "One more craving to satisfy before going back to the trail." He signaled their waiter and ordered a chocolate shake.

Hannah held up her empty glass. "Make that two."

The waiter looked at Alex. "Should I make it three?"

Alex raised his hands in defeat. "What the heck? I'll take in some pity calories for you two."

As they finished their milkshakes thirty minutes later, Alex said, "We're going to take you to the trailhead tomorrow. What time do you want to leave?"

"The sooner the better. Before I can change my mind. How about 6 AM?"

"Sounds good. Then we can get back to San Francisco at a decent hour."

"Shall we waddle back to the hotel?" Between his stiff legs and overfull belly, waddle was all Bob could do at this point.

Message from Bob: *Jessica: I have a ride to the trailhead at 6AM tomorrow!*

Message from Jessica: *Bob: Great:)*

26

On the Trail Again

2022

Day 13

August 17 - Bishop to Le Conte Canyon

Alex parked his car as close to the Bishop Pass trailhead sign as he could. He reached over and offered his hand to Bob. "Thanks again for helping Hannah. I hope you make it to Mt. Whitney. You deserve it."

"I don't know about that, but thanks."

Alex pulled the trunk release. "I'll let you and Hannah say goodbye outside."

Bob and Hannah walked back to the trunk and raised the lid. His knees buckled and his shoulders drooped when he looked at his pack, now containing over six days of food. He and Hannah looked at each other, then looked at the ground and fidgeted. Conversation at dinner last night had flowed freely. Their bursts of laughter drew looks of scorn by patrons who typically reserved them for families with rowdy children. But now that they were alone, words escaped them. So many words competed for their tongues, but none made it out of their mouths. They settled for a hug to bide their time. When Hannah backed away, she pulled something out of the trunk. Bob leaned his head back to focus on the furry black object now in front of his face, a black bear about the same size as Marty.

"Is that your new trail mascot?" asked Bob.

"Yeah, but only after you take him to Mt. Whitney. Marty needs a friend to protect him. I named him Boo the Bear. He should remind you of our first meeting at Tuolumne Meadows, where a bear said *Boo*, and you saved my hike before it began."

Bob placed it in the palm of his hand. "Four more ounces to lug around." Bob drooped his shoulders again. Hannah smiled.

"Thanks. I'm sure Marty gets lonely sitting in my pack most of the day. Maybe he called the marmot near Thousand Island Lake to carry him away to freedom." They both smiled.

Hannah placed her right hand on his left shoulder. "Be careful and have fun for the three of us: me, Cathy, and yourself."

"Whoa. That's a lot of fun. I hope my old heart can handle it."

"One more thing—send me updates on your satellite device."

"OK. I'll be in touch when I return to civilization. Take it easy, like the doctor prescribed."

"One photo before you go." She removed Marty from his pack. As she handed Marty to Bob, she told Marty and Boo, "Now you two get along out there."

Hannah guided him to the trailhead sign, where he held up the mascots on each side of his face and smiled.

* * *

The trail was the same, but the experience was entirely different. Two days ago, Bob was concerned, exhausted, and rushed. All those feelings had been diminished in town. Hannah was getting better. He had slept well and ate well. And he could set his own pace now that his trail family was scattered.

He remembered the descent from Bishop Pass taking forever. The ascent would be tougher and take longer. Each of the lakes had looked the same while coming down, but now he noted the differences in their colors and shapes. The final climb through the jagged rocks near the summit seemed to use up all the reserves he had built up over the past two days. Despite the lack of views at the summit, he felt obligated to take a photo of Marty and Boo by the sign. He wanted to save his lunch break for the wonderful viewpoint overlooking upper Dusy Basin, which he had passed by quickly in his haste before.

When he descended from lower Dusy Basin, the mountains on the other side of Le Conte Canyon pulled him down the switchbacks. When he reached the long water slide to the left of the trail, his knees encouraged him to take a ride. *You'll be down there in no time. Yeah, but I won't be alive to tell anyone about it.*

Around 4 PM, he crossed the JMT to visit Sally's cabin. He heard her before he saw her. "Look who's back. I knew I'd see you again." Seconds later, he saw her sitting on the porch in a rocking chair.

"How is Hannah?"

"She's much better. Her memory is mostly back, and she's on her way home with her father."

"Good to hear."

Bob stepped on the porch and sat next to Sally.

"I have good news too. My ranger buddy at Bench Lake ran across those party animals. They didn't admit to anything at first. But I found a luggage tag with one of their names while going through the trash you picked up. It must have fallen off one of their backpacks. When the ranger saw the same name on their permit and challenged them, one of them cracked. They're off the trail now."

"Wow. Nice work. I remember one guy wasn't too keen on the idea. He must have been the one who cracked."

"So, are you headed to Whitney after all?"

Bob shook his head. "You too? Cathy must be talking to me through all the wonderful ladies I meet on the trail. Jessica. Hannah. Now you!"

"It's nothing supernatural. We just know how much this means to you."

"Well, I have to resupply at Onion Valley, so I'll at least make it that far. I'll decide on Whitney when I get there."

"If you've made it this far, you can make it to Whitney. Just take your time."

"Thanks Sally. I appreciate what you do for us backpackers. It can't be easy."

She looked off in the distance. "I can put up with a lot with a view like this from my front porch."

* * *

Mark and Jessica climbed the trail along Middle Rae Lake, the second of three Rae Lakes. A couple of hikers walked toward them on a social trail. They appeared to be leaving camp–kind of a late start, but not a bad place to spend the entire morning. Based on their recommendation, Mark followed the short path to a flat, sandy spot on the top of a hill. In one direction, the Painted Lady showed off her bands of white, black, and yellow over the southern part of Middle Rae Lake. In the other direction, a white granite monolith, Fin Dome, towered over Lower Rae Lake. It was only early-afternoon, but how could they pass up a campsite like this?

After they set up their tents, Jessica went down the hill to explore the shoreline while Mark laid down on top of his sleeping pad with the door flap tied open. If he leaned to his right, he could see the Painted Lady without leaving his tent. In what seemed like a few minutes later, his whole body twitched, and he woke up. Where was he? Why was he sleeping outside? He looked at his watch: 4:10 PM. Oh yeah. Rae Lakes. He couldn't believe he had slept that long. He climbed out of the tent and stretched his arms over his head, but didn't see Jessica. He peeked in her tent. Not there. He looked down at the sandy beach below. A couple was creeping into the cold water, but he saw no sign of Jessica. Where could she be?

He replaced his camp shoes with his hiking shoes and explored the other side of the hill. Not there either. Maybe she wandered over to explore the upper lake. After a few minutes of hiking up the trail, he heard a shrill voice screaming the dreaded words, "Bear, Bear!" Jessica was sprinting toward him on the trail, 150 feet ahead. An enormous bear charged her from the slope on her right with two cubs following in its wake, thinking their mother was playing chase. Well, it was a chase, but it wasn't a game. Jessica must have surprised mama bear, who was now shooing Jessica away from her cubs. Mark ran toward Jessica–and the bear. When he reached Jessica, he shoved her behind him. "Stop running. Just stay behind me." A solo hiker approached from the same direction Jessica had come.

Mark yelled, "Stop! Bear cubs."

Jessica's fingernails dug into the flesh above his hips, and her head peeked around his chest. "Jessica, let go." He needed to be free so he could make himself look big and scary to the bear.

Mark yelled, "Go Bear. Go away, Bear!" He raised his arms and clapped his hands. "Go, bear!"

The other hiker also yelled, but used harsher language. He followed Mark's lead and waved his hiking poles in the air. Finally, mama bear got the message and walked toward the trees above the trail. The cubs were interested in all the commotion and hesitated. Mama bear waited for them to turn back toward her before leading them into the trees.

Mark tried to turn around, but Jessica was wrapped around him like the tortilla surrounding her peanut butter at lunchtime. "Whoa. That was scary."

"Are you OK?" He patted her on the back.

Jessica released her death grip. He could finally breathe normally again.

"I believe so. That bear came out of nowhere."

"I just woke up. I'm so sorry I left you alone."

"That's OK. You can't watch me all the time. When you had been sleeping for fifteen minutes, I headed off to explore the upper lake."

They started walking back toward camp, turning their heads to the right after every few steps.

"Your mother doesn't need to find out about this." Mark winked.

Jessica zipped her lips with her fingers.

"That a girl."

Message from Bob: *Hannah, Jessica: Back on trail!*

Message from Mark: *Bob: Watch out for bears at Rae Lakes. Seriously!*

Message from Jessica: *Mom: We got to Rae Lakes early. Did some exploring. Should be at the trailhead tomorrow*

* * *

Dear Cathy,

I'm back on the JMT! I am now camped just south of Sally's cabin. We had a pleasant talk before I made camp. It seems like you're speaking to me through my trail friends. They are just as persistent as you were. I can't blame you. I didn't always listen to you, especially about your trips, so maybe you're trying out some other voices. Keep it up; it helps.

Climbing Bishop Pass took a lot out of me. I felt as drained as the last time I was there. But the beautiful descent has reinvigorated me. The scenery today served as a synopsis of the first half of the trail: the lush meadow and ponds like in Lyell Canyon, the blue lakes like Garnet and Evolution, the walls of mountains, the bridge over the waterfall like Fish Creek, and the water slide down the sloped granite.

The Golden Staircase awaits. Mark and Sally have warned me against climbing both it and Mather Pass on the same day, so I will camp at one of the Palisade Lakes. Believe it or not, I'm trying to listen more.

Love, Bob

203

27

Saved

2021

August 27 - Houston, TX

Bob dragged the big box through his front door. It was too big to be the hiking shoes he ordered a few days ago. The label showed the Fresno County Sheriff's Office to be the sender. His stomach rose toward his throat and his head spun, so he sat on the floor and laid his head on his arms on top of the box. The sheriff's office had called a few weeks ago about Cathy's backpack. His mind froze when they asked what they should do with it, so he took them up on their offer to ship it to him as is.

When his head stopped spinning, he stood up slowly and paused to make sure it was safe to walk to his office. He returned with scissors and cut the thick tape sealing the box closed. The heavy and awkward package had survived the trip with surprisingly little damage. When he opened the first flap, the musty smell forced him to turn his head to the side. He shouldn't be surprised. Backpacks are often abused in the backcountry. They pick up sweat, dirt, sunscreen, food residue, and worse. And this one had been in the water and probably set aside where it couldn't dry quickly. It must be filled with mildew.

After moving the box to the garage, he opened the other flaps and removed the pack from the box. Sure enough, even the outside of the pack had black stains. Why did he even have them ship it? Nearly everything was ruined, and if not, would forever remind him of the tragedy and his failures that led to it. He should just set it by the curb next to his trash cans on Saturday. As he guided the pack back into the box, he noticed a bulge in the side pocket. After setting the pack back on the ground, he reached into the pocket and pulled out a marmot. Marty! His fur was matted and had a few black splotches. *I almost tossed you out with the trash.* The water filter and the stove could be replaced, but not Marty. He was with Cathy when she died. Marty could help him show Cathy the trails remaining on her bucket list.

He brought Marty close to his nose and cautiously sniffed him. He closed his eyes and dropped him on the garage floor. Marty was beyond his cleaning capabilities. He needed professional help. *I'm sure they've seen worse.*

28

Listen and Learn

2022

Day 14

August 18 - Le Conte Canyon to Upper Palisade Lake

Unlike most SOBOs, Bob actually enjoyed the Golden Staircase. This was due in part to Mark's advice, which relieved Bob of the expectation of also climbing Mather Pass later in the day. His legs could recover by one of the Palisade Lakes overnight versus immediately being asked to repeat the strenuous climb. He admired the craftsmanship of the trail designers and construction crews. True to the name, most of the steps were similar in height to those on a standard staircase versus the twelve- to eighteen-inch steps seen on some parts of the trail. A few exceptions at the turns of the switchbacks tested his knees and thighs. Cobbles were used sparingly on small sections where the trail crossed fields of large boulders. Wildflowers thrived where small springs seeped from switchback to switchback, giving him a close look at their blooms without having to bend over. The higher he climbed, the longer he stopped to admire the incredible view of the valley from which he had come. With sweat dripping from his nose, he struggled to comprehend how it was once full of glacial ice.

The numerous false summits would have been frustrating without the surprises awaiting him around each turn of Palisade Creek. Waterfalls fell through small gorges. Wildflowers thrived where springs emerged in open areas exposed to full morning sun. Bands of black rock invaded the white granite. If he were a geologist, this section would have taken forever. He was almost sorry to see the bottoms of the Palisade mountains when they appeared over the last hump.

From the narrow foot of Lower Palisade Lake, the lake widened and the mountains on each side rose into the sky. Mather Pass was not yet visible. It was only noon, but someone had already set up their tent near the trail. The owners of the tent would have to endure a long afternoon in the sun. Only a few short trees dotted the shoreline, providing very little shade. Bob enjoyed his lunch with his bare feet resting on coarse sand in six inches of water. Since this end of the lake was so shallow, the water was cool and refreshing versus freezing and biting. What the heck! Might as well go all in. With no jagged rocks on the bottom, he let the sand squeeze between his toes as he walked into the deeper water.

As he approached the other end of the lower lake, Mather Pass came into view, further reinforcing Mark's advice. It was still so far away and so much higher, essentially another Golden Staircase. Without Mark's note, Bob knew he would have driven himself over the pass at any cost. A couple of empty tent sites appeared just off the trail to the right. The upper lake was now several hundred feet below. The sites were fully shaded by a thick clump of trees and would remain so through sunset. Yet ten feet away, there was a mound of rock with an unobstructed view of Upper Palisade Lake, Mather Pass, and part of the lower lake. But where was the water supply? Walking down the steep slope to the lake was not practical or safe. However, when he stood still, he heard trickling water. He set his pack and poles down to claim the site and wandered farther up the trail with a bounce in his step. Two hundred feet away, he found a stream falling down the mountainside and crossing the trail. That sealed it. This would be his home for the night.

He lamented not bringing his water bag while searching for the water source, since he would have to return after setting up his tent. So many things to keep track of out here. No wonder my mind is so exhausted.

Dark clouds moved toward him from the other side of Mather Pass as he set up his campsite. So much for enjoying the sunset over a cup of hot chocolate after dinner. Instead, he had an early dinner while sitting on the mound of granite, watching the dark clouds dance in the sky above the lake. Instead of racing up the pass to beat the lightning and hail, he could slip into his tent at a moment's notice with a full belly. If the previous weather patterns held, he would be able to enjoy the view in the morning as the sun lit up the mountainside on the far side of the lake. And if the wind stayed away, the peaks would reflect perfectly off the surface of the water.

Message from Bob: *Mark: Golden advice for Palisade Lakes:)*

* * *

Mark and Jessica's last day on the trail would be difficult, even with fresh legs after a lazy afternoon at Rae Lakes, aside from the bear encounter. Two passes stood between them and pizza. Glen Pass was reputedly one of the toughest on the trail, especially when approached from the north. Kearsarge Pass would be much easier since another trail cut over to the pass before they lost all their hard-earned elevation. Those continuing on the JMT would descend gradually past the trails to Bullfrog and Charlotte Lakes and then descend steeply to Bubbs Creek.

Jessica's mood had soured during dinner last night. Even though she was almost sure to achieve her goal of completing their section hike, he sensed she wanted more, perhaps Mt. Whitney. She hadn't said as much; even she had limits on how far to push him.

Mark nipped at Jessica's heels for the first time in days as they wound their way up the steepening trail to Glen Pass. Her pack was the lightest it had ever been, but her shoulders sagged as if they were loaded with a bunch of rock souvenirs. Fortunately, the scenery was quite engaging and diverse. The view of Rae Lakes was different every time they turned around. Several dark blue tarns appeared on their right. They didn't appear to have names, but some were larger than a few of the named lakes they had passed. The Painted Lady and some of her neighboring peaks were striped with color. Mark commented on the interesting scenery during their numerous breaks in an attempt to raise Jessica's spirits.

Jessica finally perked up as they reached the pass, which was a 100-foot walk along a knife-edged ridge from which they could see both sides below. She took her pack off and walked back and forth along the ridge, pausing to catch the views through the notches between the large rocks. They ate peanut butter directly from squeeze packs as they looked down on Rae Lakes and tried to identify their wonderful campsite and the trees from which mama bear had begun her chase.

A couple of smaller tarns greeted them on the other side. They scrambled down to the first one to fill their water bottles since they weren't sure they would find other water sources before Kearsarge Pass. Shortly thereafter, Jessica stopped at the junction with the Kearsarge Pass trail. Mark stopped beside her and grabbed her hand since he couldn't put his arm around her and her pack. She stared down the JMT instead of looking up at him.

"This is our turn. I'm so proud of you, Jessica. You've made it much farther than we originally planned."

"I know." She still stared straight ahead. "I just wish we could go all the way to Whitney."

"You'll have other opportunities. You did great for your first backpacking trip."

Mark gently pulled her hand toward the other trail. He let go and led her down the trail so he wouldn't make her feel rushed following closely behind. She could stop and enjoy her final views as long as she needed. And the views rivaled the best on the JMT itself. Bullfrog Lake was first, then the Kearsarge Lakes, which resembled Rae Lakes from this distance. Instead of being framed by the Painted Lady and Fin Dome, the Kearsarge pinnacles formed the backdrop for the lakes. If they ever had the opportunity to finish the southern section of the JMT, these lakes would make an excellent first camp after climbing Kearsarge Pass.

The trail was steep only for a short section before the pass. Large blocks of granite towered above. They looked like they could tumble on the trail at any time, but Mark knew they must have been there for decades, if not centuries. They ate their last trail lunch on top of the pass. With Kearsarge Pass being a popular day hike from the Onion Valley trailhead, they shared it with nearly a dozen hikers and a few fat marmots. They had no assigned lunch left in their food bags, so they munched on the most appealing scraps remaining. They washed them down with the last of their water. Stopping at the tarn had been a good call, as they hadn't found any water sources since then.

Mark pried Jessica off of her rock bench and lifted her pack so she could ease into it. They would need to get water soon. Big Pothole Lake teased them just over the pass, but it was well below the trail. They still had not found water a mile later. Even though the trail surface was smooth, Jessica's head was down. She stopped abruptly, and Mark ran right into her pack.

"You two should watch where you're going."

"Brock!" yelled Jessica.

"What a surprise." said Mark.

"It was hot at the trailhead, so I just decided to hike up to meet you."

"There's some shade just ahead. Let's talk there."

They started walking downhill but immediately faced three mules heading toward them. The man sitting on the first mule pulled on the reins, and the mule shook his head to the side a couple of times. He pointed to the downhill side of the trail.

Mark stepped to the side and looked back to check if Jessica had done the same. "Sorry about that. Where are you headed today?"

"Charlotte Lake. Delivering resupply packages for some hikers and a few things for the ranger."

Jessica said, "Cool. Hikers can do that?"

"Almost every day. Saves a long hike to town and back."

"Dad, if we had done that, maybe we could have made it to Mt. Whitney."

Mark smiled, "You may not have had enough, but I have. We did very well for our first backpacking trip."

Brock began walking, staying as far from the mules as he could without falling off the trail.

Mark and Jessica followed. Jessica raised her hand, but the pack leader was watching her closely. "Please don't pet the mules. You might spook them."

After removing their packs and exchanging hugs ten minutes later, Brock reached into his day pack and removed three large plastic bottles of Coca Cola. Jessica and Mark swiped two from his hands.

"Your timing is perfect. We are completely out of water," said Mark.

Jessica rubbed the cold bottle on her cheeks and forehead, then twisted off the cap and let the fizzing drink tickle her nose. She took a small sip and closed her eyes. Mark wasn't so patient. He took three quick gulps before pausing to let the burning in his mouth and throat subside. The sugar started to bring him out of the trance the dusty switchbacks had lulled them into.

"Where's your mother?"

"She's down at the trailhead. I think she was going to drive to the campground to find some shade. You wouldn't believe how hot it is down there."

Mark stared at Brock. He was proud and relieved. The troublesome Brock had not resurfaced with his return to the city. His appearance with the drinks may have been spontaneous, but still magic. And being spontaneous meant it was genuine, not contrived like so many of his reactions in the past.

"Have you heard from Bob and Hannah?" asked Brock.

Mark said, "Only by satellite messages, so not much. Hannah is fine and on her way home. Bob seems to be struggling, but he returned to the trail. I don't know if he will finish or not."

"He's gonna finish," said Jessica, as she turned toward her father. A precious sip of her drink sloshed out of the bottle onto her leg.

"And what makes you so sure?" asked Brock.

"He's just got to. I won't let him give up. Neither will Hannah. I bet she's the one who got him back on the trail."

Brock looked at Mark and raised his eyebrows. "OK, if you say so."

"So what else exciting has happened, other than Hannah getting hurt? See any bears?"

Jessica looked at Mark and giggled.

Brock responded with a quick chuckle. "What?"

"Can you keep a secret?" asked Jessica.

"Sure. What?"

"Well, there was a bear at Rae Lakes. But you can't tell Mom. She'd never let me hike again."

"I won't tell. Did you get a good picture?"

"Are you kidding? I was running for my life. A mama bear and two cubs. I guess she thought I was a threat. But come on, even the cubs outweighed me."

"No. Get out of here." Brock looked at Mark, who confirmed the story with a nod.

"Fortunately, Dad woke up from his nap just in time and remembered to look big and make lots of noise."

"Your Mom doesn't need to know about that nap either." Mark winked at Brock.

"Wow. Sounds like you two had a great trip." Brock looked at Jessica. "I'm so glad you got to finish. I knew you would make it. Not sure I would have."

Mark stood up. "Shall we go rescue your mother from the sun?"

Jessica hopped up, all fueled up with a large dose of sugar. She reached for her pack, but Brock handed her his nearly empty day pack. "My treat, sis.'"

Mark beamed. *Thank you, Bob. Thank you, Trail.*

Message from Jessica: *Bob: We made it! And so will you! Brock met us on the trail and carried my pack down. Nice to have my old big brother back. When do you expect to get to Onion Valley?*

* * *

Dear Cathy,

I'm actually feeling pretty good tonight. I slept well last night and didn't overdo it today. The Golden Staircase was tough, but it kept me entertained. I am camped far above Upper Palisade Lake. Mather Pass shouldn't be too bad on fresh legs in the morning.

You and my trail family are advising me well, getting me back on the trail and encouraging me to pace myself. Please keep it up. I need all the help I can get. This trail is beautiful, but also littered with obstacles. I wonder what will be next.

Love, Bob

29

Cobbles

2022

Day 15

August 19 - Upper Palisade Lake to Lake Marjorie

Bob's optimism for an easy climb to Mather Pass lasted thirty minutes. He should have known better by now. The initial climb from his campsite was gentle, but then section after section of trail filled with cobbles slowed his pace to a crawl. The cobbles ranged in size from lemons to grapefruit and shifted under his feet no matter how carefully he stepped. The sound of the rocks grinding against each other as he stepped gave him the chills. He would have fallen several times if not for his hiking poles providing two more points of contact. Unnecessarily high steps seemed to mark corners of every switchback. His poles and arms helped his quivering thighs and aching knees lift him over the steps. He took a break after every couple of switchbacks, as much to relieve his growing frustration as to inhale more oxygen. How can two ascents so close together (the Golden Staircase and Mather Pass) be constructed so differently? He knew they were built at different times, but it still felt good to blame someone for his misery. The only thing more frustrating than climbing a trail like this was descending one. If the other side of the pass was the same, he might only make five miles today.

It took him two hours to climb the remaining 1,000 feet in elevation to Mather Pass. Bob leaned on his poles shoved up in his armpits while he caught his breath. A much younger male hiker was packing up to descend the trail Bob had just climbed. "That tough, huh?"

Bob never quite knew what to say in these situations. He wanted to be truthful, but he didn't want to discourage oncoming hikers with the unpleasant realities ahead. He usually erred on the side of telling it like it was. "Yeah. Lots of cobbles and big steps. But the hike along the lakes is wonderful. Then, you know the Golden Staircase is ahead, right?"

"Yeah. Glad I'm going down that one. Your descent won't be bad. Pretty gradual, only a few small sections of cobbles. Have a great day."

Bob removed the food bag from his pack. He tried to improve his mood with a large snack, macadamia nuts followed by a dried tropical fruit mix. Pinchot Pass was ten miles from here, plus another mile or two to a decent campsite. Since yesterday's decision to stop before the pass had worked out so well, he would try to camp at Lake Marjorie, just short of Pinchot Pass.

* * *

Bob walked toward Lake Marjorie's rocky shore with his rehydrated mashed potatoes and bacon bits and his water bottle. As he approached the shore, a couple of pikas turned their heads and darted into gaps between the rocks. He had read before the trip that the gray and brown hamster-like creatures with oversized ears were part of the rabbit family. Their ears were round versus long and floppy, and they scurried instead of hopping; he would take the biologists' word for it. He had seen them a few times before, but never long enough and close enough to take a picture.

He sat down and began eating while staring across the lake. The water deepened quickly and must be icy at this elevation. It was much too late for him to find out. The rocks surrounding the lake were nearly white, but up ahead he saw red and brown, probably indicating the presence of iron in the rock.

Out of the corner of his eye, he saw movement. He turned his head quickly, and a pika ran out of sight. Bob set his dinner pouch down and took his phone out of his pocket. A minute later, the pika reappeared and stared at him. He lifted his camera slowly, and the pika surprised Bob by staying put. He held down the shutter button to enter rapid shot mode, knowing that many of the shots would be blurry as the pika surveyed the area for danger. Another one appeared in front of him. He turned his head slowly, and again, it stayed in place. After staring at him for nearly a minute, it pulled up some vegetation growing in a crack of a rock and ran back to its well-hidden den. They must be foraging for the long winter ahead.

Marmots were fun, intriguing, and cute in their own way, but pikas were the cutest animals on the trail. And he had finally figured out how to observe and photograph them. They scattered with any sudden movement, but if you just stopped and stood still, they would come back out and let you admire their beauty.

Bob was getting chilled, so he headed back to his tent. He arrived at the same time as a ranger did. The ranger stared at him for a few seconds and tilted his head. "Wait a minute. Are you Bob Riley?"

"Yes." Bob squinted his eyes. "Oh. You must be the ranger from Bench Lake."

"Yes. Josh. Sally described you to a tee, just like those guys we busted for making a mess in the hut. Thanks for your help with that."

"Oh, it's nothing. You and Sally did all the work. I just wish I had said something to them at MTR so the whole incident wouldn't have occurred."

"I'm glad you told Sally. We just don't have any patience for those who disrespect the trail."

"Do you know how the young lady that fell is doing?"

"Much better. I hiked in to Bishop to check on Hannah, and she was feeling much better."

"What a great trail friend. I'm glad she's OK." Josh looked at the ground for a few seconds, then back at Bob. "By the way, Sally told me how she was hurt—"

Bob held his palm up. "I know. I feel really bad about that. I didn't mean for her to go up there, but I never should have mentioned it."

"OK. Thanks again. I'll let you get on with your chores. I need to get back to my cabin. Good night."

Message from Bob: *Hannah, Jessica: Mather Pass was so hard. Camping at Lake Marjorie. I'm worried about getting over Glen Pass. What did you think, Jessica? Expect to be at Onion Valley in three days.*

Message from Jessica: *Bob: If you can get over Mather, you'll get over Glen. Kearsarge is a piece of cake after that.*

Message from Hannah: *Bob: Nice job. My headache is finally gone. Just take it one day at a time. You'll get there.*

* * *

Dear Cathy,

My decision to stop at Upper Palisade Lake yesterday looked even better by mid-morning. Mather Pass almost beat me all by itself. Sure, it was tough on my legs and lungs, but even tougher on my mind. The trail surface was atrocious, so I had to focus on each footfall instead of my breathing and pace. And just to rub it in, I watched a young guy fly down the trail while I ate a snack. How he didn't bust an ankle, I'll never know. Youth, I guess.

I am camped at Lake Marjorie. I'm now starting to wonder if I should have given you a stuffed pika instead of a marmot. But then again, they're probably even harder to find than Marty was. They are so cute. What did you think of them? I imagine they look too much like mice for some people.

Three more passes until my resupply at Onion Valley: Pinchot, Glen, and Kearsarge, each around 12,000 feet in elevation. Pinchot shouldn't be too bad, but many say Glen Pass is the toughest. If it is harder than Mather Pass, it may be the end of this trip. I don't know if I could handle two passes and Mt. Whitney after that. Everyone says if I made it this far, I can make it to Mt. Whitney. But they're not here. They haven't been hiking for two weeks. They don't feel the deep fatigue. Just like I didn't appreciate what you were going through. Your calls for help should have told me, but I wasn't listening close enough. However, I will give it my best effort. I owe it to you.

Love, Bob

30

The Lady and the Fin

2022

Day 16

August 20 - Lake Marjorie to Rae Lakes

Bob had company on the top of Pinchot Pass, not fellow backpackers but a couple of bold marmots. Instead of laying Marty on a rock for a photo in each direction, he took selfies holding Marty, and then Boo, next to his face. He didn't think the marmots would dare mess with a bear, but he was taking no chances after the incident near Thousand Island Lake. As he returned them to the safety of his backpack, he realized that he hadn't even thought about taking their picture on top of Mather Pass. He must have been in a real funk. He vowed to maintain a more positive attitude today.

His snack was constantly interrupted by the tag team tactics of the two marmots.

You go tug on his backpack strap while I circle around the other side.

Charge from the right. I'll sneak in and pick up what falls out of his bag when he shoos you away.

Go knock over his water bottle. He'll probably drop the whole bag of nuts.

He wished Mark, Jessica, and Hannah were here to make it a fair fight.

Between marmot attacks, he studied the reds and browns of the surrounding peaks, which added a little spice to the gray and white that had become almost ordinary after two weeks. He looked down at the large unnamed lake sitting at the bottom of an extensive slope of reddish-brown talus. The darker surroundings made the lake appear to be a deeper shade of blue than Lake Marjorie. Different, but just as beautiful. The views on this trail rarely disappointed!

The initial descent from Pinchot Pass was straightforward. However, as the trail followed the Woods Creek drainage, it became very rocky and seemed to wander up and down pointlessly. Steps as high as his knees were commonplace, forcing him to a complete stop to lower himself with the support of his hiking poles. In a few cases, he had to sit on the top of the step to make his way down. Where possible, hikers had created easier paths around the enormous steps.

He was breaking his vow to maintain a positive outlook. Fortunately, Woods Creek brought a smile to his face when it turned into a slip 'n slide as the water flowed over a broad incline of smooth rock. It was shorter than the one along the Bishop Pass trail, but more tortuous. He couldn't help but think of his favorite water park from his youth. Shortly thereafter, he heard voices–lots of voices, and the Woods Creek suspension bridge appeared in front of him. Several hikers were splashing in the water below and drying off on the rocky creek bank.

The bridge must have seemed like overkill to many hikers looking at the knee-deep water, but Bob was thankful. Having hiked along a massive creek channel all day, he knew the flow could become much more dangerous during heavy snowmelt or after a rainstorm. If only there was such a bridge at Evolution Creek! Just one more bridge like this, and he and Cathy would be hiking together; if not on this trail, then another one on her long bucket list.

A hiker stood still in the center of the bridge. From below, she appeared to be admiring the stream underneath, but when Bob climbed the stairs to the landing, he saw she was frozen with fear. She gripped one side of the wire handrail with both hands, turning her head from one end of the bridge to the other. Bob looked for partners of hers on the other side, but saw none. A sign on the landing said, "One person at a time." Yeah, but he was thin, and she was small. *It should be OK, right?* If other hikers lined up to cross, she might panic even more.

Bob folded his hiking poles and attached them to his pack. He wasn't afraid of heights or water, but he took tiny steps in the middle of the grating so as not to create big motions for the lady holding on for dear life. When he reached her, he stood still, holding the handrail with one hand and placing the other on her shoulder. "Hi. My name is Bob."

She said, "I can't do this." Her voice wavered. Bob could barely hear her over the water rushing below.

"I understand. You might not be able to do this by yourself, but I'm going to help you. OK?"

"I don't know."

"What's your name?"

"Ashley."

"Ashley, which way are you going?"

She nodded in the direction Bob came from.

"Northbound. OK. I'm going to turn that way. I want you to grab the sides of my backpack one hand at a time. OK?"

"OK."

"Great. I'm going to walk slowly, just like when I came out here. Hold on and do the same. And just look straight ahead at my backpack."

Ashley nodded.

Bob shuffled his feet when he felt her grab his backpack. After about thirty feet, the motions increased. She tugged on the left side of his pack, causing him to stumble and increase the motions even more. She let go of the pack and grabbed the handrail again. He heard metal hitting the rocks below and looked down. Oh no! Ashley had dislodged one of his hiking poles, and it had fallen in the creek. Fortunately, no one was swimming directly below, but he couldn't hike without his poles. How would he handle all those giant steps or cross the streams without bridges? One of the onlookers sitting on the beach rushed into the creek and retrieved the pole. He held it up with one hand and gave Bob a thumbs up with the other. Bob's heart rate subsided by half, and he returned his attention to the woman he was helping. Her heart must still be pounding.

"Ashley. Let's try that one more time. The closer we are to the end, the less the bridge will move. You can do this."

They repeated their moves from before and resumed progress. When Bob got within ten feet of the end, he increased his speed, hoping she would keep up. When they arrived on the fixed landing, he turned around and grabbed one of her hands while she grabbed the handrail with the other. She climbed down the steps right away, placing two feet on each step and gripping the both handrails the entire time. Bob followed her down. She turned and gave him a hug and wouldn't let go. He felt tears soak through his shirt. "Thank you so much. That thing is terrifying." She backed up and wiped her eyes.

"Yes, I understand how it can be for some. But, hey, you made it. You won't see another one like it all the way to Yosemite."

"Thank goodness."

"Hey, can you do me a favor?" Bob took off his pack and reached inside.

"Sure."

He pulled out Marty and Boo. "Will you hold up my two trail mascots so I can take their picture with the bridge in the background? I don't dare take them out while on the bridge."

She smiled, and Bob snapped the picture while she still found his comment funny.

"Thanks. Why don't we sit down and drink some water, then you can continue."

The hiker who had retrieved his pole arrived and handed it to him. "Thanks. I can't hike without these."

"No, thank you. She'll never forget you."

Bob now had a photo to remember her by.

* * *

Bob crossed the bridge at his own pace, trying his best to shed the effects of Ashley's panic so he could enjoy the experience. Once on the other side, he pondered the decision Ashley had forced him to put off. Camp here or continue on? The graphic warning sign just past the bridge implied that a visit by a bear was inevitable. He had hiked nine miles so far, a bit on the low side. From here, the trail rose six miles to Rae Lakes, where Cathy's second to last rock would be placed. A fifteen-mile day was beyond his comfort zone, but it would allow him to reach a hotel room in Independence the following day. Each day and night in the backcountry, setting up and packing up camp and struggling to sleep, took a toll beyond the miles hiked. The call of town food and a real bed were too strong. *Rae Lakes, here I come.*

For the next four miles, appreciation for the shade of the thick forest replaced his frustration with the rocky trail along Woods Creek in the hot sun. Small, and not-so-blue, Dollar Lake marked the end of the shade as he neared tree line. When he climbed above the lake, Fin Dome dominated the horizon to the right, even though a mile away. Ten minutes later, it hovered over Arrowhead Lake. Then, it stood behind the first and smallest of the Rae Lakes, Lower Rae Lake. Fin Dome is a monolith of white granite resembling Devil's Tower in Wyoming, and as its name implies, the dorsal fin of a fish. Unlike many mountain peaks, its symmetry gives it a similar appearance from multiple angles. Bob imagined the rainbow of colors he might see tomorrow morning as the sun rose above the mountains. Straight ahead was another icon of the trail, the Painted Lady, showing off her bands of white, black, and yellow. While many hikers sought to camp near Middle or Upper Rae Lake to be closer to her, he preferred the view of Fin Dome from the Lower Lake. Camping here would also shave a half-mile off the already long day of hiking.

* * *

Bob's evening was short, but memorable. He freed Marty and Boo to enjoy the view while he ate dinner. Initially, he faced Fin Dome, but found himself turning his head to the left every few minutes to peek at the Painted Lady.

Both were iconic, but so different. If he had arrived earlier, a bath and laundry would have been in order. They were easy to skip knowing he could take care of both in town tomorrow, with hot water and soap instead of cold lake water.

If tonight ended up being his last night on the trail, what a way to end it. But would it be his last day? His body screamed, "Yes!" For most of the day, his mind had concurred. But Cathy's voice was urging him on. And Hannah and Jessica were unrelenting in their encouragement. In the end, he approached the decision as he had in Bishop; he would see how well he recovered on his day off in Independence and go from there. Either way, he had to get off the trail to resupply.

Before he retired to the tent for the evening, he considered where to place Cathy's rock. The Rae Lakes covered a vast area. He could place it anywhere from where he sat now to the top of Glen Pass. He preferred a view of Fin Dome, so he scanned the immediate area for an inconspicuous resting place. But would that be Cathy's preference? Most photos of Rae Lakes showed the Painted Lady in the background. He wasn't sure why, perhaps the additional colors and texture. He suspected Cathy would prefer to be with her instead. He removed the rock from his pack. Sure enough, the Painted Lady was prominent in the image painted on the rock. He would find a place on the way out tomorrow, closer to the Painted Lady. Perhaps he could find one with a view of both Painted Lady and Fin Dome.

Message from Bob: *Hannah, Jessica: Made it to Rae Lakes today. Love Fin Dome. Planning to make it to the trailhead tomorrow. I really need a day or two in town to recover. Will call you from there.*

***

Dear Cathy,

I pushed myself hard to Rae Lakes today so I could exit over Kearsarge Pass tomorrow. It was a long day, but very worthwhile. I understand why you looked forward to this spot so much. Fin Dome and the Painted Lady bookend the lakes, but you can never see them and all the lakes at once. Most people identify the Painted Lady as the crown jewel of the area, but I prefer Fin Dome. Which do you prefer? I still need to pick a spot for your special rock.

I am so ready for town. My skin and hair need hot water and soap. So do my clothes. I won't have as many choices for food as I did in Bishop, but I hear there is a food truck with good Mexican food. Sounds like a good way to satisfy hiker hunger. And it will be so nice not to have to pack everything up in the morning and put it on my back. Two passes tomorrow will be tough, so I will need the added motivation. I'm a little anxious about Glen Pass. I hear it may be even tougher than Mather, but I will get over it one way or another. I have to!

Stay close while I am in town. I'll need your support to finish this hike off. I'll face two tall hurdles to returning to the JMT. As much as I want to finish, the comforts of town will make it hard to leave. Hannah won't be there to make sure I get to the trailhead. And there's the long climb back over Kearsarge Pass. Once I get back to the trail, I'll have little choice but to finish. So, please help me to help you finish by getting me back on the trail.

Love, Bob

31

Magic

2022

Day 17

August 21 - Rae Lakes to Kearsarge Lakes

Bob set his alarm for only the second time while on the trail to reduce the risk of storms delaying his arrival in town. He was facing his second two-pass day of the trip, but the Glen-Kearsarge combination was more formidable than Donohue-Island. He hiked around a hill on the side of Middle Rae Lake before he first glimpsed Upper Rae Lake. From here, the Painted Lady was both impressive and intimidating. The trail followed a narrow strip of flat ground between the shoreline and a rock wall about twenty feet high. The wall was filled with nooks and crannies, perfect hiding places for marmots and pikas. Perhaps he should put Cathy's rock in one of those holes? But then he looked up and imagined the view of the lake from the black tip of the Painted Lady. There was no way he could climb that high, but he might be able to reach her shoulder. That would be a much better place for the rock. *I will get you as close as I can, Cathy.*

Glen Pass lived up to its reputation. It was long and steep, with more cobbled sections than he cared for. However, the diverse scenery helped to pass the time and distract him from the strenuous effort required. To the north, Rae Lakes waited for a goodbye kiss. The Painted Lady showed off her intricate color bands as the trail wound around her side. The graceful lady resembled an ancient pyramid, leaning back from Rae Lakes, with bands of white, gray, black, and yellow. A pointed black hat on top left a spooky last impression.

When he reached a large tarn on the right, he saw the relatively flat approach to the large black band on the Painted Lady, where he hoped to leave Cathy's rock. Unfortunately, the rocks between him and that spot were much larger than they appeared from below. He stepped from rock to rock until he was about 100 feet off the trail. His poles kept sliding down between rocks and getting stuck. It was just a matter of time before he broke one, so he took his pack off and laid down his poles. He grabbed Cathy's rock from his pack and put it in one of the large pockets on his cargo pants. He continued up the talus slope, using his hands to help maneuver himself around the larger boulders. About fifteen minutes later, the talus ended at the steep rock face of the black band. This would have to do. He had been so focused on finding stable rocks to step on that he hadn't been checking the view of Rae Lakes. All three lakes were visible from here, and Fin Dome peeked around the mountain to his left. *Perfect!* He placed the rock up against the black band. It would rest on the Painted Lady's shoulder forever, or at least until the next rockslide.

When he returned to his pack, a marmot was licking the grips of his poles. They found anything salty to be irresistible. It continued licking until Bob was ten feet away, then scampered across the rocks and dipped into one of the larger gaps. More marmot spit—and a couple of tooth marks about an inch apart. He must have been doing more than licking.

The climb to Glen Pass ended with a 100-foot walk along a jagged spine of rock. He wondered how Ashley, whom he had rescued from the Woods Creek bridge, made it past here. Looking back to the south, he could only see parts of the Upper and Middle Rae Lakes, and Fin Dome was now behind the peak in front of him. The view was much better from the spot where he left Cathy's rock. Bob didn't see any marmots, so he set Marty and Boo free and took their photos facing Rae Lakes and the dark blue tarn to the south. He walked down the ridge and took a photo of both with the Painted Lady hovering over their heads.

"Oh. How cute. Do you want me to take a photo of you with both of them?"

Bob wondered how he didn't notice the other hiker earlier. "Yes. That would be nice. Thanks." He handed her his phone.

"No problem. What are their names?"

"Marty the marmot and Boo the bear. Special people gave them to me."

"I've seen plenty of marmots on the trail, but no bear yet. What do you want in the background?"

"How about one with Rae Lakes and one with the Painted Lady?"

"Perfect."

After she took the two photos, she asked, "Can you take one of me with them?"

Bob hesitated at the odd request, but saw no harm in it. She was probably just trying to capture her unique experiences on the trail so she wouldn't forget. "Sure."

Bob handed the mascots to her and grabbed her phone. He took photos with the same two backgrounds, but her poses were much better than his. He always deleted half the photos of himself because of his awkward poses or contrived smiles.

"Thanks." She tossed them back to him in quick succession. He caught Boo with no problem, but Marty bounced off his hand and went straight up. He raised his hand to grab him, but batted him back toward the other hiker instead. She jumped to her right much more quickly than he could have and grabbed Marty just before he flew over the side. Bob leaped forward and grabbed Marty from her hand. She stepped back in surprise.

"Oh sorry. It's a long story. Let's just say that Marty has used up most of his lives on this trip."

"It's OK. I should have been more careful. It is pretty much straight down on both sides of the trail."

"Thanks for the photos."

"No problem. I'm going to head down now. Trying to make it over Pinchot Pass today."

"Wow. Good luck."

Bob removed a pouch of almond butter from his food bag and secured the bag and his mascots in his backpack. Marmots could appear at any time out of the infinite nooks and crannies in this massive pile of rock. As usual, he had packed too much food. A little extra was prudent in case of unforeseen delays, but he was lugging around at least two unnecessary pounds.

When he returned to the tree line, the environment changed dramatically. Instead of the shady forest of tall pines leading to Dollar Lake, he walked through a forest of widely spaced and squat foxtail pines. He had seen foxtails for days, but always mixed in with other types of trees, typically forming a dense forest. Here, with the wide spacing and lack of undergrowth, he could see for hundreds of feet through the forest. Thin branches of needles resembled foxtails or bottlebrushes. The bark of the healthy trees was deep red, but the dead ones had lost their bark and displayed a tan grain full of swirls. Branches on the dead trees looked like little arms attached to a thick torso, reminding him of the eerie forest in the movie *Snow White*. Only here, they were welcoming, instead of foreboding. Ancient and magnificent trees.

The mountains to the south were more menacing than ever, with sharper peaks, even whiter granite, and fewer trees. Would he have enough left in the tank to see them up close?

The trail to Kearsarge Pass veered to the left. Just past the sign, three people sat on a log. One leaped forward and ran to him with open arms. "Bob!" Jessica knocked him backwards, and his pack nearly pulled him down to the ground.

"Jessica? What are you doing here?"

"We're here to help you finish the trail." She grabbed his hand and pulled him toward the log from which she had leaped. Mark and Brock stood up, and each shook his hand. Mark helped him lower his pack to the ground.

"What the heck? I didn't expect to see you again for—maybe forever."

Mark said, "We got all your messages, and you seemed to need a little boost."

"Are you getting back on the trail already?" asked Bob.

Jessica raised her lower lip and looked at Mark. "I wish, but Dad wasn't quite up for that. Then Brock suggested we bring your resupply to you on the trail."

Mark said, "We were initially planning to meet you at the trailhead, but then Brock said, 'Why don't we carry it over the pass? Make it as easy as we can for him.'"

"Basically, we're your resupply mules," added a smiling Brock. "And we brought you a few town treats as well."

Bob patted Brock on the shoulder. Jessica sat down and pulled on his arm until he sat between her and Brock.

Mark said, "We figured if you didn't have to hike down to the trailhead and all the way back over Kearsarge Pass, you would find it easier to continue. But you don't need to decide right now."

Mark nodded to Brock, who pulled a couple of soft-sided coolers from his backpack. From one, he grabbed a couple of cans of beer for Bob and Mark and Coca Cola for Jessica and himself. The fizzy pops of the cans being opened were music to Bob's ears. Out of the other cooler, Brock pulled club sandwiches, fresh bread stuffed with meat and cheese that wasn't dehydrated and garnished with fresh vegetables. He laid out bananas and apples and a bag of BBQ potato chips on a towel.

"Where's Linda?"

"She's still recovering from the first hike. I think she's had enough for the summer," said Mark.

"She did great for her first time backpacking. You all did."

Bob felt the buzz from the beer almost immediately, as the alcohol rushed through his famished stomach to his brain. He devoured half of a sandwich as fast as he downed the first beer. Brock pulled out another beer from the cooler and handed it to him. Scraps of meat fell to the ground at Bob's feet. The squirrels and marmots would enjoy their own feast once he and Mark's family departed.

"Y'all are too much," Bob said, as he leaned his head back and patted his quickly filling stomach. Jessica stared at him as she ate her sandwich. Bob ate a banana in three bites in between the halves of his sandwiches. His pace slowed as his tank approached full.

"Our pleasure," said Mark.

Bob looked at Brock. "So, are you a hiking convert now?"

"Not really, but it's just a day hike for us and a way to thank you for what you did for me—for all of us."

"And Mom and I made all these sandwiches," said Jessica.

"Be sure to thank your mother for me. They're delicious, and that's not just hiker hunger talking. They really are."

"Have any of you heard from Hannah?" Bob asked.

Jessica grinned, then admitted, "Maybe."

Bob leaned over and bumped her shoulder. "Have y'all been ganging up on me again? How is she doing?"

"Feeling better every day. She threatened to drive down here if our scheme didn't work."

Bob shook his head, then smiled.

Jessica continued, "So—now that your belly is full and you're half drunk, what have you decided? Hike out with us and go home, stay a night or two in Independence, or take the food in Dad's pack and continue on?"

"Jessica," Mark said. "Give him some time to relax."

"It's OK, Mark. I've had days to think about it. The passes are getting harder, and the lack of sleep is wearing me down. By the way, thanks for the tip on not climbing the Golden Staircase and Mather Pass on the same day."

"You're welcome. I don't know what got into Jessica that day." Jessica smiled.

"And now this wonderful lunch reminds me of what real food is like. I just don't know. I was going to make the call after resting in town for a day."

Brock said, "We brought all the food and supplies you need for four or five days." He patted the pack sitting between him and Mark. "You won't need to hike all the way back up here. Believe me, this side of the pass is easy, but it's a long way up the other side."

Mark said. "How about this? Why don't you exchange your trash for your new food, hike down to Kearsarge Lakes, and take the rest of the day off. Wash up. Take a nap. Get a good night's sleep. From there, you only have three long days, or four easier ones, to reach Whitney Portal. And if you wake up tomorrow still exhausted, you can exit over Kearsarge Pass then."

Bob sat in silence, gazing at Mark, then glanced at the others. Jessica leaned so far forward he thought she would fall off the log. He then looked at the Kearsarge pinnacles, spears of granite reaching toward the bright sun. The Kearsarge Lakes were just below, but they weren't visible yet.

"What would Cathy want you to do?" Jessica asked.

"Unfortunately, she didn't get a second chance. Who knows if I will?"

"This will be the easiest resupply you ever get," said Brock.

"OK. You win!"

Jessica stood up. Bob pointed an index finger at her. "I see where you get your persistence from." She stepped over and gave him a hug. For a change, his head was below hers. "I like your idea, Mark. Deep down inside, I knew it would be hard to hike up Kearsarge Pass again after the comforts of town. If it weren't for Hannah, I wouldn't have made it back over Bishop Pass. Y'all have removed that obstacle. Maybe it will be enough."

Tears filled Bob's eyes. He rose, stood in front of Mark and Brock until they rose and gave each of them a quick hug. "I can't thank y'all enough. I wouldn't have continued if you hadn't made it so easy."

"A small fraction of what you did for us and Hannah: giving Jessica the medicine she needed, donating food at MTR, helping Brock turn himself around, and getting help for Hannah—OK, we better transfer all this stuff so you can get going. And we have a long walk back to the car."

Bob removed the bear canister from his pack and gathered all the trash and his leftover food. He also handed over the bag containing his used toilet paper, hidden deep in his back mesh pocket. Brock looked reluctant to take that one, but Mark reached over and grabbed it. Then Mark gave Bob a couple of shopping bags full of food and toiletries.

"Take these bags and pack your bear canister in comfort down by the lakes. Oh, here's a fresh power bank too, since you won't get to charge yours in town. And a full tank of gas for cooking."

"Thanks, I forgot about those." He removed the used ones from his backpack and handed them to Mark.

Remembering the couple of pounds of extra food he had been carrying the past few days, he looked through the bags and held out a couple of handfuls of food.

"Do you have any more Cokes? I'll trade you."

Brock pulled a Coke from the cooler and took the extra food. It would be warm by dinner time, but twenty minutes sitting in one of the Kearsarge Lakes would fix that. Nature's refrigerator. Jessica pulled one more thing from the cooler. "And here are some fresh brownies for dessert tonight. I know you would prefer ice cream, but it wouldn't have survived the trip."

"Thanks. You're so sweet. Well, I guess this is goodbye for now. Wish me luck."

"This isn't goodbye. You need to help me get to the top of Whitney next summer. Keep sending messages so we can follow you," said Jessica.

Since Bob hadn't planned to camp in this area, he consulted the map on his phone. There were two routes to Kearsarge Lakes. One would take him up toward Kearsarge Pass before descending to Kearsarge Lakes. The other would descend a bit farther on the JMT before following the Bullfrog Lake trail. Even with his two beer buzz, the choice was simple. His legs decided for him. Bullfrog Lake was on the way, but unfortunately, camping had been prohibited there for years.

* * *

Bob finished setting up his tent in the shade an hour later, with the door facing one of the Kearsarge Lakes. The Kearsarge pinnacles rose so high above the lake that Bob could not see the sky through the door. The shade would make the sorting of his new food and repacking of his bear canister more tolerable. He planned to do so in his tent to avoid trouble with the marmots and squirrels. The shade would also allow for a comfortable afternoon nap.

Mark's plan for the day had sounded so peaceful, but Bob's afternoon off was surprisingly busy. He waded into the shallow end of the lake to refresh himself and rub off some of the sweat and dirt on his skin and hair. With no clouds in the sky, he rinsed his hiking clothes and laid them out to dry while taking a nap in his shorts. Before he fell asleep, he took a selfie with Marty and Boo lying on his pillow on each side of his head. After two hours of sound sleep, he sorted his food and toiletries. Despite the feast at lunch, his hunger returned by dinnertime. The Coke he left in the lake during his nap made his backpacker meal much more satisfying. He might have taken in more calories than he burned for the first since leaving Bishop.

What had appeared to be a long, difficult day at breakfast turned into a short, magnificent one. Glen Pass tested him, but it was the only significant ascent of the day. Mark's family had rejuvenated him. The fresh food and cold beers put a dent in his hiker hunger and helped him relax, but their care and generosity had a greater impact. It was nothing short of magic. When he had left Rae Lakes in the morning, he was prepared to say goodbye to the JMT, at least for this year. Their words had been urging him on for over a week, but their actions made the difference.

Message from Bob: *Hannah: Mark's family saved my hike. Thanks for your support. Mt. Whitney, here I come!*

Message from Bob: *Jessica, Linda: The brownies were delicious!*

Message from Hannah: *Bob: Great news. I knew Jessica and Brock could do it!*

* * *

Dear Cathy,

The trail provided me with magic today! Perhaps just enough to get us over the finish line. Mark, Jessica, and Brock brought me a fresh meal and my resupply to the junction with the Kearsarge Pass trail. I was so pleased to see Brock with them. Evidently, it was all his idea. My messages must have told them I was likely to leave the trail for good at Onion Valley. Maybe you sent them a message too.

It all happened so quickly. I wasn't ready to decide whether to proceed. Mark advised me to take the rest of the day off by Kearsarge Lakes to rejuvenate myself and decide in the morning. But, I've made up my mind. I will go on. We will go on. How could I stop now with all this wonderful support? Plus, I suspect Jessica will be waiting at the trailhead tomorrow, just in case I decide to quit.

Kearsarge Lakes are beautiful, kind of a cross between Marie Lake and Rae Lakes. Instead of Fin Dome and the Painted Lady watching over me, I now have the Kearsarge pinnacles.

I am still deeply fatigued, so it won't be easy. But over the last twenty-four hours, I have been able to rehydrate (including a couple of cold ones brought by Mark and Brock), refuel, clean up, and get some rest. I hope it is enough to get me through the next three or four days to Whitney Portal. If the weather is good, I should cross the mighty Forester Pass tomorrow, reach Guitar Lake the following night, and Mt. Whitney the next morning. Stay with me. I imagine Forester Pass will sap all the energy I recovered today.

Love, Bob

32

Blood, Sweat, and Tears

2022

Day 18

August 22 - Kearsarge Lakes to just south of Forester Pass

The euphoria from yesterday vanished in the thinnest air yet on the trail. After a short but steep descent to Vidette Meadow, Bob hiked several relaxing miles in the forest, gaining elevation slowly. He knew it couldn't last. The final push to Forester Pass, the highest on the trail at 13,160 feet, was long. The trail surface was outstanding, and the scenery rivaled the best on the entire trail. Bob used every single calorie from his beer and brownies to get to the top. And Mt. Whitney was almost 1500 feet higher! How could that be? How would he do it? Cathy will help. That's how. She has to. We'll be SO close!

Unlike most of the passes he had summited, Forester was covered with hikers basking in their achievement, quickly forgetting the drained legs and overworked lungs that led them there. Their legs would remind them of the climb on the way down, but their lungs would recover. Several backpackers cheered as he put a hand on the sign and lowered his head. As others joined the cheer, he raised his hiking poles in triumph. Finding a comfortable place to rest was as difficult as finding a campsite at the end of a long day. He asked another solo hiker if he minded some company, and the hiker motioned to a boulder next to him. "Thanks. That was tough."

"When you catch your breath, look over the other side. It's nothing like what you just came up."

Bob took Marty and Boo out of his pack and asked his new buddy to take a photo. He posed by the sign, resting his two mascots on the top. The sign indicated he was leaving Kings Canyon National Park and entering Sequoia National Park. He would be hiking in the park all the way to the summit of Mt. Whitney.

Bob stepped over to the other side of the pass, placed one on each shoulder, and smiled.

A couple of women sitting nearby said, "How cute? They must be special. What are their names?"

As Bob turned around to face them, his weary legs stumbled when he didn't lift his foot high enough to clear a rock. He tried to plant his poles to regain his balance, but his hands were holding plush instead of poles. Marty went flying over the heads of the women as he tried to brace his fall. He managed to hold on to Boo, who was crushed between his hand and a rock. The man who had taken his photo and one of the women helped him up.

"Careful. Are you OK? Ooh, your glove is turning red. Looks like you cut your hand." She took Boo and said, "Put pressure on it while my friend gets her first aid kit. Her friend opened her pack and removed a few items before finding her kit. She pulled out a couple sizes of bandages, an alcohol pad, and antibiotic ointment. The guy brought him some fresh toilet paper. Bob removed the glove and couldn't find the cut under all the blood. He folded the toilet paper and pressed it hard against his palm to stop the bleeding and soak up the mess.

"Did you hurt anything else?" the man said.

Bob stretched out each leg and bent his elbows and wrists. "I don't think so." He glanced down. Boo was covered in dust, but his stuffing was still intact. Marty? "Where's Marty?" He spun his head around.

"Marty? Who's Marty?" asked one of the women.

"My stuffed marmot."

"Oh. Something flew over my head. Maybe that was him." She looked over the side, then shook her head. "Let's get you patched up, then we'll look for him. It's pretty steep over there."

"Oh no." He tried to stand up, but she pushed him back down by his shoulder. "Bandage first."

Bob removed the saturated, dark red wad of paper, dropped it on the ground, and saw a half-inch slice on his palm. The bleeding had slowed, but not stopped. He pressed more toilet paper on the cut and increased the pressure. More cheers. Wait a minute. Were they making fun of him? That wasn't very nice. Another hiker approached from the south. Instead of holding up his hiking poles for a celebratory pose, he held up Marty in one hand. "Did anyone lose this?" Even louder cheers. Several hikers pointed at Bob, and the hiker brought Marty to him.

"There he is! I thought I lost him when I fell. Thank you so much."

"No thanks necessary. I'm just glad I didn't fall. I was focused on the narrow trail, trying not to peek over the side, when this thing hit me in the head and fell on the trail. Six inches to the left or right, and it would still be tumbling down the mountainside."

Bob held up Marty and whispered, "I don't know how many lives marmots get, but that's your third on this trip, Marty." Those who heard him laughed. He walked back to his nurses, and they applied antibiotic ointment and a bandage.

"Thanks so much. Let me get a bandage to replace it."

"Don't be silly. We have plenty. You'll want to change it out a couple times a day, so you'll need them more than me." She crossed her fingers.

* * *

Though Bob's leg muscles had recovered enough to begin his descent, he allowed his nerves another twenty minutes to do so, using the time to eat more. Usually he shoveled nuts in his mouth, eager to get back to the trail, but this time, he savored every single one. The trail ahead gave many hikers shaky legs, even if they hadn't just fallen and nearly lost one of their trail friends. He felt bad about startling that hiker with Marty, almost making him fall from the sharp ledge.

He used his hiking poles extensively on descents to relieve the stress on his knees. With his injury, every time he put pressure on his right pole, it would squeeze his fresh cut. The cut would begin bleeding again if he didn't change his grip. But that must wait until he was past the sketchiest part of the trail.

After a few short and steep switchbacks to the right, the trail wound back under the pass, then passed through a gully surrounded by loose rocks. This must be where Marty fell. The gully still held traces of snow near the top. In heavy snow years, the snow extended over the trail, making it one of the most treacherous sections on the 211-mile trail. The trail then followed a ledge around the sheer rock wall on his left. He would soon be invisible to those watching from the pass. The ledge looked like it had been chiseled out of the rock wall by a giant, but Bob figured that explosives must have been used instead. He hugged the rock wall on his left, alternating his eyes between the trail at his feet and fifty feet out so he wouldn't be surprised by an oncoming hiker or a brave marmot.

He arrived at the bottom of the mountain wall sooner than he expected. Unlike the other side, this side was steeper, but shorter. He looked back at the nearly vertical rock face he had descended and wondered how the trail architects ever thought they could build a trail there. Even having just come down, only the zigzagging hikers above allowed him to locate the upper portions of the trail.

Now that the trail was wider and the slope gentler, he felt comfortable tinkering with the grip on his hiking poles. He used his thumb and fingers to hold the very top of the handle, instead of the normal full grip involving the palm. His fingers and wrist would be sore by morning, but he couldn't think of a better option. His glove was still red from the initial bleeding, so he couldn't tell if the bleeding had resumed. Taking his glove on and off to check would do more harm than good, so he continued on.

> **Message from Bob**: *Hannah, Jessica: Forester was long and tough, but I made it. Marty almost didn't; my fault again. Two more days. I can't imagine climbing 1500 feet higher than today, but I will find a way.*

> **Message from Jessica:** *Bob: I knew you could do it. Just remember–Whitney Portal has ice cream. Call me from the summit.*

> **Message from Hannah:** *Bob: Congratulations! Heard about your resupply. Wish I could have been there, but you know, doctor's orders:(You're going to make it now.*

* * *

Dear Cathy,

Only two more long days, but the finish line should draw me in. Despite the constant flow of hiker traffic, there was a continuous party on top of Forester Pass. The new arrivals replaced those departing with unspoken instructions to cheer future arrivals. Marty almost bit the dust again. Actually, he did bite the dust when I tripped and flung him over the top of Forester Pass.

I sliced my palm on a sharp rock when I fell, but it could have been much worse–a broken ankle, twisted knee, knock on the head–all of which would have ended my hike, just like Hannah's. My fatigue played a role in the fall. If I had fallen on the initial descent from the pass, the result may have been tragic. I wouldn't survive a fall as readily as Marty did.

The hike tomorrow contains enough interesting sights to ward off some of the increasing anticipation. First up will be the Bighorn Plateau, then Crabtree Meadow, and finally Guitar Lake. Guitar Lake is one of my most anticipated sights on the trail. It really is shaped like a guitar, and the atmosphere must be electric with so many people staging for their summit of Mt. Whitney. Please remind me to take my time as I become more fatigued and distracted. Forester Pass ate up the rest of the boost Mark's family provided. Only you can boost me now. Are you ready for the summit? To finally finish what you started last July?

Love, Bob

33

Strummed to Sleep

2022

Day 19

August 23 - South of Forester Pass to Guitar Lake

No bighorn sheep patrolled the barren Bighorn Plateau, but Bob saw a dozen marmots grazing on the sparse grass like a herd of cattle. He hadn't expected to find them here with the absence of rock piles to hide in. From all the holes he saw, he presumed they tunneled their dens under the few boulders that were present. A single tarn held on to the last of the remaining snowmelt. The Great Western Divide was visible far to the right. Mt. Whitney was now visible straight ahead. Instead of a sharp peak rising high above the rest, the summit sat at the end of a long ramp. Unlike Fin Dome, Mt. Whitney's shape changed drastically from different perspectives. Some thought it would beckon them all the way to the summit. However, since it was only hundreds of feet higher than the neighboring peaks, it often vanished behind them while hiking far below. The summit would not even be visible from his intended campsite tonight at Guitar Lake.

* * *

Between Wright Creek and Crabtree Meadow, the skies darkened and occasional wind gusts blew sand in his face. He no longer needed his sunglasses for the glare, but he kept them on to keep the sand out of his eyes.

Crabtree Meadow was filling fast with campers when he arrived. Some had planned all along to begin their assault on Mt. Whitney from here, especially those arriving from the south. They could set up a base camp here and hike to Mt. Whitney and back the following day with only the essentials on their back. When they returned to Crabtree Meadow, their campsite would be set up and waiting–a rare treat for thru-hikers. Others were setting up camp earlier than intended to avoid being caught in the brewing storm. Bob considered stopping here, but that would lead to an eighteen-mile day to Whitney Portal and a mid to late morning summit. If the weather was threatening early in the afternoon today, it could be bad in the late morning tomorrow. He pushed on and picked up the pace. Guitar Lake was only three miles away. He would be relieved if he could just set up his tent at Guitar Lake before it started raining.

Forty-five minutes later, he arrived at Timberline Lake at the same time as the rain. He had come so close; just one and a half more miles. He found shelter under an ancient foxtail pine near the shore. The large drops dimpled the surface of the lake, but only a drop or two per minute hit him. The rain turned to ice, pea-sized hailstones. He had seen what hail could do to cars and roofs back in Houston, and didn't want to find out what they would do to his skin. Hailstones bounced off the ground beyond the coverage of the tree and rolled down the slope to the shoreline. He took off his pack and sat with his back against the tree trunk. The tree provided such good coverage that he could probably set up his tent without it or himself getting very wet. He would probably do so if he weren't just a few feet from the water and if camping was allowed here. If the storm continued too long, he might not have a choice. The thought of turning into Nick disgusted him.

The hail turned to a light drizzle thirty minutes later, so Bob put on his rain gear and pack cover and resumed hiking. Fortunately, thunder and lightning had not accompanied the hail. Guitar Lake was fully exposed and not a good place to camp during a thunderstorm. The low spots on the ground had turned white. If he didn't look too closely, the hail could pass for snow.

Bob arrived at Guitar Lake around 6 PM to partly sunny skies. His gamble had paid off. Cathy had helped him through the grueling eighteen-mile day. The most convenient campsites were already claimed, but they would also be the noisiest ones tonight and early in the morning. Many hikers would depart at one or two in the morning in order to view sunrise from the summit. Bob was more pragmatic; it would be cold and dark then. Not only would the darkness increase his chances of falling, but he wouldn't be able to enjoy the views from his high perch. Sure, he would experience some of the views on his descent, but he wouldn't be returning to the initial part of the trail. Instead, he would duck over the other side of the ridge toward Whitney Portal.

He settled for a campsite high above the lake. Gathering water would require more effort, but finding privacy for using his WAG bag would be easier. Yes, he must now poo in a bag. The environment at this elevation was too fragile to handle the waste from so many hikers congregating every night. The ranger placed a supply of the bags next to the trail at Crabtree Meadow. Even after three weeks on the trail, he rarely hit the cat hole he dug ahead of time. This would be interesting. Usually, he used a stick to scrape his steaming, stinky mound into the hole, but that wouldn't work with these bags. Some hikers altered their diet the day before or even resorted to Imodium.

As the evening progressed, the noise increased. But since no individual voices were discernible, it was easier to tune them out. During dinner, he stared at Guitar Lake and the Hitchcock pinnacles beyond. The Hitchcock Lakes sat at the bottom of the pinnacles, but they weren't visible from here. He could admire them for hours on the climb to Whitney in the morning and the subsequent return to Trail Crest. Bob wasn't in a hurry to enter his tent. Sleep would be difficult, so why fight it longer than necessary.

His clothes were as stinky and dirty as they had ever been. He had rinsed them out a couple of days ago, but it was a poor substitute for the laundry he had planned to do in Independence. The same for his skin. Though he had seen a couple brave souls dipping themselves in Guitar Lake earlier, he dismissed the idea. He expected the water to be frigid at this high elevation and couldn't risk beginning his last day in wet clothes. The opportunity to clean up in Lone Pine, a twenty-minute ride from Whitney Portal, would help motivate him to finish tomorrow. There were a few camping areas on the descent from Mt. Whitney, but few thru-hikers could bear to stop so close to the end.

Message from Bob: *Hannah, Jessica: At Guitar Lake. It's beautiful. I can't see Mt. Whitney from here, but I saw it earlier from Bighorn Plateau. Hard to imagine I'll be up there tomorrow–and I WILL be up there. Please stay with me.*

Message from Jessica: *Bob: No doubt now! You got this. Wish I could be there too. Maybe next year.*

Message from Hannah: *Bob: One more day! Enjoy the moment with Cathy. Let me know if you need anything. See you soon:)*

* * *

Dear Cathy,

I'll keep it short tonight and leave you a message from the summit.

Thank you for guiding me to this point. I would not have made it without you. Yes, many others helped along the way: Mark, Jessica, Hannah, Brock, the lady on top of Forester Pass, the guy who recovered Marty by Thousand Island Lake, and Sally. But without you, I wouldn't have even begun. I'm confident about making it to the summit and plan to savor the experience. Where I really need your help is on the long, brutal descent. Stay with me to the end; the JMT officially ends at the summit, but the journey doesn't.

Love, Bob

34

Redemption

2022

Day 20

August 24 - Guitar Lake to Whitney Portal

Though Bob didn't aim for a sunrise summit, he knew it would be difficult to sleep after those who did started preparing to leave. Most of his neighbors tried to be quiet, but in the absence of any other noise on a calm morning, the tent zippers and gas stoves were alarm clocks he couldn't snooze. He left his tent around 5 AM, after pretending to sleep for the previous hour. At least he was able to sleep a couple more hours after the first departing hikers woke him around 1 AM.

The headlamps of the hikers on the switchbacks to Trail Crest looked like shooting stars in slow motion. High above them, he could see the real stars, more than he had ever seen before. He planned to leave at first light, so he enjoyed his hot creamy coffee and last serving of oatmeal for at least a month. They would keep him alert and fueled for the steep climb to Trail Crest.

When he could see the hikers who had turned off their headlamps, he lifted his pack and began his four-and-a-half-mile journey to the pinnacle of the trip, both in altitude and achievement. After a half-dozen switchbacks, he saw the long and slender Hitchcock Lakes sitting under the pinnacles, and Guitar Lake took its namesake shape. He had slept where a guitarist's arm would rest while strumming.

He hiked at a slow, steady pace and took few breaks. After two-and-a-half miles, he arrived at Trail Crest, which was essentially a pass between the east and west sides of the ridge leading to the summit. It was a bustling spot considering the elevation of 13,746 feet, higher than all the official passes on the JMT. On the other side of the ridge, hikers toiled on the infamous ninety-nine switchbacks, which would test his knees on his descent. Hikers from both sides met at Trail Crest to finish the last two miles of their climb together. Most of the elevation gain for the day was done.

Most hikers from the east carried light day packs that the backpackers could only dream of. But they were huffing and puffing much more than the thru-hikers who had been acclimating for two to three weeks. Bob removed his pack and nibbled on trail mix while watching the traffic. Those who had been on the summit for sunrise were coming down, creating tight, two-way traffic on the narrower sections of the trail. A collection of backpacks and bear canisters lined the rock wall at the beginning of the ridge. Bob was reluctant to leave his pack here for the marmots to chew, so he compromised by leaving his bear canister.

Dear Cathy,

Quick update. At Trail Crest. Finished with the second hardest part of the day and ready to begin the easiest—the final two miles to the summit. The 6,000-foot descent will be the hardest.

The trail followed the west side of the ridge that led to the summit. The rocky surface and the sheer drop of over a thousand feet demanded his full attention. The amount of ice left on the trail from yesterday's hail storm surprised him. His first steps on the icy sections were tentative, but he found that the hail had filled in the gaps on the rocky trail, actually making it easier to traverse.

He stopped walking when he wanted to admire the unique features along the trail and relish the ever-changing views. For the first time, he noticed the dark blue clusters of flowers and dark green foliage of skypilots. They were one of the few plants that broke up the stark landscape. He passed rock towers made of large blocks of granite leaning on each other on his left. From a distance, it appeared that just a nudge would cause them to tumble. But as he passed closer, he realized they would likely stand for hundreds, if not thousands, of years–or until the next earthquake.

Halfway along the ridge, he thought he saw the roof of the shelter on the summit. He squinted, blinked his eyes twice, and squinted again. Yes, that was it! The summit had a broad, relatively flat back side, so it would not be obvious from this angle. The shelter would be his beacon, not for route finding, but for managing his anticipation.

Massive spires resembling canine teeth appeared on the right. On his map, they were labeled as the Needles. The last one, Keeler Needle, was just a hair shorter than Mt. Whitney itself. Views to the east teased him through the troughs between the Needles. The most adventurous hikers scrambled to the top of one or more on their way down from Mt. Whitney, knocking out several 14,000-foot peaks in a day. For most hikers, though, Mt. Whitney demanded their full attention.

The top half of the shelter was visible now. The trail disappeared. He adjusted his stride to hit the large, flat slabs of white granite and the patches of sand in between. Hikers fanned out as they climbed the final five hundred feet. With all his focus on his footfalls, he was at the shelter before he knew it. Instead of being circular, like Muir Hut, it was rectangular. The rocks making up the walls were much smoother, which would make it much more difficult to climb on the corrugated metal roof. Memories of Hannah's fall flooded his mind. She should be here with him.

Along the nearest wall of the shelter, a crowd of proud hikers surrounded the cabinet containing the summit register, so he bypassed it and walked another fifty feet in search of the summit marker. A parade of hikers posing for pictures gave it away. The four inch diameter brass plaque was attached to a large slab of granite. The summit area was covered in these flat slabs, approximately five feet by five feet and six to twelve inches thick, stacked on top of each other at different angles. The rock was as white as the sand on a Florida panhandle beach or in White Sands National Park. Hikers explored the summit by hopping from slab to slab. He removed his pack and laid it on a slab out of the way.

He hopped over to the eastern side of the summit, careful to stay a safe distance from the precipitous drop. He sat, looked at 180 degrees of the view to the east, bowed his head, and closed his eyes. Tears built up under his eyelids, trying to force them open for an escape. When he opened them, a gusher of tears fell to the granite, creating dark gray spots the size of quarters.

Dear Cathy,

We made it! It was hard, so hard. Not just today, but the entire three weeks. But we made it! How I wish you could sit next to me right now, so I could put my arm around you, tell you how proud of you I am, and share our impressions of the countless features of the endless view. Through the glare, I can barely see the dry and dusty Owens Valley where I will stay tonight. A small, indigo blue lake fills a bowl down to my left. Down to my right, I see parts of the ninety-nine switchbacks which I must descend shortly. To the far right is my favorite part of the view, the series of Needles guiding the way to the summit. The shelter behind me reminds me of my trail family, which I miss dearly. Perhaps I can enjoy this moment with them in the future. Surprisingly, I don't see any marmots. They may hang out on the less-crowded, northwestern part of the summit, dashing in and out when hikers get careless with their food. Speaking of marmots, I have photos to take and a register to sign. Another update is coming soon.

Bob removed Marty and Boo from his pack and zipped it back up to keep the real marmots out. He set them on a slab to capture a photo with the expansive view to the east in the background. Next, he placed them on each side of the summit marker. A gentleman with a British accent offered to take his picture.

"Thank you for asking. I'd love that."

He handed his phone to the stranger and held up Marty and Boo in his hands on each side of his cheeks. They all showed their wear: Marty's matted fur, Boo's dusty fur, and Bob's dirty, bristled face with sunken eyes.

"Thank you so much. And one for you?"

"No. Thank you. I've had plenty."

Bob hopped back to the shelter and entered the open door. It was a small room, maybe ten feet by ten feet, so there must be another room or two inaccessible to hikers. Except for the roof, the interior reminded him of Muir Hut. The fireplace was plugged, and a plaque described the history and purpose of the shelter. The steady flow of people in the small area made him claustrophobic after being in wide open spaces for so long. He walked out and made his way to the now unattended cabinet. The bottom of the cabinet was covered in stickers, several layers thick. He grabbed a pencil and wrote: *Bob and Cathy Riley, August 24, Houston, TX, At Last!* After staring at the entry for a few seconds, he added *Marty and Boo* under their names. He wanted to linger and read more of the entries, but sensed others gathering over his shoulder. He fetched his pack and took it to the quiet, northwest side of the summit.

Dear Cathy,

I told you I would be back soon. I found some peace and quiet, looking to the west from where I came. I can't see Guitar Lake or the Hitchcock Lakes from here, but I have plenty of time to enjoy them on the two-mile walk back to Trail Crest. I am placing your last rock where I sit now, where it can rest in peace. The area around the summit marker and shelter are too crowded.

You are now officially a summiter—your name is on the summit register next to mine. You deserve as much of the credit for enduring this journey as I do. Without me, you weren't able to finish the first time. Without you, I wouldn't have finished this time. I did the best I could. I hope it's enough.

* * *

Message from Bob: *Hannah, Jessica: On top of the world. Cathy and I had a blast. Couldn't have done it without you and Mark and Brock. Now the hard part. My knees may never forgive me.*

With all his photos and notifications complete, Bob looked in his food bag so he could catch up on his food intake. The effort and excitement of the morning had kept him from eating enough. Instead of eating his typical peanut butter or fish for lunch, he would just snack from here to Whitney Portal where a hamburger awaited him. After eating some cheese crisps and dried fruit, he treated himself to a snack Mark must have snuck into his resupply, praline-covered pecans. How did he know it was one of his favorites? The sugar would provide an instant energy boost to begin his descent, but the nuts would stick with him throughout the long afternoon.

When he grabbed his water bottle to wash down his first few bites, he found an empty one first. He pulled the other one out of his pack; it was only a quarter full, barely enough to wash down his snack. Where did it all go? He had filled up both of his one-liter bottles before leaving this morning. But that was almost five miles of hard hiking ago. And he still had another five miles to Trail Camp, where he might find the next water source. He had become so accustomed to carrying between one and two liters that he hadn't bothered to figure out the mileage to the next water source. In hindsight, he should have filled his two-liter dirty water bag as well. But water was so heavy!

Bob knew the descent would be long, hard, and painful. Now, the first five miles would be without water. Most passes on the JMT required 2,000-3,000 feet of descent before the trail rose toward the next pass. Today, he faced a 6,000-foot descent over eleven miles. At least there would be no pass to climb tomorrow. As daunting as it seemed, he sympathized with those summiting via a day hike from Whitney Portal. They faced the same descent, but had already climbed that same 6,000 feet, much of it in the dark.

When he reached the first icy sections along the ridge to Trail Crest, he noticed piles of hail on the rocky slope to his left. His dry mouth got him thinking. The ice is white. No one could pee up there. There's no trail above. He didn't see any marmot footprints. Why not grab some hail to suck on while he hiked by? He took off his filthy sun gloves, cleaned his hands with hand sanitizer, filled his mouth, and hiked on. The first few mouthfuls were refreshing. Subsequently, his mouth became numb, and he flirted with brain freeze, but he kept eating hail until Trail Crest. Another gift from the trail.

He repacked his backpack with the bear canister he had left behind, and crossed over the ridge to descend the ninety-nine switchbacks. This side had been in the sun all morning, so the hail had all melted. He lost count of the switchbacks around fifty-six.

At the bottom of the switchbacks, hikers were busy setting up and taking down tents at Trail Camp. This camping area was much less scenic than Guitar Lake and probably even noisier. He made his way across the camp to find the source of the water filling the nearby pond. With the number of campers around, filtered water from the pond was probably dirtier than the hail he had been eating earlier. He filtered two-thirds of a liter, drank it, and filtered two more liters. There were many water sources below here, so his water concerns were over.

Just after Trail Camp, some attractive campsites were perched above Consultation Lake on the right. About halfway down, he hiked through Outpost Camp, nestled in the trees next to a beautiful waterfall. The final designated camping location was at Lone Pine Lake. Despite his burning desire to finish the hike, he sat on the shore and soaked his aching feet. Over the far end of the lake, he saw the Owens Valley. The upcoming section of trail must descend steeply. At least his feet would be numb for some of it.

His first sighting of the parking lot delighted him until he realized how far down it remained. He kept walking, ignoring the fatigue in his legs, until he saw the brown wooden frames, the Portal through which he would end his epic journey.

He rounded the last corner and headed straight for the gates. But he no longer noticed them. He only saw a smiling face, framed by dirty blonde hair on top of a tall, thin body, with her arms raised in the air. Hearing his name in her shrill voice flooded his eyes yet again. She didn't move. She must want her hug after he finished, not a foot before. He was too tired to change his pace, so he continued shuffling his feet, causing her to lean forward in anticipation. He passed through the final gate, dropped his poles, and gave her a hug. When she backed away, he removed his pack for the last time. He pulled Boo out of the side pocket and handed it to Hannah. She held the dirty plush bear against her cheek.

He walked to a couple of boulders lining the parking lot thirty feet away and took a seat. Hannah followed him and sat on the other.

"You shouldn't have," Bob wept.

"I had to," Hannah declared.

They sat in silence for thirty, forty seconds.

"So, how did Cathy like the summit?"

"She loved it. I loved it. But it's the journey we will remember most: Jessica, Muir Hut, Marie Lake, the bear at Tuolumne Meadows, Marty's near-death experiences, Forester Pass, cold beer at the Kearsarge Pass junction, Brock's transformation, Sally the ranger, and now you at the finish line."

"And you made us all better people."

"To think, I could have enjoyed so many journeys with her before she passed if I had just listened."

"She's still with you. I heard your conversations at night. But she might need to share you with your new trail family. By my count, I still have 74 miles of the JMT to finish."

"I know just the young lady to accompany you!"

Author's Note

I sincerely hope you enjoyed the story and that it motivates you to get outside and experience your own adventures. Please **leave a review** where you bought this book. They really help others discover and enjoy it as well. Thank you in advance.

As a bonus for you, I have created a **Photo Album** showing many of the key scenes in the book and some of the intriguing wildlife the characters encountered, including the Muir Hut, Garnet Lake, the Woods Creek suspension bridge, and Mt. Whitney. To obtain the photo album or a free novella in the Bucket List Hike series, please visit my website.
  (https://strivingforsafety.mailerpage.com/fiction)

For updates on new releases, free bonus material, and highlights from my own travels, please sign up for my newsletter here.
  (https://strivingforsafety.mailerpage.com)

My website is https://strivingforsafety.mailerpage.com/.

You can also follow me on:
  Facebook
  (https://www.facebook.com/profile.php?id=100087842125447)
  LinkedIn
  (https://www.linkedin.com/in/arnold-marsden-14170180)

You can email me at arnold@strivingforsafety.com. I love to receive feedback from readers on my books and their travels.

Acknowledgments

Thanks to the following generous people for providing valuable feedback on drafts of this book to make it a better read and help me become a better author: Lori Downs, Ethan Gallogly, Richard Lewis, Mary Hamilton, D.A. Galloway, and many others.

About the Author

Arnold lives in Fulshear, Texas, USA, just outside of Houston. He worked as a Health, Safety, and Environment (HSE) professional for over thirty-five years helping to prevent injuries, save lives, and protect the environment. Since retiring, he continues to hike and backpack in some of the most beautiful parks and wilderness areas in the country and has begun an author career, writing both fiction and nonfiction.

Glacier Chalet Surprise is his second novel in the Bucket List Hike series and was inspired by his own visit to Glacier National Park in 2019. *Muir Trail Magic* was the first novel in the series, inspired by his own hike of the trail in 2021 and 2022. Stay tuned for future releases following Bob, Cathy, and others on hiking, backpacking, and sightseeing adventures in the National Parks and other nature preserves. Though fictional, he hopes that the books help you prepare for your own adventure, relive a past adventure, or experience the area from the comfort of your own home.

In his nonfiction books on industrial safety management, he shares valuable lessons learned from his career to help others save lives. His first book was *Don't Let It Fall: Stop Dropped Objects, Save Lives.* His second, *Safety First! Really?*, was published in February 2023.